THE GREATER GLORY

A NOVEL BY

DAVID F. RUPPERT

The Greater Glory

Copyright 2012 by David F. Ruppert

All rights reserved. No part of this book may be reprinted or reproduced or utilized in any form or by any electronic, mechanical, or other means, including photocopying and recording, or in any information storage or retrieval system, without permission from the author.

ISBN: 0-6156-7741-X
ISBN-13: 978-0-6156-7741-5

This is a work of fiction created solely from the author's imagination and is not based upon or derived from any actual persons, living or dead. Any such resemblance is purely coincidental.

A.M.D.G.

PART I

Chapter 1

Peter Gallagher hadn't seen a Jesuit priest wearing a black cassock for nearly thirty years, and he never had seen one lying in a pool of his own blood.

During his fifteen years with the force, the Washington, DC, homicide detective had worked many brutal scenes, but the sight of the dead priest, in the early hours of that Tuesday morning, surprisingly shook him like no other he had worked before.

"What do we have, Ty?" asked Gallagher, as his partner, Lenwood Tyrone Johnson Jr., sauntered casually up a minute after Gallagher's arrival. Johnson was above average in height, very fit, with a clean-cut, urban fade haircut. The end of his tie was tucked into his blue button-down shirt military style, keeping it out of his way while he worked.

With a latex-covered hand, Detective Johnson pulled his notepad a bit closer to his eyes. "Father Edward Sachs, forty-two, a resident priest here at St. Gabriel for the last couple of years. According to the rectory housekeeper, Maria Rosario, Father Sachs arrived back around ten thirty this evening before apparently going up to his room on the third floor of the rectory. A little after eleven p.m., the housekeeper and the pastor, Father Damien Thomas, heard a crash. Apparently both were in the rectory kitchen on the first floor at the time. They mounted the stairs, found the window to Father Sachs's room open and the good father lying on the driveway below. They then called nine-one-one."

"That's all?" Gallagher asked, a slight terseness in his voice. His lithe, six-foot frame shifted uneasily, as he nervously fidgeted and loosened his own tie that the heat had suddenly made uncomfortable. He worked to mat down his thick but shortly cropped schoolboy haircut that was still wet from the rushed shower taken before his arrival. His blue-green eyes not shifting from the sight of the body.

"Give me a break, Pete. We've only been here thirty minutes, for Christ's sake." Johnson moved back toward the body of the priest, where he gave directions to the crime-scene investigators and the other uniformed police who were securing the site. Portable floodlights were already in place, as was a crowd of onlookers, who were unaccustomed to such excitement on the streets of Georgetown during a warm summer night.

Gallagher looked up at the third-floor window of the gray, brick, antebellum building as another investigator took photos from the window, down onto where the dead priest lay uncovered.

Detective Johnson returned to where Gallagher stood. "Poor bastard. Not like it was some gangbanger who bought it. Tough to see something like this."

"You think he could've jumped?" asked Gallagher.

"Doesn't look like it, Pete," responded Johnson. "Appears he may have fallen through the window screen." Johnson looked toward his partner. "It's a bit of a short drop for someone wanting to do himself in, don't you think?"

Gallagher waited while dismissing the possibility of suicide then redirected his thoughts. "I want to talk to the housekeeper and the pastor."

Gallagher and Johnson walked up the stone steps of the rectory and into the kitchen, where a sobbing housekeeper and a shocked parish pastor sat around a wooden table.

"Father Thomas?" Gallagher asked the man, who sat with his arm around the Latino woman.

"Yes."

"My name is Detective Peter Gallagher, DC police. Can you tell me what happened?" The priest looked up as Gallagher directed a female officer to take over the job of looking after the housekeeper.

The priest placed his hands on his face and rubbed his strained and tired eyes. "Mr. Gallagher, I'd like to pray over Father Sachs. Would that be possible?"

"Father, our investigators are working to ascertain what may have happened. As soon as they're done, I'll be happy to oblige. In the meantime, can you tell me what happened?"

"Of course. Maria and I were in the kitchen tonight around eleven, as we usually are. I'm a bit of a creature of habit, and Maria makes me a glass of hot milk around eleven before I go to sleep." Gallagher shot a quick glance toward the old stove and noticed the small saucepan on the now-cold burner; a half-finished glass of milk sat on the counter nearby.

"Go on."

"Well, as we were sitting here, we heard a crash. Sounded like something had snapped. Sort of like the sound of cracking wood. I yelled up the stairs to see if everything was okay. There was no response. Then I walked up and knocked on Father Sachs's door. Still no answer. I opened the door and saw the window was open and the screen missing. I went to the open window. It was then that I saw Father Sachs lying in the driveway below. I must have screamed. Maria ran up to find me. I picked up the phone and called for help." Father Thomas rubbed his hands over his face again. "It was horrifying."

Gallagher placed his hand on the priest's arm before turning back to Johnson, who was standing behind, listening and taking notes. "Ty, let me know when the boys outside are done and tell them not to remove Father Sachs until Father Thomas can have a moment for prayers."

"Understood," responded Johnson, as he moved away from the kitchen.

Gallagher turned back toward the shaken frame of Father Thomas. "What time did Father Sachs return to the rectory this evening?"

"A little before ten thirty."

"And were the three of you the only ones in the rectory tonight?"

"Yes. Normally, there are five priests in residence here. Father Clifford, however, is on sabbatical in Rome—been there since February and doesn't return until the fall. Father Desoto is teaching at Santa Clara University for the summer. And Father Benjamin, a visiting priest, is back home in Uganda doing missionary work. Right now it's just myself, Father Sachs, and Maria here."

Gallagher worked as quickly as he could to flush out what Father Thomas knew before the priest had time to think. He relied on this tactic, which often had resulted in identifying inconsistencies when formal statements were made. While sincerely hoping the priest before him was innocent, he hadn't ruled out foul play. "Anything else you can remember? Anything at all out of the ordinary?"

Father Thomas thought for a second. "Nothing. It was the same as every night this week. Father Sachs would come in around ten thirty, I'd be drinking milk by eleven, and then everyone was asleep."

Johnson had returned to Gallagher's side. "Pete, they're almost done out there. If the father would like to say some prayers, he can go ahead. The coroner is almost ready to remove the body."

"Mr. Gallagher, may I go ahead and gather what I need?"

"Yes, Father. Please do. When you're ready, Detective Johnson here will escort you."

"Thank you," said Father Thomas before heading for the stairs to retrieve a stole and his prayer book.

Gallagher looked at Johnson as the priest left. "What did they find, Ty?"

Johnson looked perplexed. "They haven't found any prints. Not a single print. If Father Sachs had been trying to open the window, there would have likely been something."

"Well, maybe he opened the window and fell without getting a hand on the screen. Wouldn't that explain it?" asked Gallagher.

"Yeah. But what I'm telling you is that there are no prints on the windowsill at all. Not a one."

Gallagher digested the comment slowly, but now the shock of his having first seen the dead priest nearly an hour before was overwhelmed by the shock of what might now follow. "Oh, Christ."

"Yeah, Pete," said Johnson. "Either Christ opened that window or Father Sachs's death is looking less and less like an accident."

Chapter 2

The death-scene investigation didn't wrap up until nearly dawn the next day.

The body of Father Sachs was now pending an autopsy, and formal statements from both Father Thomas and the Latino housekeeper were scheduled for early that morning.

Gallagher sipped on a coffee at one of the several desks in a large office space shared by the members of the homicide squad. He looked up when Johnson arrived.

"Hell of a night, Pete," said Johnson. "You're in early. You get any sleep?"

"No. By the time we wrapped up, it was nearly five, so I just came here and showered. I figured I'd better just push on through. The captain is already in."

"What's got him in so early?" Johnson walked over to the coffee pot and poured himself a cup.

Captain Irvin Drexler opened his office door, stuck out his head, and summoned the two detectives to his desk. Gallagher and Johnson took final sips of their coffees, shared a quick look, and entered Drexler's office.

"What do we have, Gallagher, on the dead priest?" inquired Drexler. Drexler was in his early fifties, thin and tall with a short, dated Afro haircut that only stood to highlight his receding hairline. His chocolate black face was taught and his voice craggy—both from years of too much smoking that he had only recently given up.

"Very little, I'm afraid, other than the preliminaries. The coroner is scheduled to conduct the autopsy this morning. The parish pastor and the rectory housekeeper should be here shortly to give their formal statements. We should know more after that." Gallagher held tight on the lack of fingerprints and his own suspicions.

The captain looked down at his blotter and the seemingly hundreds of tasks he had on tap for the day. "Okay, then. Get back with me later today. And make sure you two do a full check of the rectory again. We all had a late night. I want you to have another look with fresh eyes."

"Yes, sir," responded Gallagher.

As they left the captain's office, Johnson glanced at Gallagher. "What's the play here? Why'd you hold back about the prints?"

"Ty, I want you to conduct the interviews this morning. Something in my gut doesn't feel right. That little voice, I guess."

"Okay. Anything you want to share?" asked Johnson, his curiosity heightened.

"Not yet. Not enough to sink my teeth into."

Father Thomas and Maria Rosario arrived by nine a.m. and were placed in separate interview rooms. Gallagher watched both of them through the one-way glass and listened intently as Johnson worked through the chronology of events and the preliminary statements of the night before. There was nothing unusual, nothing that didn't comport with the stories both witnesses previously had provided.

Father Thomas, wearing a short-sleeve black clerical shirt, black pants, and Roman collar, seemed even older than he had the night before. A wiry man of about seventy, he looked closer to eighty, Gallagher thought. His statements and recounting of the events of the previous evening were forthcoming and clear, and this fact began to wear away on Gallagher's personal suspicions.

Rosario's interview produced similar results; nothing she said was inconsistent with her statements the night before. Putting her age somewhere around fifty-five, Gallagher noticed that the woman appeared distinctly calmer and more collected than the last time he'd seen her.

Johnson stood from his chair in the interview room where Maria Rosario sat with her hands respectfully in her lap. Gallagher watched as Johnson informed her that he would return shortly and that the interview was nearly finished. The door to the room opened, and Johnson emerged into the surveillance area, where Gallagher waited anxiously to hear his partner's thoughts.

"Well, what did you think?" asked Johnson.

"You beat me to the question. You were in there with them."

Johnson let out a slight sigh. "Either they're telling the truth, or that's the best damn criminal conspiracy I've ever seen. Everything clicks with last night's statements. No sense of defensiveness or deception that I could see. All above board."

Gallagher raised his eyebrows and shrugged. "Okay. Get the statements typed up and have them sign 'em. I'll drive Father Thomas and Ms. Rosario back to the rectory when they're ready."

"Roger that." Johnson went back in with Maria Rosario to wrap things up.

Gallagher appeared calm while looking from behind the glass, although he was unable to shake the feeling that there was much more to the death of Father Sachs yet to be uncovered.

Chapter 3

The ride from the precinct was relatively swift. Gallagher again thanked both Father Thomas and Maria Rosario and offered his heartfelt condolences to the parish for the loss of the young priest. His passengers were open and warm in responding to his comments.

"Father?" asked Gallagher, as they rounded M Street onto Wisconsin Avenue. "I'd like to see Father Sachs's room again, if you don't mind. I apologize for the intrusion again today, but I'd like to make sure I didn't overlook anything last night."

"Mr. Gallagher, what are you looking for exactly?" said the priest.

"I'm not sure yet, but perhaps something in there might shed some light on how Father Sachs fell from that window. It's mostly routine. Shouldn't take long."

"Of course. Whatever we can do to help, we certainly will."

Gallagher entered the rectory with Father Thomas and Maria Rosario around one p.m. Father Thomas offered him something to eat when they arrived, but he politely turned him down. He was anxious to again see the room where the apparent accident had taken place. "I'll join you shortly, and perhaps we can chat for a bit, Father," he said.

"Yes. I'll be here. Come find me when you're done."

The parish rectory building was old, built around 1857, on ground that once had been the site of the old church cemetery. The ceilings were high with wood paneling liberally used in the construction, giving the place a formal, solemn feel. The wooden staircase was commanding, and the boards under the dated carpet creaked and moaned as Gallagher ascended them to reach the third floor.

Gallagher stopped at the door to Father Sachs's room and broke the police seal before entering. The room seemed different than it had the night before. In the heat of the night—not to mention the circumstances of a dead priest—he had failed to appreciate the layout. Like other rooms in the rectory, it had the same high ceilings of the floors below. The room was simply decorated. A single bed sat against the wall next to a nightstand with an old, cheap lamp.

Gallagher turned on the lamp before walking over to a large wardrobe. He opened it and noticed the precision of the clothes hanging in it. He found apparel that was neatly folded, and three freshly pressed, black cassocks hung smartly together. The rest of the room contained a small work desk; a worn Oriental carpet; and a wall of built-in bookshelves nearly full with volumes that ranged from modern banking and finance to old leather-bound books on Latin, Greek, and theology.

The desk was set against another wall. It sat just adjacent to the window through which Father Sachs had fallen the night before. The leather top was clear, aside from a gold crucifix set directly in front of where one would sit. Gallagher stared at the cross and the figure of Christ. He looked out the window and onto the driveway below then turned back to the room. Nothing unusual, he surmised, aside from the striking order and discipline of the room.

His eye caught the black, leather briefcase that sat aside the desk on the floor. He sat down at the desk chair and placed the briefcase on his lap. Inside there was nothing out of the ordinary. He found a daily planner, legal pads, a calculator, and Georgetown University building-access and library cards.

Gallagher pulled the planner from the briefcase and opened it. Father Sachs's commitments and tasks were abundant, with parishioner meetings and other groups, along with dates and times when he was due to say Mass or hear confessions.

Gallagher also noticed very quickly other notes—some placed on calendar days—that were not so clearly decipherable. Initials and numbers and letters were used in no particular order, something Gallagher assumed was some sort of shorthand. He turned to the previous day in the planner.

Five thirty a.m.: rise, spiritual exercises
Six a.m.: run
Seven a.m.: prayer, preparation for Mass
Eight a.m.: Mass—main church

He noticed nothing unusual until he saw the entry for eight p.m.

Eight p.m.: C004S
Ten p.m.: rectory
Ten thirty p.m.: spiritual exercises, prayer
Eleven p.m.: lights out

He turned to the previous week's entry and found the same "C004S" written for eight o'clock Tuesday night. The code also appeared at least once a week in the preceding twelve weeks and, for the week prior to his death, daily.

Over the next thirty minutes, Gallagher found more things that interested him; the daily planner was the first of many discoveries that did nothing but create more questions as to who Father Sachs was and, most important, why someone might have been motivated to see the young priest meet with an untimely and painful death.

Chapter 4

Father Thomas was sitting at his desk writing when Peter Gallagher descended from the third floor. The short-sleeve black shirt and Roman collar the priest had donned earlier had been replaced with a white Lacoste polo shirt, open at the neck. A small cross hung from a gold chain, giving him more of an air of a professional tennis player than the picture Gallagher would have expected from the pastor of an established Roman Catholic parish.

Father Thomas looked up as Gallagher stood in the doorway. "Mr. Gallagher. How did it go?"

"Did I disturb you, Father? I apologize."

"I was working on a homily for Sunday. I need to start on the funeral arrangements for Father Sachs." Father Thomas sighed. "I suppose I'm trying to put them off as long as I can." He capped his pen and set it in front of him then sat back.

"Father, if it's not too much trouble right now, I wonder if we could chat for a bit." Father Thomas's curious look struck Gallagher as suspicious.

"Please sit down. Can I get you something?"

"Just an ice water, Father. Thank you."

The priest stood from his desk as Gallagher settled into the leather chair that sat before it. Father Thomas called out from the doorway of his study, asking Maria Rosario to bring in two waters. Gallagher faintly heard a *"Si, Padre"* in response.

Father Thomas settled back into his desk chair. Gallagher could see the defensive posture through the man's outward attempt at relaxation. The priest clearly was waiting for the first serve to come across the net.

"Father," Gallagher began in a friendly and somewhat hushed tone, "I'd like to know more about Father Sachs, what he did here, and anything else you can offer."

Father Thomas sat forward in his chair and placed his arms on the desk before him. His fingers interlocked and noticeably clenched with an uncomfortable tension. "What exactly are you looking for?"

Gallagher flashed a subtle smile. "That's the second time you've asked that question today. Is there something you're afraid to tell me, or for me to find out?"

Father Thomas appeared to go gray before the flush rushed back to his face. "You know, Mr. Gallagher, I'm not sure I like your tone. I think I've been nothing but cooperative. Are you accusing me of something?"

"Should I be?" Gallagher responded, then waited, hoping the unexpected heat would clear from their conversation.

Father Thomas eyed Gallagher but said nothing, as their exchange was interrupted by the arrival of Maria Rosario and two glasses of ice water. The housekeeper handed one to Gallagher and the other to Father Thomas, while seeming to sense the tension that filled the room.

"Thank you, Maria. If you could please close the door on your way out."

"Si, Padre," said the housekeeper, who gave Father Thomas a look of concern that Gallagher sensed without having to turn around. The door closed.

"I didn't come here today to accuse anyone of anything. I'm merely trying to look into the death of one of your priests at a time when you and Ms. Rosario were, apparently, the only ones present," Gallagher said. "That being the case, I suggest we dispense with the subterfuge. Tell me about Sachs."

"What do you want to know?"

"Well, you can tell me about his background, what he did for you and the parish, and who he interacted with on a daily basis," started Gallagher. "But I want to begin with his uniform."

"I'm sorry?" responded Father Thomas. "You said, 'his uniform'?"

"Yes. You see, Father, I'm a product of Jesuit schools myself, and I haven't seen a Jesuit wearing a black cassock for some time. I noticed that you don't wear one." Gallagher paused and sipped his water. "So let's begin there, shall we? Why was that young priest wearing a black cassock?"

The story that Gallagher heard over the next hour was more revealing; Gallagher hung on every word about the young priest that Father Thomas brought forward from his lips.

From just outside the door to Father Thomas's study, so too did Maria Rosario.

Chapter 5

On the drive back from the St. Gabriel rectory, Gallagher received a call from Ty Johnson. He patched it through to the cordless speakerphone in his car.

"Pete, the autopsy results came in on Father Sachs. They came back clean. No drugs, no alcohol. Shit, even his cholesterol was low. Father Sachs was as healthy as a horse."

The results didn't surprise Gallagher. If anything, they only gave him reason to investigate with even greater zeal.

"You still there?" asked Johnson.

"Yeah, still here. What was Sachs's height and weight?"

Gallagher waited while Johnson rustled through the paper report from the coroner.

"Ah, says here six foot three and a hundred and ninety-five pounds."

"Pretty big guy," said Gallagher.

"Yeah, so?"

Gallagher ignored the question. "Ty, you almost done over there?"

"I could be," responded Johnson with increasing curiosity.

"Come over to my place when you're ready. We can talk over a couple of steaks and some drinks."

"Hey, brother, must have been a hell of a discussion at the rectory today. You don't have to twist my arm. I'll be there in an hour or so. Let me just call the wife and let her know."

"See you then. And bring the autopsy report and the case file."

"Will do." Johnson hung up the phone.

17

During the remaining minutes of his drive back to his apartment building, Gallagher's thoughts focused on the profile Father Thomas had provided on Father Sachs and the information he'd received from Johnson: a priest the size of a respectable professional football player, the brain of an Ivy League professor, and the personal habits of a military officer. Dead. Sachs could have avoided the life of a priest. He could have had any woman he wanted in Washington, a grand house, wealth, and power. But Sachs chose none of those paths, Gallagher pondered. Instead, he chose another path. A path few men would have taken had they the same natural talents and abilities.

Gallagher knew that a man like Sachs—so meticulous, so strong, so intelligent—was not one to casually meet a fatal accident. There was little doubt in the detective's head that something else was going on. But even if, at the end of the day, Sachs's death did turn out to be an accident, Gallagher would be damned if he didn't exhaust every possibility that it might be otherwise. Failing to do so was not something he could accept nor, thought Gallagher with an uncharacteristic religious sentimentality, would God.

Chapter 6

Captain Irvin Drexler was already on edge when Peter Gallagher and Ty Johnson arrived the next morning with bloodshot eyes and slightly throbbing heads. The two detectives had been up again most of the night digesting the limited official information they had gathered on the Sachs case, along with a couple of T-bones and more than a few drinks between them. They looked rough, and this only set Captain Drexler off further when they plopped before his desk sipping strong coffees.

"I'm shutting down the Sachs case. Ruling is going to be an accident," Drexler said. The pronouncement jolted Gallagher and Johnson into sobriety.

"Sir, what the hell for? It's been less than forty-eight hours. We need more time," shouted Gallagher, nearly spilling his coffee. Johnson only got in a "boss" before Drexler unleashed.

"Yeah, and what the hell do we have, huh? We've got nothing from the statements. We've got nothing from the coroner. We've got no physical evidence at the scene that indicates anything other than what this death was—an accident. A tragic, unwanted accident. The DA has no case. Shit, Gallagher, you're a former DA, for God's sake. You know how this works. Not only that, but I got the goddamned mayor calling to tell me to wrap this up—and you two coming in here this morning looking like you just spent your last night on shore leave before going back to sea for a year. I've got three other bona fide homicides since last night, and we're short on resources. You tell me why the fuck I should continue this investigation. More time, my ass." Drexler had exhausted himself and sat back to catch his breath.

Johnson was the first to respond. "Boss, you got to hear what Pete thinks about this case. He sold me last night on his idea that there's something worth pursuing here."

"Oh, yeah? From one look at you, Johnson, it seems like Gallagher poured enough booze in you last night to sell you the London Bridge." Drexler turned to Gallagher. "Okay, hot shot. See if you can sell your shit to me."

Gallagher liked Drexler, although they locked horns from time to time. Drexler was a Washington native who had grown up black and poor and hungry for success. Gallagher knew Drexler was smart and behind the emotion, lay a well-reasoned and open-minded police officer through and through.

"Okay, sir. What we know is this. Edward Sachs, SJ—Society of Jesus—was sent to St. Gabriel parish two years ago. His appointment wasn't without considerable controversy and was done over the strenuous objections of the Jesuit leadership in Washington and specifically St. Gabriel Parish. St. Gabriel and its Jesuits, it seemed, had been a thorn in the side of the Archdiocese of Washington for many years, and we think Sachs may have been brought in to bring the parish into line."

"What the hell does that mean? You're talking to an old Washington black Baptist," said Drexler. "My understanding of religion is some old uncle getting up saying, 'Praise be the Lord' while the hundred in the pews start dancing." Johnson chuckled at Drexler's crudely descriptive ethnic stereotype. "Shut up, Johnson," the captain barked.

Gallagher pressed on while trying to provide the additional background Drexler was looking for. "In 1959 Pope John the Twenty-Third called what became known as the Second Vatican Council. The council continued on for another six years. Its mandate was to bring the Roman Catholic Church into the 'the modern age.' The Catholic Mass was changed, the old Latin shelved, and the laity—the non-clergy—were empowered."

"Gallagher," said Drexler. "Get to the point."

"As a result of the council's actions, many Catholic churches around the world began to see the guidance coming from Rome as license to embrace a more liberal approach toward the Church and its teachings. St. Gabriel in Georgetown was one of those parishes.

"The social unrest of the late 1960s and early 1970s only added to the atmosphere that fostered an even greater resolve and mission of the more liberal elements within these Catholic parishes. As it turned out, St. Gabriel became more and more a concern for the Archdiocese of Washington.

"According to some research Ty and I did last night, in the late 1960s some of St. Gabriel's priests openly defied the Church's teachings on birth control. That was the first of many theological dissensions to come out of the parish. In later years the Archdiocese of Washington undertook a number of investigations into the parish, including investigations of accusations of liturgical abuses.

"We think Father Sachs's appointment may have been an effort to turn the theological tide at St. Gabriel. The parish didn't want that. And I think someone killed him because of it."

Drexler was reluctantly intrigued by Gallagher's theory but still skeptical. "You got all this crap from the statements of that old priest, the Mexican woman, and the Internet?"

"Sort of, sir. But yesterday I had a long conversation with the pastor, Father Thomas, after taking him back to the rectory."

"And he told you all of this too?"

"Not exactly. I pieced together most of the theory from what little we really know at this point," Gallagher said. "But Father Thomas did tell me about Sachs's appointment and that there was objection as to the protocol used by the Jesuit order in making it. All he said is that he'd had doubts that Father Sachs was 'a good fit' for the parish."

"You want me, against my better judgment, to keep this case open based on that? Can't do it, Gallagher. This sounds like nothing more than pure church politics. Shit, what the hell city do you think this is?" Drexler was losing interest again.

"Thomas also said that Sachs had his hand in all sorts of matters within the parish. I confirmed this with the files and papers I found in Sachs's room yesterday." Gallagher changed track. "Did you know Sachs was a lawyer? The guy had a JD and an MBA from Harvard. He also was working on a PhD in modern Church history. According to Father Thomas and the files, Sachs was working with a number of people and on a number of projects at St. Gabriel. Apparently he was involved with some financial matters as well. He spent a lot of time doing research in the parish records—digging around quite a bit."

"Even if I find your theory interesting," Drexler said, "that still doesn't explain the lack of any evidence that something or someone, other than fate, killed that priest. Let's say, for a second, I give you the benefit of the doubt. And say there is something that would equate to motive. We still don't have opportunity. No one was there at the time of death, other than one old white priest and an aging Latino woman, neither of whom could come close—even together—to overpowering a priest who was built, according to the coroner's report, like a Redskins player."

The room fell quiet as Drexler pondered the facts, his sharp mind processing the information the detectives had given him. "All right. I'll give you two another couple of days to see what you can find to confirm this hunch of yours. But unless you find something compelling, I'm going to close this case. Are we clear?"

The detectives signaled their understanding and stood to leave. As they reached the door, Drexler stopped them. "Gallagher, why would I get a call from the mayor on this case? What the hell is so special about this church?"

Gallagher and Johnson turned around. "We don't know, sir," responded Gallagher. "How often does the mayor call you about a case your people are working?"

Drexler paused then answered, a concerned tone in his voice. "He doesn't."

Chapter 7

When Peter Gallagher had left the St. Gabriel rectory after talking with Father Thomas the day before, the parish pastor had acceded to the detective's request for further and unfettered access to people and records at the parish. The fact that Gallagher once had been a district attorney had paid off during the conversation with the old priest. In no uncertain terms, Gallagher told Father Thomas that both he and his housekeeper remained "persons of interest," and it would be in their best interest to assist the DC police in the matter. Of course, Gallagher also knew at that time that he would have to get the okay from above to continue the investigation, but he had gambled and won on that issue and now had the opportunity to take advantage of the carefully cajoled invitation from the parish pastor.

Back at their desks, Gallagher and Johnson sucked down more coffee while decompressing from the meeting with Captain Drexler.

"Now what, Pete?" asked Johnson, loosening his tie a bit.

"Check on the information Father Thomas gave on the three other priests who weren't present. Get a hold of them if you can. Find out what they know about Sachs and Thomas and the parish. Perhaps there's something there that we didn't get from good Father Thomas. Then continue on with our research from last night. Go over to the archbishop's residence and see what you can get on the relationship between the Archdiocese and St. Gabriel. Then check out Drexler's comment on the mayor. I'll check in when I get a chance."

"And what are you going to do?"

Gallagher picked up the daily planner he had taken from Sachs's room the day before. "I'm going to run down the leads from this. I'll see who Sachs was working with at the parish, dig around some more, and try to find an answer to Drexler's other question as well."

"You mean, who might've had the opportunity to kill Sachs?"

"No," said Gallagher. "I mean, what the hell is so special about this church?"

Chapter 8

It was quiet in Georgetown when Gallagher arrived at St. Gabriel around nine thirty Thursday morning. The streets were deserted, and the heavy humidity of the air lent a peaceful stillness to the neighborhood. It was summer, and the hustle and bustle of the academic year had abated following the Georgetown University commencement exercises and the release of grade-school children for summer recess.

The detective found a parking spot directly across from the main church. The parish occupied nearly half a city block, with the main church as the centerpiece. Made of white stone, the church had a Roman quality; four large columns stood at the front, supporting a triangular-shaped portico under which great wooden doors sat closed. Two redbrick buildings flanked the house of worship that Gallagher correctly assumed to be the parish school. A stone retaining wall and heavy, black, ornate iron fencing surrounded all the buildings.

The main church felt imposing as Gallagher crossed the street with his mailbag-style attaché slung over his shoulder by its canvas strap. The building sat above street level yet so close to the sidewalk that it towered over the casual observer as one approached.

As Gallagher stood at the bottom of the steep set of stone steps that led to the church entrance, his eye caught sight of the two heavy brass plaques fastened to the iron fence. The first noted that St. Gabriel had been the house of worship for President John Fitzgerald Kennedy. The second summarized the building's history and indicated that the church had been built before the Civil War and the interior had been renovated in the late 1970s.

The stained-glass window above the wooden front doors was old. The acronym "IHS" within it was familiar to Gallagher, who had spent nearly two decades in Jesuit institutions of learning. It stood for "*In Hoc Signo*," Latin for "In This Sign," the trademark for the Society of Jesus.

The first sight of the interior of the church surprised Gallagher a bit. It was clear the church had been renovated, as the plaque out front had just informed him, and the extent of the renovation was evidently total. The interior was stark white, aside from the brown wooden pews and rectangular stained-glass windows. Both looked as though they were about the only things unchanged since the church had been built more than a century-and-a-half before.

Without thinking, and without having set foot in a Catholic church for a number of years, Gallagher genuflected and slipped into a pew near the rear. He sat and took in the rest of the interior.

The high altar must have been dismantled during the renovation in the late 1970s, the heavy marble moved down below where it once sat. A bench had replaced the high altar, and Gallagher assumed this was where the celebrant now sat when conducting the Mass. Above the bench hung an unusual glass cross upon which a figure of Christ was not to be found hanging. A purple drape hung behind the cross in an open space behind which there was no wall. There was no communion rail; it too had been removed along with the pulpit, the tabernacle, the side altars, and other staples of Roman Catholic churches once seen the world over.

Upon closer observation, from his seat in the back, the detective noticed a modernesque statue of the Virgin Mary placed off in a corner, and the once-centerpiece tabernacle now relegated to a secluded left alcove off the main altar. To the right, a mirror alcove of the one on the left looked to contain a baptismal font of some sort. Both side alcoves were carpeted. Portable, stainless-steel bleachers had been folded up against the walls in front of each.

As the lingering smell of recently extinguished candles from the daily eight a.m. Mass hit his nostrils, he noticed the activity taking place in the sanctuary, where four women worked in silence. Slipping from his seat, Gallagher made his way to the front of the church.

"Good morning," he said to a late-middle-aged woman with frizzy red hair that was intended, but failed, to cloak the unfortunate signs of alopecia; a pair of reading glasses was tucked into the red frizz.

The woman turned, a look of disinterested surprise on her face. "Good morning. Can I help you?" asked the woman. She held a jar of some kind, filled with a blue liquid, in her hands.

"Yes, ma'am. I'm Detective Peter Gallagher of the DC police. I'm here looking into the death of Father Sachs." He quickly flashed his badge.

"Yes?" the woman responded.

"Would you mind if I asked you a few questions?"

"If you must, but I only can spare a few minutes. As you can see, we're busy this morning. This situation has been rather inconvenient."

"Inconvenient, you said?" asked Gallagher.

The woman set down the jar of colored liquid, brushed off her hands, her demeanor suddenly changing. "I'm sorry, Detective…Gallagher, wasn't it?"

"Yes, ma'am."

"Please don't call me ma'am, if you could. I find it an anachronism." The woman held out her hand. "I'm Rachel Goldman-Scott, chairperson of the St. Gabriel Jewish Society. I also am a member of the Committee on Liturgy for the parish. I apologize for my testiness, but we've been instructed by Father Thomas to remove some of our treasured ornamentation from the church in preparation for Father Sachs's funeral in a few days."

Gallagher now noticed the multicolored standing banners that were being removed from the main altar. "I take it that jar you were holding is also part of the project?" he asked.

"Yes, Detective. It's a ceremonial urn that's part of the display you see in front of you." Gallagher looked over to see an arrangement of pedestals of varying heights on which sat other jars that contained liquids of various colors. "The arrangement took us weeks of planning and research at the Center for Liturgy. They symbolize the liquid quality that is life. The colors represent

God's diversity and ever-changing nature." The woman beamed with pride as she gazed on the display. "You may also notice the banners hanging down the frescoed columns on either side of the altar."

Gallagher looked up. "The writing almost looks like Hebrew."

"Very good, Detective. The liturgical committee commissioned these last year. They impress the true Jewish heritage upon which the Catholic identity was founded." She appeared sour again. "And we've been told to take it all away for the funeral. Frankly it's an injustice."

"I see. So this was requested by Father Thomas…to take down these items?"

"That's right. We've been told the funeral Mass for Father Sachs will be the old, oppressive Latin Mass and that our liturgical decoration apparently isn't appropriate for the event." The woman pursed her lips.

Gallagher abandoned the other questions he had for the time being, as he'd already been provided a sense of the answers he would have received. "Thank you for your time, Mrs. Scott. Can you tell me where the Center for Liturgy is located?"

"It's Ms. Goldman-Scott, Detective. I'm rather proud of that fact. And you can find the Center for Liturgy out the door and down to the left, first door on the right." The woman pointed to the doors on the left-side alcove. She turned her back and reengaged with the dismantling of the ceremonial urns. She watched out of the corner of her eye as Gallagher genuflected to the tabernacle before slipping out through the doors she had directed him toward.

Once outside the church, he riffled through his attaché and pulled out a crumpled Marlboro. He lit it quickly and stepped down three stairs. He stood in a small walkway that ran between the side of the main church and the back of the parish theater. To his right, a small, open area of blacktop was penned in by the other buildings: a parish-meeting hall, which looked of new construction; the side of the theater; and the gray rectory building. Off to his far right stood the back white wall of the original St. Gabriel Church, which was once the convent for the nuns who ran the school but who, like everything else it seemed, had long since become extinct.

The original church, built in 1794, also had been renovated, Gallagher had learned the night before when he and Johnson had done their research. Gallagher took another drag of his cigarette and looked up at the window of the rectory from which Father Sachs had tumbled to his death.

Stubbing out his short break, he took a deep breath and walked into the Center for Liturgy, hoping for a bit warmer of a welcome than the last one he'd received. Gallagher, however, already sensed this was a long shot.

"Good morning," he tried again on an older woman who sat behind a desk. The woman looked up as the detective moved closer. She was at least seventy, with white hair, large rimless glasses, and the body of a linebacker. Her expression matched her physical appearance. Gallagher felt as if he had walked back in time. The only thing missing, he thought, was a nun's habit.

"Good morning," said the woman. Gallagher viewed this as a small victory.

"My name is Detective Peter Gallagher of the DC police. I was wondering if I could ask you a few questions. I'm looking into the death of Father Edward Sachs."

The woman remained stoic. "How can I help you?"

"I was wondering if you could tell me a bit about Father Sachs—" began Gallagher before being interrupted by yet another middle-aged woman entering the center in almost a full gallop. She wore an expensive, professional suit; her hair short and perfectly coifed. An expensive watch and huge diamond ring dressed her hand. Her eyes were defiantly angry and hostile.

"Excuse me!" the furious woman said to Gallagher then turned toward the woman with whom he had attempted a dialogue. "Liz, don't say anything to this man."

"And you are who, ma'am?" inquired Gallagher.

"Who I am is frankly none of your business. What is important is that I am an attorney with Hartson, Bennett, and Lang, and I'm fully aware of our rights under the law." The woman turned again toward the first. "Thank goodness I stumbled into the church when I did, Liz. Apparently this man has been harassing other members of the parish about Sachs. Rachel was very upset when I saw her minutes ago, and she informed me that he was coming over here to continue with you. I rushed right over."

Although Gallagher was now beyond the pale, he sequestered his primal reaction momentarily to attempt a parlay. "Ma'am, I'm not sure where your emotion is drawn from, but I can assure you that nothing of the sort you're now accusing me of has occurred. I am merely here to inquire—"

"We are all fully aware of why you are here, Detective. And I can say with total confidence that neither myself nor Liz has anything to provide you."

Gallagher set lose his inner dogs. *Enough of this nonsense,* he thought. "First, ma'am, I'm here on an official investigation into the death of Father Edward Sachs, SJ. Second, I don't give a rat's ass where you work or how prestigious your firm is. Third, I've been given plenary authority by the pastor, Father Damien Thomas, to investigate any aspect of this parish I deem necessary. Finally, you can walk out that door, or I can either have Father Thomas escort you off the premises or call in a squad car to take you downtown to face charges of interfering with an official police investigation. Your choice, lady!"

The woman looked as though she would collapse on the spot. It was clear to Gallagher that she was used to getting her way. The woman said nothing, composed herself, and gracefully left the Center for Liturgy.

As Gallagher turned toward the woman behind the desk, he noticed she too was nearly white and clearly intimidated as a result of his assertion of authority. "You're Liz then, I take it?"

The woman nodded hesitantly then spoke with clear deference. "Yes. Elizabeth Connor. I work here as the executive assistant to Father Jacobs of Georgetown University, who leads this Center. How may I help you?"

His ire now cooled, Gallagher asked about Father Sachs. Elizabeth Connor informed him that the priest had been a very charming man and that he had often utilized the Center's library for his research. She stood and pointed to a row of three small, wooden study carrels. "It's the one on the right," she informed him. "Feel free to look around, and let me know if there's anything else I can assist you with."

"Thank you," said Gallagher, as he walked over and sat down at the carrel reserved for Father Sachs's personal use.

The carrel was full with materials and the upper shelf lined with books. The tabletop inside the carrel contained neatly stacked papers of no particular importance, Gallagher thought. He combed through the papers, finding only information on church statistics: the number of American and worldwide adherents to Roman Catholicism, Mass attendance figures, the draft of an instruction manual for altar boys, and a full roster of names of the same.

He also noticed the articles on the recently permitted use of the old Latin or Tridentine Mass, which the Pope had been vigorously advocating. He found more statistics on vocations as well as demographics on the student body at nearby Georgetown University and other Catholic institutions of higher learning, including his own alma mater, Fordham University in New York. Nothing struck him as unusual.

After thirty minutes, Gallagher stumbled across a DVD that was marked with what appeared to be another code, written with a black marker—"Ref: 4 C004S." Curious, Gallagher pulled a small laptop from his attaché and turned it on. The DVD whirled after he inserted it. Gallagher pulled out his earphones, plugged them in, and turned up the volume. The video had been semi-professionally edited, he could tell, when a title popped up *An Easter Celebration of the Eucharist at St. Gabriel Parish.*

The video appeared to be shot from the balcony of the main church from where he had just come. Contemporary piano music played as the processional got underway. Gallagher was somewhat surprised by what he watched. Down the main aisle of the church came what appeared to be ballet dancers in white leotards. The dancers were being led, and followed behind, by men and women who waved long, flexible plastic poles with colored streamers attached.

To Gallagher, the scene was more reminiscent of rhythmic gymnastics from the Olympics than the beginning of a Roman Catholic Mass. He looked on as Father Damien Thomas came into focus on the screen, walking behind the dancers and banner bearers, shaking hands and hugging members of the congregation, as if he were running for office. The video continued.

After some ten minutes of processional theatrics, the camera zoomed in on Father Thomas standing above the main altar "bench" flanked by two older women wearing white robes. The faces came in clearer now, and Gallagher could see the dour face of Elizabeth Connor as one of the two acolytes. He raised his eyebrows then subtly glanced at Connor where she now sat just feet away. She was watching him intently. Gallagher forced an awkward, closed-mouth smile and turned back to the laptop screen.

He quickly shut off the video and slipped the DVD into his bag after Connor finally moved and walked over to the bookshelf on the other side of the room.

Okay, then, Gallagher said sardonically to himself. He looked up again at the books.

The choice of books seemed to be tied to the other materials Gallagher had reviewed. There were books on Church statistics, some older volumes on the Second Vatican Council, and newer ones that commented on the liturgical reform that had flowed from it.

He continued to look at the remaining volumes for a minute more, noticing that one author held a prominence on Father Sachs's reading list—*Lest We Go Before*, a book that focused on instilling spirituality in young Catholics; *Vatican II and the Promise of a New Era*, which explored the liturgical reforms of The Second Vatican Council; and *God's Open Hand*, a discussion on women and homosexuals within the Catholic Church. Gallagher noted the author as one Clarence J. Symanski, SJ.

The detective opened his attaché to retrieve the just-reviewed DVD and the daily planner he'd taken from Father Sachs's room. The initials "C" and "S," found on the DVD and in the planner schedule, were there, but the "004" gave him pause. Brushing the thought aside, he slipped the three books from the shelf, tossed them into his bag, and pulled his cell phone out to check for any messages from Ty Johnson. There was nothing, yet.

Before Gallagher could stand and make a wanted exit, a hand from behind unexpectedly and forcefully grabbed him.

Chapter 9

Peter Gallagher jumped as the hand touched his shoulder, his nerves on edge from the morning's interactions and still tired from the two previous late nights. His mind calmed instantly, as he viewed an extremely attractive young woman smiling widely. She was in her mid-twenties, with blond hair tucked behind her ears, highlighting understated but expensive pearl earrings. She wore a light blue Lacoste polo shirt and a casual khaki-colored skirt that went well with a physique that resembled that of a swimmer or tennis player or both.

"Hello," said the woman. "I'm sorry for frightening you."

"Not at all." Gallagher was immediately drawn to her wide smile and natural beauty. "I'm Peter Gallagher."

"I'm told you're here looking into the death of Father Sachs," the woman said. "Liz Connor just told me. I was dropping off some stuff from the Center that I found while cleaning my classroom this morning, before leaving for summer vacation. The children are done with the school year."

"You're a teacher then?"

"Yes, fourth grade. Just finished my first year of teaching," said the woman before continuing. "I'm sorry. Where are my manners? I'm Laura Miller. I teach over in the lower school." She paused. "Father Sachs's death was truly tragic for this parish and the school. The children adored him."

Elizabeth Connor watched the two as they spoke, her aging face showing open disapproval.

Twenty minutes later at a small coffee shop down the street, Gallagher and Laura Miller sat chatting pleasantly together. Gallagher hadn't learned much about Father Sachs since sitting down with Miller ten minutes before, their conversation largely having been focused on Laura's students and how challenging her first year of teaching had been. Although he had only known Miller for a few short minutes, he felt he could confide in her. She was poised and sophisticated; extremely sharp and polished, but Gallagher was struck at how down-to-earth and relaxed she appeared to him. She gave off not a hint of pretentiousness, although, from what Gallagher had gathered, she was the product of an extremely affluent and privileged upbringing.

Gallagher sipped his coffee, which had gone lukewarm. "Laura, you said earlier that the children adored Father Sachs. Can you tell me more about that?"

"Down to business now, hey, Detective?" responded Laura with another of her trademark smiles that melted Gallagher. He looked down to avoid betraying his admission.

"I've got to tell you, Laura, you're the first and only person from the parish I've enjoyed talking with so far. And I figure you might be able to offer some better insight than what I've been given already." Gallagher paused. "But please call me Peter."

Laura took a sip of her coffee. "Like I said, Peter, the children adored Father Sachs. He'd only been with the parish for about a year prior to my starting with the school. He was immensely interested in the students: their studies, their sports, their spiritual development. By the time I arrived to teach, Father Sachs had coached the boys' basketball team to its first championship ever and was turning the girls' team into a powerhouse as well. The girls made it to the semifinals of the playoffs this year, and Father Sachs promised them a championship to match the boys next year. He was a hell of an athlete, and the boys especially idolized him.

"Father Sachs was also very much involved with the students' academic development and always stressed the need for excellence, whether on the playing fields or in the classroom. The children responded and were motivated to learn." Laura began to soften and cleared her throat, as the emotion welled up.

Gallagher interjected. "So it would seem that Father Sachs had a very positive influence on the parish? However, I sensed a clear sense of hostility in some of the people I talked with this morning when I mentioned Father Sachs by name."

Laura's face became stern and serious. "I'm sure there was," she said. "Father Sachs had caused a great deal of discomfort to a number of people in the parish, and there was a move afoot to have him transferred."

"What do you mean?" inquired Gallagher.

"Well, for one, he thought it a good idea to begin having the school boys serve at Mass."

"Not sure I follow. As an old altar boy myself, I don't see the problem."

"Father Sachs began to recruit boys from the school as altar servers, and there was a surprising flood of interest. As I said before, Peter, the schoolboys idolized him. Father Sachs began to train the boys to serve at school Masses, and the interest and pool of available boys became so abundant that he began to utilize them for weekday and Sunday Masses that he celebrated at the parish."

"And this caused a problem?"

"Not at first, until some individuals at the parish began to realize this was here to stay. Father Sachs had limited the service on the altar, when he celebrated Mass, to just boys, no girls. He also undertook an effort to provide each boy with his own black cassock and white surplus—an effort he funded out of his own pocket when the parish refused to do so. There were ruffled feathers to say the least."

"You mean it was a threat to the parish agenda?"

"Well, yes. There were calls from angry parents of girls, asking why their daughters weren't able to join the spirited army of Father Sachs's altar boys. There were complaints from a number of women at the parish who were serving as adult acolytes. They saw the effort as a threat. Father Thomas, the pastor, was under fire, but he had little ground to stand on from a Canon Law perspective—Father Sachs was a trained lawyer and well within the rules of the Church to limit the servers for his Masses to boys, and there was no Church prohibition on the wearing of cassock and surplus."

Laura continued, "The situation got even worse when a Turkish diplomat called to complain that one day his son—a student in the fifth grade—had come back home to the Washington embassy after school and informed his father that, not only did he want to convert to Catholicism in order to serve as an altar boy but also wanted to become a priest like Father Sachs."

"I see." Gallagher changed course. "What about this Committee for Liturgy? I met a Rachel Goldman-Scott this morning at the church. She wasn't a friendly lady."

Laura laughed. "Yes, that was another sore spot."

"Tell me."

"Well, Father Sachs wasn't a fan of the Center or the Committee for Liturgy. But more important, he had a great passion for traditional church architecture. He had been researching in the parish archives."

"Researching what?"

"He was looking at the original designs of the parish buildings—the original church and the current main church, mostly. Father would oftentimes bring in pictures to show the students of the interior of the churches before they were renovated. He was working on a campaign to restore the interior of both churches to their historic integrity."

"And I take it this was perceived as another threat?" asked Gallagher.

"Like no other. You see, he wasn't only a smart man but also a charming one. He had begun to gain some preliminary support for the project. He even had some pledges to donate considerable sums, should the project get approval. So for women like Rachel Goldman, Father Sachs was the devil incarnate."

"Ms. Goldman-Sachs said she was the head of the St. Gabriel Jewish Society. Is she a Jewish convert to Catholicism?"

"Oh, heavens no. Their connection to the parish is through their spouses, who are Catholics. Rachael Goldman is the wife of Congressman Perry Scott from Connecticut."

Laura chuckled as she noticed the blank look on Gallagher's face and reached over and put her hand on his arm. "You look lost, Peter. Let me try and help explain a little better. My family has been members of this parish forever and a day."

Over the next hour, Laura had all but confirmed Gallagher's theory on motive in the death of Father Sachs. It was clear that Sachs had likely been a marked man.

Gallagher glanced at his watch and was shocked at how much time had passed without his realizing it. "Let me ask you this, Laura. Please don't take this the wrong way, but you don't seem to fit the profile of someone who's a part of this parish. Quite frankly, why are you still working there? I realize I'm not a practicing Catholic, but I did grow up in the Church and, to be quite honest, the parish seems to go out of its way to be almost anti-Catholic. Why hasn't the archdiocese stepped in and simply removed the Jesuits from the parish?"

"Wow!" said Laura. "That's quite the list."

"I'm sorry. That didn't come out right."

"Don't be. Those are fair questions, and I agree with you. Part of my decision to work at St. Gabriel was that I was a student there too. In fact, I've received all of my education over the last two decades within a three-mile radius of where we're sitting—first as a student at St. Gabriel, then high school at Georgetown Visitation just up the street, and then at Georgetown University for my undergraduate and graduate degree in teaching.

"My four older sisters were also students at St. Gabriel, and this was the parish we attended on Sundays with our parents. Some of the stories my sisters tell of those years in the late seventies and early eighties—which I have no recollection of—are downright weird, if you ask me: circus performances at Mass, rock bands, rabbis and imams doing the homilies. But those were the times, I guess. But I also had faith that things would change. Father Sachs was the embodiment of that hope for me.

"As to why no one has been able to do anything officially, the archdiocese is in a difficult position and has been for many years. On the one hand, they have real and—if you ask me—justifiable concerns about what goes on here. On the other hand, St. Gabriel has one of the most educated and affluent groups of parishioners in the city. I've already told you about the son of the Turkish diplomat and Congressman Scott. That is just the tip of the iceberg.

The parish is replete with powerful lawyers, doctors, and political appointees. You name it. And they have big wallets and lots of clout."

Gallagher took a moment to digest this information. "So your father must be a senator then?" he asked tongue in cheek.

"No," she said with another characteristic smile of bright white, perfect teeth and the genuine warmth coming from striking blue eyes. "Actually he's the ambassador to Ireland."

Shock poured over Gallagher's face as Laura laughed out loud. "You're serious," he stated.

Laura just smiled. "Yep. My family is part of the power base for St. Gabriel's cloak of apparent theological invincibility."

Gallagher laughed then turned serious. "Laura—" he began to ask before she interrupted him.

"Yes, I'll help you on this case. More important, I think you're right."

"That the parish is anti-Catholic?" Gallagher asked lightheartedly.

"I meant something else," said Laura with a look so serious it made Gallagher nervous.

"Right about what, then?"

"That Father Sachs was murdered."

Chapter 10

A distinguished and impeccably dressed older man sat without emotion, looking at the hired giant who sat before him. "So you did not find it, then?"

The hulk of a man sat rigidly. "No. It was not in the room."

The well-dressed man pondered the answer in silence. "And what about this detective?"

"He's asking many questions but seems to be finding no answers."

"So the police have nothing, correct?"

"Correct."

"Then this may just go away for the time being. We can't even be sure that it even still exists," said the gentleman, thinking. "But in the end, we must be certain."

The giant said nothing and waited for his orders.

"Make sure the police come up empty, and then wait for further instructions."

"Yes, sir," the giant grunted.

"But if they do get onto the scent…" The well-dressed man quieted then looked at the giant and answered the question on his massive face. "Then we may need to remove them as well."

Chapter 11

The picture that had developed in Peter Gallagher's head as he drove back to the station from Georgetown troubled him, and he had no idea how he would deal with it other than to dig deeper, if he could. He had made the most of the first half of the couple days he had left to find a thread—any thread—that could point to what both he, and now Laura Miller, suspected as the cause of Father Sachs's death.

Gallagher was jolted from his thoughts by the sound of a screeching car as his own ran a red light on M Street. He dialed Ty Johnson.

"Johnson."

"Ty, it's Pete. What do you have?" said Gallagher, now keeping a closer eye on the traffic in front of him.

"Pete, finally. Been trying to reach you for the last hour. I was worried when you didn't pick up. You okay?"

"Yeah. I was working on some leads." Gallagher faulted himself for not monitoring his phone while he had been with Laura. "What do you have?"

"I got an opportunity to meet with a Monsignor Quinn over at the archbishop's office. The file on St. Gabriel is four inches thick—and that's just one of the files. Seems like our preliminary research the other night was just a taste, but an accurate one. Over the years there have been numerous investigations that include dissident priests, liturgical irregularities, and even questions regarding the school's curriculum. The archdiocese wouldn't share the files, and without a warrant, the best I could do was take notes. The monsignor was generous with his information, though. Too much to tell you on the phone. You on your way back soon?"

"In the car now. Look, what about the other priests?"

"No time yet, partner. It was too early to call the priest on the West Coast before I went over to the archdiocese. I need to track down the priest from St. Gabriel who's in Rome. The one in Africa is going to be tough, as I assume he's in the bush somewhere. I'll work on them this afternoon."

"What's Drexler's schedule look like?"

"He's here. Busy as hell," said Johnson.

"Okay. Let's grab him when I get there."

"You get something over at the parish, Pete?"

Gallagher chuckled. "You could say that." He shifted tone. "We need a sit-down with the boss to compare notes before he gets a chance to reconsider his decision to let us continue with this investigation. Considering what we have so far, it may buy us some more time."

"You sound pretty intense, Pete."

"That priest was killed," responded Gallagher. "I can feel it."

Chapter 12

That night, Peter Gallagher awoke at a little past eight thirty, on the couch in his apartment in Northwest Washington. One of the books by Clarence Symanski lay open on his chest, and a spot of wet saliva lay next to his head. He sat in a fog for only a moment before realizing he must have dozed off.

Captain Drexler's stern mood when Gallagher and Ty Johnson had sat down with him earlier that day had remained tense. His quick temper fired several times as Gallagher explained to him where he thought things were heading on the case. But Drexler had given the two detectives just another forty-eight hours before sending them home to get some rest. Gallagher was more than grateful for both the reprieve and the rest, he thought, as he pulled himself into a seated position and rubbed his hands over his eyes.

The two Symanski books Gallagher had digested over the last few hours now bounced through his head and painted a more complete picture of the current state of the Roman Catholic Church and the Jesuits in particular. It was a picture more akin to a political party than a religion, he assessed—a rationale for finding God and meaning through society and laying out reasons why God had failed the same. Gallagher assumed that Father Sachs had been studying these ideas and this modern thinking for some reason, and it was perhaps the reason he was killed. Even so, the whole thing made little sense.

Gallagher picked up the phone while thumbing through more of the book he had been reading.

"Hello."

"Laura? Hi, Pete Gallagher."

"I was wondering when you would call, but I didn't think you would call so soon. How are things going with the case?"

"Slowly," he said, now coming to the realization that perhaps his case was sputtering out. "Are you free tomorrow?"

"Yes. I think so. Summer vacation and all that."

"Good. Can we meet at the parish? Say, around nine?"

"And I thought you were calling me for a date," Laura said with a giggle. "Sure. What do you want to do?"

"Ah, er, I...," stumbled Gallagher, a bit taken aback by Laura's comment that rushed to his face in a flush. He worked to shift back to the purpose of his call and avoid over-complicating things any more that they had to be—at least for the time being. "Do you have access to the parish archives you mentioned? The place where Father Sachs was doing his work on the parish buildings?"

"Yes. I can get us in. I have a key." Laura's voice grew more serious. "Why don't we meet in the Center for Liturgy and then we can walk over to the parish archives?"

"On second thought, can we meet at the coffee shop instead? I think it would be better to keep my return visit quiet, especially after my not-so-warm welcome yesterday. We can sit and chat, and I can tell you what I'm looking for so we can get in and out of the archives as quickly as possible," Gallagher said.

"Okay. It's a date. Nine it is. See you then."

"Thanks, Laura. Goodnight." He waited a second after ending his call with Laura before dialing again.

Ty Johnson picked up on the second ring. "Pete, that you? You woke me up, you shit."

"Sorry, partner. I dozed off myself. Just got up. I need you to track down someone."

"Sachs case?" Johnson asked, already knowing the answer.

"Yeah, but I need you to do it quietly."

"Okay, who now?" asked Johnson, reaching for a pad and pen.

"It's another priest. Symanski, Clarence John, SJ." Gallagher glanced at the back of one of the Symanski books. "He may be local. Check around."

"You and your fucking priests. All right. But what's with all the cloak and dagger? Why don't we just do a normal shakedown through the computers?"

"I learned my lesson today over at the parish. Walk softly and carry no visible stick. I don't want to tip anyone off. Too many prying eyes and angry people already, and I don't want to give Drexler any excuse to shut this investigation down prematurely."

"I got you," said Johnson. "Can it wait until the a.m.? I'm shot."

"No problem. Call me on my cell when you get the info," said Gallagher sympathetically. "Thanks, Ty. I appreciate all of this."

"All part of the contract," said Johnson. "By the way, I got a call back from a Father Desoto in California. Wants me to call him back tomorrow. Also, I got a scheduled call with the priest in Rome—Clifford—at seven a.m. our time."

"Let me know what they say. What about the priest in Uganda?"

"No luck on Father Benjamin. My guess is he's going to be a no-go, but I'll try the American Embassy over there and see if they know how to get a hold of him. If that doesn't work, I think it's a dead-end. Sorry."

"Well, just see what you can get. That's all we can do. Get some sleep."

"I was trying. Later."

Gallagher put down the phone and picked up the Symanski book he had been reading when he had fallen asleep. His thoughts drifted to his own days under the tutelage of the Jesuits at Fordham Prep and the last time he had practiced his own Catholic faith with any certainty.

But Peter Gallagher couldn't really remember when there had been any real certainty nor, more introspectively, why there hadn't been.

Chapter 13

Laura Miller looked even more beautiful than Gallagher had remembered when she arrived at the coffee shop at a little past nine Friday morning wearing a yellow coat and green rubber boots. Her hair was wet from the rain that had descended on Washington just after midnight. She smiled as she spotted Gallagher, shaking off the rain from her coat and stomping her feet on the mat just inside the door.

"Well, hello there, Mr. Detective," said Laura, fastening her umbrella closed and tossing a small backpack into an empty chair at the table. "What's with this rain?"

"How are you?" Gallagher asked, his stomach in knots like a schoolboy on a first date. "I got you a coffee…cream no sugar."

"Soaked," Laura said. "Oh, you're a sweetheart. Thank you. You okay?"

"A bit tired, but I'll make it. Thanks again for meeting on such short notice. I hope you didn't have to change your plans."

"Not at all. My schedule is free for the next couple of days—trying to unwind and all that." Laura sipped at the coffee. "It's good to see you again. In fact this is all rather exciting given the circumstances. So what do we need to do today, sir? I'm all yours."

Ten minutes later, Gallagher and Laura shared an umbrella as they walked down the street toward the parish, both quietly enjoying the closeness but careful not to let the other know.

When they turned into the parish driveway, the area where Father Sachs had met his death was surprisingly busy. A flower truck was unloading its contents, and a catering van was attempting to enter. Gallagher spotted Father

Thomas at a distance, running in the side entrance to the church after holding the door open for one of the flower shop's delivery boys who was carrying a large arrangement.

"The funeral is tomorrow," Laura said. "So much for the quiet and unnoticed arrival."

"I should have thought about that."

"Come on, Mr. Detective," Laura said with another subtle smile as she tucked her arm under Gallagher's and led him quickly toward a door to the Parish Center, which was located directly behind the rectory. "No one is going to notice us with all this activity going on."

Gallagher took notice of the modern architecture of the Parish Center. "Looks like a new building."

"Yeah," said Laura. "They finished it about a year ago. Took over a year to build. Expensive too. But as I told you yesterday, the parish has plenty of deep pockets."

"Evidently," said Gallagher. Laura kept control of his pace and direction as they slipped quietly into a small hallway.

"I think we made it unnoticed," said Laura. "Another thirty minutes and this place will be really busy. I think the funeral reception will be held in this building." Laura let go of Gallagher's arm and pulled down the hood of her raincoat. "This way." Gallagher followed.

At the end of the hallway, Laura opened a door using one of the keys on her ring. The door led to a concrete landing from which a metal spiral staircase led down below. "This goes to the basement where the archives are," she said.

"This isn't part of the new construction, is it?" asked Gallagher.

"No. This has been here for a while. They reinforced the floor and installed a climate-control system when they built the new Parish Center, but other than that, this part of the parish is original." She pulled a flashlight from her pocket and guided them down the stairwell. "It's pretty spooky down here. Not much light."

"I see you came prepared."

"Done this before. Father Sachs took the class down here once or twice. The kids thought it was cool. Careful, Peter. These metal steps get slick when they're wet."

"Yes, ma'am."

"Good, now we're getting along real well."

Gallagher smirked to himself. The air at the bottom of the staircase was dry and refreshingly cool. A heavy wooden door stood before them and a smaller metal door secured with a padlock sat adjacent. "I would've expected it to be pretty damp down here," he said.

"Well, it should be, but they installed a dehumidifier." Laura pulled her key ring out and began to open the wooden door as Gallagher noticed the ventilation system that must have been a part of the climate control. "Got it," she said, as she opened the door and turned on the overhead lights.

The room was surprisingly large, with metal shelves nine feet high lining the room. Boxes were stacked neatly on the shelves. Gallagher wondered why such an old part of the parish should be so large given the depth. "This is quite a place. Rather impressive considering its age and how far below ground we must be."

Laura stood with Gallagher while he looked around the room. "Yeah, it is pretty impressive. Apparently this was part of the famous Underground Railroad used to ferry slaves from Maryland, Virginia, and the District of Columbia up North."

Gallagher looked at Laura with a sense of amazement.

"Surprising, I know," she said. "There are supposed to be all sorts of little tunnels and hiding places down here, although that seems to be largely legend—I haven't seen any. Still, when they dug the foundation for the Parish Center a couple of years ago, they found the remains of buried slaves. And in the old church—what used to be the convent—the upper balcony was reserved for slaves so they could attend Sunday Mass. Here. Let me show you."

Laura threw off her raincoat and hung it on a nail in the cinderblock wall. "Put your coat there, and follow me."

Gallagher did as told then followed Laura around a corner and over to a wooden worktable. Laura pulled a string to a single-bulb light above. "This is where Father Sachs used to sit and go through photos and do his research." She pointed to a picture clipped to a corkboard hanging above the table. "This was taken just after the start of the Civil War." The picture showed what appeared to be a group of African Americans standing on a balcony above a congregation of well-dressed white parishioners.

"Amazing," said Gallagher. "I'm very impressed. This is like a private history tour."

Laura tucked her hair behind her ears and looked at Gallagher. "What?" she asked, as Gallagher stared at her without knowing it.

"Sorry." He blushed and turned away from Laura. "What was Father Sachs interested in down here?"

Laura smiled coyly. "Well, as I told you, Father Sachs largely worked on his church architecture project down here, but there are all sorts of other records here as well. Financial data, sacramental records—you name it. However, as you can see, Father Sachs wasn't the type to leave his work scattered about. There are no boxes here."

"How do you know what he was working on?"

"Follow me." Laura slid past Gallagher and walked around the corner into an aisle flanked by two stacks of tall shelving and seemingly hundreds of boxes. "Father was pretty secretive at times. He didn't like people to know what records he was delving into. That was pretty smart, if you ask me. Why bring unwanted scrutiny on himself, especially when everyone was looking for a reason to get him transferred out of here?" She walked down the row and glanced to the left and right.

"Well, then, how do you know what you're looking for?"

"One time I caught Father Sachs off guard when he was restacking some boxes. We sort of had an understanding that I would keep his filing system to myself. We trusted each other." Laura fixed her gaze on a box that seemed no different than all the others that lined the shelves. "Here! You see?"

"What am I looking at?" asked Gallagher.

Laura pointed to a step stool. "Do me a favor, Peter, and bring that over here."

Gallagher moved the step stool over to Laura. She stood on it and pointed to a box on the third shelf. "You see that? That little cross cut into the box?" Gallagher squinted and then noticed a mark that looked like it had been made with a penknife. "Father did that to the boxes he was working with," she said. "Here, help me get this down."

Peter Gallagher and Laura Miller spent nearly three hours below ground poring through boxes of materials that were marked with the elusive symbol. Gallagher remained convinced, as they went through the materials, that they would find something that would shed light on someone who might have had a reason to murder the young priest. After they entered the fourth hour, however, both Gallagher and Laura became increasingly tired and hungry and didn't have a single lead.

Gallagher stood on the step stool and placed one of the boxes into the precise location from which it had come. It was heavy, and he was having difficulty wedging it between the two others that had flanked it on the shelf. He moved an adjacent box, and it fell to the floor.

"Shit," he said as his patience gave way some more.

Laura ran around the corner to see the box's contents lying on the floor. "What the hell are you doing? Trying to get yourself killed?"

"Help me pick this up. I think we're done."

After a few minutes, the contents of the fallen box were back inside and the lid secured. Gallagher picked up the box and started to slide it back into place in front of another that sat directly behind. He squinted as Laura looked on.

"Well, are you going to put it back up there or not, Mr. Detective? We should clean up and get out of here. You can buy me lunch." Laura looked curious when Gallagher didn't respond immediately but kept his focus.

"Hand me your flashlight," he said.

Laura pulled the light from her back pocket and handed it up. "What is it?"

"You sure we've gone through all of the boxes that Father Sachs marked?" He turned on the flashlight.

"Pretty sure. We put back all the boxes already. I didn't see any others," responded Laura, her curiosity now visible.

Gallagher threw the flashlight down to Laura, who caught it without thinking. He struggled to reach the box handle. He took a foothold precariously on one of the lower shelves and reached further.

"Peter, be careful. Don't bring down the entire shelf."

"Got it," Gallagher said, his breathing a bit heavy. He slid the box forward and pulled it down.

"What is it?"

"Another Sachs box. But this one has *two* small crosses on it."

"Well, I'll be damned. What good little eyes you have."

Gallagher and Laura carried the box to the worktable and opened it, both of them equally anxious as to what might be inside.

"Just more pictures," said Laura, picking one up. "Here. This is the old church. Here's another of the rectory." She turned the picture over. "1862, it says."

Gallagher dumped the contents onto the worktable and tossed the box on the floor as Laura began to spread the materials out before them.

"Oh, my gosh," said Laura, as she pulled out a photo from the pile. Gallagher looked over. "This is a picture of my father from the 1970s. Would you look at those sideburns?"

"Who's he standing with?"

"I'm not sure." Laura turned the picture over. "Says here: Father Murray Gibbons, Mr. Richard Miller, Congressman John Duffy, Senator Forbes Raybeck, and Glenn Hartson."

"Hartson?" said Gallagher. "He's not a lawyer by any chance, is he?"

"Yes, I think he was. He's dead. His father was a founding partner of Hartson, Bennett, and something."

"Lang."

"How do you know that?"

"Part of my parish 'orientation' yesterday. I'll tell you later. It's not important," said Gallagher, as he pulled out another photograph.

"Here's one of Father Thomas," said Laura. "Boy, he was young when this was taken. Looks like some sort of vacation picture…like a safari or something. There are palm trees everywhere."

Gallagher examined the photo of Father Thomas, who stood posing with two other men and a young boy. All were wearing tropical clothes. Two of the men, including Thomas, had long hair and scraggly beards. And one of them, who stood beside Thomas, looked familiar. "What does it say on the back?"

"Nothing here." Laura took a closer look at the photo. "This older guy is Father O'Brien."

"And who is he?"

"A former St. Gabriel pastor. He baptized me. He was the pastor here from the late 1960s to early 1980s. He died a few years back."

"You recognize anyone else?"

"Can't say that I do. This other young guy next to Father Thomas looks familiar," said Laura, "although I can't place him right now."

Gallagher's mind triggered. He reached down and pulled *Lest We Go Before* from his bag and handed it to Laura. "Does this help?" She looked at the cover then turned the book over. The resemblance to the author's photo was immediate.

"Father Symanski. This guy used to teach at Georgetown long before I got there. Sort of a nut, I was told," Laura said. "Where did you get this?"

"From Sachs's carrel in the Center for Liturgy."

The sound of feet moving down the metal spiral stairs echoed into the archives room. Gallagher and Laura looked at each other quickly before Gallagher began to shove the contents on the worktable into his bag.

"Here. Let me do that!" Laura said nervously. "Get the box back on the shelf, now."

Gallagher grabbed the empty box and dashed around the corner and into the aisle from which it had come. He ascended the step stool and moved to place the top on the box. He looked inside to ensure that he and Laura had taken all the contents. It was indeed empty. The door to the archives opened, but Gallagher wasn't visible to the entrant.

"Ms. Miller?" asked a voice.

"Father Thomas, so good to see you. What brings you down here this morning?" asked Laura.

"I should ask you the same question," Father Thomas responded. "Is someone else here?" he yelled out to the room.

Gallagher fumbled with the box before getting it back in place. He descended the step stool and moved it away from where he had been using it, while he answered, "Father Thomas, is that you? It's Peter Gallagher." he rounded the corner from the archive aisle and faced Father Thomas directly. "So good to see you. Ms. Miller was just showing me some of the old pictures of the parish. Very impressive."

Father Thomas wasn't duped by Gallagher's puerile attempt at innocence. "Detective, I thought we were clear that your presence at the parish was to include prior notice to my office." He turned toward Laura, her face now ashen. "I came down here to find some pictures of Father Sachs for the funeral reception tomorrow and, instead, find one of my grade school teachers giving unauthorized access to confidential parish records."

The young teacher attempted another explanation. "Father—"

Thomas interrupted coolly and with calculation. "Ms. Miller, I'm not interested in your thoughts on this matter. In fact I am most disappointed, especially considering your parents' lifelong affiliation with this parish and your own present service to it."

Miller and Gallagher said nothing, as Father Thomas, focused on Gallagher, continued. "Detective Gallagher, the DC Police will be hearing from our attorneys this afternoon, and your access to the parish is hereby revoked."

The priest turned back to Laura. "And you, Ms. Miller…it is my sad duty to suspend you from your position with the school. Final determination as to your future with us will be made before the start of the upcoming academic year."

Laura bit her lip, picked up her bag, and rushed out of the archives and up the stairs.

Gallagher moved slowly to the empty worktable and grabbed his bag without saying a word. He walked toward Father Thomas and stopped. "Father, this is my fault. There's no need to punish Ms. Miller for showing me your parish history."

"I'll make that decision in due course, Mr. Gallagher. In the meantime I suggest you start worrying about yourself."

Chapter 14

With as much dignity as he could muster, Peter Gallagher walked out of the St. Gabriel parish archives and out into an overcast sky. Laura wasn't in sight, but the activity around the parish grounds remained steady as preparations were carried out for the funeral of Father Edward Sachs.

Gallagher knew he had screwed up by not following the protocol he had agreed to with Father Thomas, but in many ways, he was glad he had done so. He quickly shelved those thoughts as his concentration focused on where Laura might have gone and what brining her into his work may mean for her future.

He walked out onto the sidewalk and down the street. He stopped at the coffee shop and looked through the large glass window. The tables were nearly empty, Laura not among the few who occupied them. He looked back up the sidewalk from where he had come then pulled out his dwindling packet of cigarettes. "I'm in trouble," he muttered, exhaling smoke.

"You got one for me?" asked Laura, who appeared from nowhere, catching Gallagher off guard.

"Laura. I'm so sorry. I shouldn't have gotten you into all of this. Are you going to be okay?"

"I'm a big girl. And I knew what I was getting into." She took a cigarette that Gallagher offered and then lit for her. "It's not your fault."

"I'm afraid it is. And my guess is this is going to get worse."

Laura placed her hand on his arm. "We'll work it out…together." She smiled then shifted focus. "In the meantime what are we going to do with all the stuff we took?"

"I don't know. Now that I think about it, we just committed larceny. I had no warrant for these."

"Well, no one knows we have this."

"I do. It was wrong."

"You *are* a serious sort, Detective Peter Gallagher."

"It keeps me safe. Or at least it used to."

The cell phone in Gallagher's pocket rang. He pulled it out and glanced at the incoming number. "Christ. The office." He answered, "Gallagher."

"Pete. It's Ty. I talked to the priest in Rome. Clifford. Not a big fan of Father Sachs. Apparently the two went head-to-head more than once. Big intellectuals, both of them. They had some spirited debates. Other than that, he was very complimentary about Sachs and seemed genuinely upset over his death. It was the same with Desoto in California. Got a hold of him about thirty minutes ago. Similar conversation. Nothing there."

"What about the priest in Africa?"

"Incommunicado. No one knows where exactly he is in Uganda. I left a message with the American Embassy in Kampala, but they can't really do anything for us other than diplomatically note the request. I'll check with them again in a day or so."

"Thanks, Ty," said Gallagher.

"By the way, that priest you wanted me to check on, Symanski—I called the Archdiocese again and talked with Monsignor Quinn. I thought since he was so helpful yesterday, he might be able to shed some light on the matter… and do it quietly."

"What did you find?"

"You were right. Symanski is local. He's retired and living at Georgetown University's Jesuit community. Apparently he had some sort of a nervous breakdown a couple of years ago. He doesn't take visitors."

"Okay, thanks. I owe you one."

"You coming into the station?"

Gallagher, nervous, wanted to avoid showing his face for the time being. "Not yet. Still working on some things here at the parish."

"Okay, then, partner. Call me when you can. I'm not sure how long I can hold off Captain Drexler. I've got another shooting this morning to look into. College kid got killed outside a nightclub. I've got to run and cover for Evan Branch who took off to take his kid to summer camp."

"When does it end?" said Gallagher.

"It doesn't, Pete. That's part of the contract."

"All right. Hang in there. Oh, Ty. Was there anything specific on where Symanski was living? A building name or anything?"

"Ryan Hall. On the Georgetown Campus."

"Thanks."

"Oh, and Pete," Johnson said before Gallagher could hang up. "I got the room number too, somewhere." Johnson fumbled with his notes.

"What is it?" asked Gallagher, as Laura shot him a quizzical look.

"Room four."

Chapter 15

It was after five p.m. when Gallagher dropped Laura off at her apartment building. They had lunched at a small restaurant on Wisconsin Avenue following their eviction from the parish archives, Laura drinking one too many glasses of wine. Gallagher was sympathetic and was frustrated that he was on duty at the time. He could have done with a few drinks himself.

Over lunch they had decided that the pictures and other materials they had smuggled in their bags would find themselves reviewed the next day, although Gallagher had ensured he had the one particular photo of the priests and the young boy for his final meeting that day. Meanwhile, Laura was in need of a good night's rest.

Tired and dejected, Gallagher summoned the resolve to press on and talk with Father Symanski—if he could find him, and if he would talk at all.

Ryan Hall was located on the campus of Georgetown University. The university was only two blocks from St. Gabriel, and the proximity gave Gallagher an uneasy feeling. He would have just as soon never venture into Georgetown again, if he could, but he knew he had to.

He arrived a little before six p.m. The sun had reappeared in the late afternoon, and the humidity was evident but tolerable as the day began its slow summer decent into dusk. There were a few people on the campus—graduate students, Gallagher surmised—but none paid him any attention. He looked down at a small handwritten map Laura had sketched for him at lunch and followed her directions.

The old, redbrick building was quiet and subdued. As Gallagher walked up to the front door, he wondered whether anyone was occupying it. There was no movement in that part of the Georgetown campus and little sound. He peered through the front-door window and spotted a desk that was unoccupied; the chair behind it was neatly pushed in and the tabletop clear, aside from an old phone. The doorbell was lit, but he hesitated to push it, noticing the flat black card reader just to its right. He thought for a moment then reached into his attaché and pulled out the pass card he had taken from Father Sachs's room the other day. He quickly looked around then swiped the card on the reader. The door unlocked itself.

"Hello. Is anyone here?"

No one answered. The building was dark inside with poor lighting, similar to interior of the St. Gabriel rectory building. The air conditioning helped to cool Gallagher's anxiousness a bit. After finding the staircase, he walked up to the next floor. There were four doors on either side. He tried the left and found two doors on one side of the hallway marked "3" and "4."

As he stood before the heavy wooden door marked "4," he heard the faint sound of classical music coming from behind it. He looked down the dim hallway to his right then knocked.

No answer. The music inside was quieted. He waited another minute then knocked again.

Thirty seconds that seemed like a lifetime slipped by without a peep. Gallagher was readying a final knock when his second attempt was finally acknowledged.

"Who is it?" a muffled voice said.

"Father Symanski?" asked Gallagher nervously.

"Who is it? How did you get up here?"

"Washington Police, Father. I need to talk with you."

"Do you have a warrant? If not, go away. Thank you for stopping by."

"Father, my name is Peter Gallagher. I need to talk with you. And no, I don't have a warrant."

"I said 'Go away.' I don't see visitors."

"Father, this is important. I'm looking into the death of Father Edward Sachs. I know he was meeting with you." Gallagher hoped his gamble would pay off, but silence met his statement. He waited.

The door opened a crack, revealing a chain lock and a dark room inside. Gallagher couldn't make out much of the man behind the door other than reading glasses perched on a noise and some white hair. The smell of scotch and tobacco was palpable.

"What do you want?"

"Father, if you could spare a few moments, I need to ask you some questions."

"The papers said Edward died in an accident."

"Yes, I know. But I think you may feel differently."

The man was silent then finally said, "Why do you say that?"

"Because I do as well."

Chapter 16

The wooden door that faced Gallagher closed briefly. He heard the sound of the chain being removed, and then the door opened again. "Come in."

The room was dark and much warmer than the air-conditioned hallway from which Gallagher had come. The air was heavy and moist; the smell of a burning cigarette mixed with the smell of sweat and alcohol. Gallagher adjusted his eyes, trying to take in the rest of the room and the man before him.

"Father Clarence Symanski?" asked Gallagher with rote formality, still trying to gather his wits and digest the cluttered and disorganized room along with the unkempt and disheveled man. The room's only light came from a single lamp under which a smoldering cigarette drew up into a yellowed shade. The window was open, Gallagher could tell, with heavy drapes blocking any light that might have dared to enter through them.

"I am," responded the priest. Gallagher reluctantly moved farther into the room, as the priest closed the door.

Symanski was tall and thin. A dirty white undershirt and black clerical trousers hung loosely on his body; his feet were bare. A wild head of thin white hair that came down like a bowl over his ears surrounded his sunken cheeks. Black-framed reading glasses sat on his nose; a chain attached to the frames dangled around his neck.

"Please sit down," said Symanski. The priest shuffled over to an old leather easy chair and threw the newspapers on its seat across the room. The chair occupied a rudimentary sitting area, including another leather chair and an antique coffee table. A half-empty bottle of expensive scotch sat on the table.

A glass with two floating ice cubes was nearly empty, guarding a half-read, cheap paperback novel.

"Thank you, Father," said Gallagher, his eyes now adjusting to the low light.

The room was much smaller than he had expected. A camp bed sat in a corner across from a desk cluttered with papers and books. Floating shelves sat above the desk, filled with more books. Another old and heavy wooden freestanding bookshelf was packed with even more. Gallagher watched as Symanski picked up his glass and settled into the brown leather chair across from him, thinking that the priest bore little resemblance to the pictures on his book covers.

"So what would you like to talk about? It's Detective Gallagher, correct?" Symanski asked, his eyes sharp and surprisingly clear.

"I'd like to talk about Father Sachs, if we could. I've been tasked to investigate his death."

"What would I know about his death?"

"Frankly, Father, I don't know. My leads are thin at best. And, from what little we have to go on, there's the likelihood that this case will be closed before we finish this conversation."

"It is Peter, isn't it?" asked the priest, topping up his drink with the bottle from the table. "Can I offer you some scotch?"

"Yes, Father. It is Peter Gallagher. And while normally I'd decline, I'm dying for a drink."

Symanski chuckled, got up from his chair, and found an extra glass. "Ice?"

"Please."

Gallagher took the glass from Symanski and waited for the priest to find his seat again. "Much appreciated, Father."

The priest sat back and pulled off his glasses, allowing them to swing freely on the chain around his neck. He gulped down half of his glass then refilled it. "Peter, it's not often that I get visitors. I have little interest in venturing out. In fact I have very little interest in most things these days."

"But you were meeting with Father Sachs before he died?"

"Yes."

"What did you discuss with him?" the detective asked.

"You mean, what did Father Sachs and I possibly have in common, other than the fact that we were both priests of the Society of Jesus?"

Sensing that Symanski's brain was sharp, Gallagher became instantly uncomfortable. "Okay."

Symanski carefully observed Gallagher's reaction then stood up again from his chair and walked to the window that was halfway open. He threw back the drapes. The unexpected action and resulting light forced Gallagher to again adjust his eyes. Ignoring the already burning cigarette under his lamp, the priest grabbed another from a crinkled pack and lit it then sat on the window ledge to allow the smoke to exit. He peered out the window in silence, smoking. "Did you know, Peter, that forty years ago there were nearly a hundred Jesuits here at Georgetown?" Symanski was quiet again, exhaling more smoke. "Now there are barely twenty."

"No, Father, I wasn't aware of that."

"The average age of a Jesuit at that time was only forty. Younger than Edward. We were all young then." He stared out the window, the sun beginning to get lower on the horizon. "Young and idealistic. Full of life." He flicked his cigarette butt out the window.

Gallagher sipped down more of his drink, trying to allow the alcohol to settle his nerves, which the old priest had tingled. He tried to bring the conversation back to the matter at hand. "Is this what you discussed with Father Sachs?"

The old priest sat down at the table and picked up his glass, looking at Gallagher with eyes that suddenly had lost their previous luster. "Gallagher. A good Irish name. My mother was an O'Hanlon. Fiery woman. Pious beyond belief but a formidable drinker as well."

"Yes, Father. My great-grandfather was an immigrant. Arrived in New York around the turn of the last century."

"Your family is Roman Catholic then, I assume?" asked Symanski, sipping his drink.

"Yes, Father. My sister and I spent grade school and high school in Catholic schools in New York. My parents were very devout."

Symanski looked at him closely. "But not you?"

Gallagher grew noticeably uncomfortable and shifted in his seat. "No, Father, I'm not a practicing Catholic."

"But your parents still are?" Symanski picked up the bottle and refilled Gallagher's glass and then, again, his own.

"Yes. They're very committed."

Symanski sat back in his chair. "Your sister? Does she practice?"

"No, Father, she doesn't." Gallagher sipped deeply on his drink. "After finishing college, she married a jerk, had two kids, and was divorced by the time she was thirty. She's largely a basket case." Gallagher was surprised at his honesty and put down his glass as a result. "As for me, after Fordham Prep and seven years at Fordham University, I took a job with the Manhattan DA's office. My father was a lawyer and a Fordham grad as well. I didn't enjoy practicing law, so I left it and New York almost a decade ago."

"I see. So you were a product of the Jesuits?"

"If we could focus on Father Sachs…"

"Is this topic uncomfortable, Peter?" Symanski moved to retrieve another cigarette. He offered one to Gallagher, who took it without thinking.

"Frankly, yes. It is." Gallagher lit his cigarette and reclaimed his drink from the table.

"But I thought you wanted to know what Father Sachs and I discussed."

Gallagher remained quiet and took a gulp of his drink as Symanski moved again to the window and drew in on his cigarette. "You see, Peter, we all have 'inflection points' in our lives. These are those rare periods when we think and reflect—oftentimes too much—on where things are, where they have gone, and where they are going." Symanski gazed at Gallagher. "For most of us, these times are only natural. They come when life shifts. The first usually comes around the age of thirty. By that time one usually has or hasn't completed formal education; they've matured; they are married or not; they have a career or not; they are fulfilled or not. The questions at this point are 'Who am I?' and 'Is where I'm going the place I thought it would be ten years ago?' I assume you had this experience, Peter, when you decided to give up the law, correct?"

The hairs on the back of Gallagher's neck stood at rigid attention. "I think that's probably true, Father."

Symanski walked away from the window, picked up his glass, and took a sip, then sat down with it in his chair. "The second period hits when we're around fifty. We have a grown family now. Our career is largely behind us. But there's still some time to plan and to dream." He took another sip. "The last is when we reach my age. We begin to ask the most troubling questions of ourselves. We ask whether what we've done in life has had meaning, if that life has produced something that we'll be proud to leave behind. We ponder our legacy and the legacy of those most important things that transcend material goods and selfish human appetites. And we must face our regrets along with the rest."

"These are the things you discussed with Father Sachs then, Father?"

"Yes." Symanski poured more scotch into his glass, his disposition becoming noticeably melancholy. Gallagher extended his own glass for a refill.

Symanski looked up after pouring some scotch into Gallagher's glass. Gallagher saw the wet lenses of his eyes, the old priest attempting to subdue them. "And I cursed Edward for forcing me to experience it."

Chapter 17

As Father Symanski explained like the seasoned professor he once was, it was a man by the name of Iñigo López de Oñaz y Loyola, more commonly known as Ignatius of Loyola, who formed a small "company" of men that became the Society of Jesus in 1540. Established from a desire to carry out the will of the Pope and defend the Holy Roman Catholic Church in the great war of Christ against Lucifer, the Jesuits—as they became known—would, arguably, grow into the most formidable force the Catholic Church has ever seen in its two-thousand-year history.

From a privileged Basque background, Ignatius of Loyola—through personal and spiritual examination and by sheer determination—built from nothing a group of men who would travel to every part of the globe…and would shape it. Shape it like a military force for the benefit of the Supreme Roman Pontiff, for whom these Jesuits took a solemn vow of obedience and loyalty. Shape it, as St. Ignatius of Loyola would famously describe, *Ad Maiorem Dei Gloriam*—For the Greater Glory of God.

For most of their elite history, the Jesuits stood as the vanguard of a Church that was under siege. Beginning with the turmoil created by the Reformation and those years following when science, math, and worldly knowledge began to challenge the spiritual sovereignty of the Roman Catholic faith, the Jesuits were there. From the palaces of European royalty to the mission fields of India and Africa and America, and into the heart of the Orient, St. Ignatius's "company" educated, ministered, and defended—even unto death—the primacy of the Catholic Faith when modern thinking threatened to undermine its timeless tenets.

The Jesuit character was forged from a martial bearing. Discipline, knowledge, and deep piety were the hallmarks of these men whose vows of poverty, chastity, and obedience transcended time and space.

Armed with superior intellect, these Jesuits became great worldly thinkers, doers, inventors, theologians, doctors, lawyers, and teachers. They built schools and hospitals and managed complex businesses. They shaped princes and peasants and captured the hearts and imaginations of a Roman Catholic Church and the world. Feared and revered, the Jesuits eventually commanded the primacy of the heart of the Roman Pontiff and became his chosen men.

From the Jesuits' formation in 1540 until the early part of the twentieth century, their character was firm and resolute—a winning formula for success that was envied and imitated by other secular organizations who saw in the Jesuits a style and ethos that could seem to do almost anything.

With their superior intellect and love of learning, the Jesuits were able to tackle challenges to the faith on the same ground that the forces against it stood. They took the battle right into the heart of the modern world, where epistemology and scientific advancement worked to bring doubt onto the Catholic Faith, threatening to extinguish it.

The arrival of the twentieth century brought change, just as the arrival of every century does. No different from the times during which St. Ignatius had formed his company of men, the twentieth century was a time of challenge for the Church. New ideas, new discoveries, new weapons of mass destruction, new roles, new countries, and new societies were now before the world and its variegated peoples. Here, in this arena, the Jesuits stood out as the logical weapon to defend the faith—just as they had always done so well since their inception, when inevitable worldly advance threatened the other worldly and timeless spiritual foundations of the Roman Catholic Church.

By the mid-twentieth century, however, the Jesuit zeal began to wane; modern thinking had steadily infiltrated the minds of even the Jesuit Order. The cracks in the once impenetrable armor of the Jesuit mentality began to reveal themselves. With the appointment of Pedro Arrupe as Father General in 1965—and the conclusion of the Second Vatican Council the same year—the

Jesuits took a new course, a course that would lead them down a perilous path with the Church and with the Supreme Roman Pontiff for whom their unquestioned loyalty was the basis of their existence.

"So you see, Peter," said Father Symanski, who to Gallagher seemingly had come to life over the last hour, "the Jesuits came to believe that the Church needed to mold itself to the world and, by so doing, they could change it for the better."

"And that's what you and Father Sachs debated over the last few months? Was this why I found all of the materials in the Center for Liturgy—materials on church demographics and statistics?"

"Probably. I'm not sure what Edward was reading specifically. But his doctoral research was focused on what he called 'a battle plan' for the Society of Jesus in the twenty-first century—a renewal of those original ideals that St. Ignatius dedicated his life to promoting."

Gallagher sat and sipped his drink, which had gone warm. "Father, excuse me for saying this, but from your books it would seem that you and Father Sachs were at polar opposites when it came to your respective views on the Church and its mission in the modern world."

Symanski leaned forward and poured the remaining drops of the bottle into his glass. "So you've read those, then?"

"I've looked at them briefly. I found your books in Father Sachs's carrel at the Center for Liturgy. Don't you hold to these ideas?"

Symanski stood up and went to the window again to smoke. It was nearly dark outside. "I thought I did, Peter." He looked out the window. "Edward was cut from a mold of Jesuit that I thought no longer existed. He questioned me, made me ask questions about myself that I didn't want to answer."

"I'm not sure I understand, Father."

Symanski moved toward Gallagher, exhaled on his cigarette, and looked at him. "Peter, have you ever asked yourself why you don't practice the faith? Ever asked why after having attended Catholic schools your entire life, you don't believe? Have you ever asked why it is that you and thousands just like you no longer practice as Catholics, while those of your parents' generation remain committed?"

"Sometimes, I suppose."

"As I mentioned when you first arrived, there were once one hundred young Jesuits here at Georgetown. And I'm sure your father, who you said attended Fordham University as well, could tell you there were just as many during his time there. Have you wondered why this is no longer the case?" Symanski sat down in his chair while Gallagher remained silent. "Well, I have. I've done a lot of thinking since Edward Sachs walked into my room a year ago."

"But your books…" said Gallagher.

"Rubbish."

The room was silent, and Gallagher felt the effects of the scotch taking firm hold.

"Tell me, Peter. Why don't you believe in the Church? What was it, during all that time in Jesuit schools, that we failed to give you?"

Gallagher sat stunned. He hadn't thought deeply about his faith—or lack thereof—for many years, and he was surprised by how quickly his conversation with this old priest had engendered a trust that made him confident to speak his mind. "There was no certainty."

Symanski poached a cigarette from Gallagher's pack, which lay on the table, and lit it. "Go on," he said like a psychiatrist with a patient, waiting for the known answer.

"Frankly it was all rather bizarre, looking back. I had nuns that would sing Simon and Garfunkel songs and priests that would tell us that God was what we wanted him to be. Everything was fungible and negotiable, nothing clear. In the process of trying to make us find meaning in the Church, if at all, the Jesuit institutions I attended only ended up instilling doubt in ourselves and in our faith." Gallagher drew in on his cigarette. "After a while I figured there was nothing to distinguish the Church from the world, so I guess I decided there was nothing really to believe in at all."

"Another drink?"

Gallagher registered a look of resignation, thinking that the old priest had a liver of iron. "Why not."

Symanski pulled a second scotch bottle from a drawer and refilled both glasses. "Do you see the picture before us that we have painted and the essence of the theological dialogue Father Sachs and I engaged in?"

The priest put down his glass and answered his own question. "You are a prime example of what Father Sachs was working to rectify—an entire generation of Catholics who grew up in this so-called "modern" Church but who left it more quickly than any other generation before it." Symanski paused. "The Church is dying. And we Jesuits, in a flash of youthful arrogance and liberal idealism, not only helped that happen but also destroyed ourselves in the process."

"Do you know what *The Washington Post* wrote a few weeks ago?" Symanski asked, before again answering his own question. "It wrote about how the Jesuits were dying out, how the legacy of the Order would be handed over to lay Catholics because there are no more Jesuit priests."

"I didn't see that, Father."

"By trying to be open and innovative and inclusive, we Jesuits ended up closing and excluding the most fundamental beliefs of Roman Catholicism—those ideals that produced my vocation and that have held people like your parents and the generations before to a practice of the faith.

"You see, Peter, I was helping Edward. That was the legacy I was leaving—helping that young, strong priest fix the mess that my generation of Jesuits was abandoning, including people like yourself, those that our own arrogance and belief in modernity ended up destroying spiritually. At St. Gabriel, Edward was working to formulate a comprehensive solution and was beginning to implement it as well. His efforts were producing results."

"Do you think someone killed him because of that, Father?"

"I don't know, but St. Gabriel is a fiercely rebellious parish. It personifies the idea that God and the Church aren't the center of the faith but that the individual is—although most there would take deep exception to that characterization. I also once championed the agenda of the parishioners there—the empowerment of the so-called special interests and the primacy of fighting social injustice. But what I've come to realize, in the sunset of my life, is that what I once championed was nothing more than a worldly political agenda cloaked and sealed with the imprimatur of the Society of Jesus. 'Moral relativism,' they call it. What we should have been doing is defending and promoting the basics: the beliefs of the Church, the saving of souls, the primacy of the sacraments, and the battle between God and the Devil.

"We once called that 'anachronistic,' 'fire and brimstone,' 'outdated,' 'unfashionable,' 'unforgiving,' 'intolerant,' 'hierarchical,' 'politically incorrect'…what have you. But those were the labels of this world not God's. And that's where we failed. We failed to follow what St. Ignatius formed us to do. And now we're dying because of it.

"But to answer your question, we are in a war, Peter. My generation, who created this mess, is dying. A war of ideas is now being waged for the heart and soul of the Roman Catholic Church. Father Sachs was on one side of that battle, and others remain committed to holding the fort against those like him. Would they resort to murder? Maybe—but not in this country. At least I certainly hope not. If so, the Church has reached its nadir. But I don't think it's quite there yet."

Symanski sipped more of his scotch and sat back, finally showing signs of intoxication and weariness, his eyelids beginning to hang heavy.

Having been lost in conversation with Father Symanski for the last three hours, Gallagher had failed to remember the reason he had arrived that evening. He set down his glass and reached into his attaché. He pulled the photo he had taken from Laura earlier that day. "Father, I wanted to show you this." Gallagher placed the photo on the table and slid it toward the old priest.

Symanski leaned forward slowly and placed his reading glasses on his nose. "Where did you get this?" He looked up at Gallagher, his eyes red and glazed but deadly serious.

"It was obtained in the parish archives this afternoon. It was in a box Father Sachs was apparently interested in. This is you, isn't it?" Gallagher pointed to the dated image of the priest that sat before him.

"Yes, it is."

"Can you tell me who else is in the picture?"

"Damien Thomas and Francis O'Brien."

"Who's the boy?" said Gallagher, pointing to what appeared to be a young native.

"His name was Thomas as well. So we nicknamed him Tio to distinguish him from Damien. He was from the village we were visiting. He kept us in fresh water and clean clothes. He was a bright and good boy. His father had been killed along with his mother. He lived with his grandmother or an aunt, as I recall." Symanski grew silent.

"What village, Father? Where was this taken?" Gallagher's interest was growing while he noticed that Father Symanski was fading.

"Nicaragua. Must have been in the mid-1970s. It was a little village called Caldera."

"Was this a vacation or something, Father?"

Symanski looked nervous, as if coming to an unwanted place in his mind. "It's getting late. Why don't you come by about the same time tomorrow?"

"Father, what are you not telling me?"

Symanski removed his glasses and sat back. "A week or so ago, Edward came in one night and asked me questions about liberation theology. He said he was researching it as part of his larger doctoral work. I was curious; it was germane to the topics we had been discussing over the last year. You see, I was once a proponent of liberation theology and had spent some time in Central America. But that was a long time ago. I haven't been back to Central America in almost two decades."

"What about Father Thomas and O'Brien?"

"Damien and I came up together as Jesuits. We were contemporaries at Woodstock Seminary and then kept in touch afterward. We were here at Georgetown together around 1973, working on doctoral theses. O'Brien was the pastor at St. Gabriel. In those days there was a robust collegiality among the Jesuits here in Washington, especially when it came to politics. Nixon was neck deep in Watergate, the feminist movement was in full swing, and the United States was still in Vietnam. We were all political activists, like I said. We Jesuits even had a sitting member of Congress, Father Robert Drinan."

"And O'Brien?"

Symanski grew more serious. "Francis was extremely bright and passionate, especially when it came to the promotion of liberation theology. He was a personal friend with a Jesuit in Nicaragua, Fernando Cardenal. Heard of him?"

"Can't say I have."

"Cardenal was a radical, a supporter of the Sandinista movement, a 'freedom fighter,' and then a member of the Communist government in Nicaragua. Francis was close to Fernando and helped establish a branch of the Central American Historical Institute—the ICHA—at Georgetown to assist with supporting the 'cause' as Francis called it."

"And you participated in this?"

"Admittedly, yes. I did. It wasn't until later that I discovered where some of the dollars raised were going and what they were funding. But Francis was extremely eloquent in rationalizing the support."

Gallagher lit a cigarette. "Support for what exactly?"

"There was never any proof, but the rumor was that some of the dollars being raised by the ICHA were financing weapons and supplies for the communist government. However, we were always under the idealistic belief, whether true or not, that somehow all of this was tied to our role as Jesuits and our mission for 'the greater glory.' Whether we were in a state of blind arrogance or had blocked out what we thought might be inconceivable, I don't know."

"What about the photo? Is that part of all of this?"

Symanski sipped the last of his drink. "I think now, looking back, yes. The picture was taken in the last few years, or even months, of the Somoza regime. The Sandinistas were gaining ground but could see a light at the end of their warped tunnel. The trip was the first I went on with that group. We spent time working with local villagers, trying to support 'the people' and enact social justice."

"How many times did you go down there over the years?"

"Maybe three times. Maybe less. I can't remember. I was very busy with teaching and doing research and writing, so I didn't have a lot of free time. But Damien went down with Francis frequently. Francis was just dedicated."

Gallagher sat quietly, thinking, then looked at his watch. "Father, perhaps we should call it a night and pick up again tomorrow, if that would be okay with you."

"That would be fine. I think I'm ready for a pillow now."

Gallagher chuckled then asked in a serious tone, "Father, are you going to the funeral tomorrow?"

"I don't know yet. I may. I wasn't asked to participate. I think I must be an embarrassment to Damien and all the other Jesuits—the crazy priest who, while they love citing my old ideas, they don't want to see or hear from now. I think it's probably better that I pray quietly here."

"This morning I heard that the funeral will be in Latin. I haven't attended a Latin Mass, Father."

"Yes. Edward was also learning how to say the Tridentine Mass. He felt a deep connection to it. Perhaps you might, as well, Peter. I tried to provide Edward with what I could remember of it, but I was having some difficulty." Symanski got up and walked over to his cluttered desk and riffled through the mess of materials on it. "Here. Let me give you this." He held a little black book in his hands. "This is an old Sunday missal. It has the order of the old Mass in it. The funeral will be a Requiem Mass, but this should help you navigate through most of it."

Gallagher stood up, accepted the missal, and grabbed his bag. His legs felt weak, his head lightening as he got up. "Thank you, Father, for your time tonight. I'll return this tomorrow." He held up the missal.

"You keep it, Peter. Perhaps it might help you find that certainty you're missing."

"Thank you again, Father. This is most kind."

Symanski reached out his hand and shook Gallagher's. "Goodnight, Peter. God Bless."

"Goodnight, Father."

"Oh, and Peter," said the old priest as Gallagher stepped into the dimly lit hallway. "As to that 'certainty,' I'm sure that in God's time, you will find it."

"Perhaps we all do, Father," said Gallagher with a smile, as the face of Father Clarence Symanski disappeared furtively back into the room.

Chapter 18

On the sidewalk, across the street from the St. Gabriel Church, Peter Gallagher watched as the casket of Father Edward Sachs was taken inside. The number of the mourners he had seen enter the church over the last hour confirmed for him—just as Laura had told him—that Father Edward Sachs had been very much revered.

Gallagher had woken with a dry mouth and pounding head earlier that morning but had pushed himself to be here on what had become a very humid Saturday. Laura also had left a message on his cell phone the night before, asking that he attend.

As the casket moved inside, Gallagher headed across the street and followed behind with the other stragglers. He stood at the back of the church, watching as the casket and the priests—all wearing black vestments—moved toward the sanctuary.

Gallagher was taken aback by how strangely different the church appeared to him that morning. The altar in the sanctuary now held upon it a gold crucifix flanked by three gold candleholders on either side. The light was low, and the smell of sweet incense wafted throughout. The detective stood transfixed by the majesty and somberness of the ritual. He watched as Father Sachs's altar boys, dressed in black cassocks and white surpluses, assisted. A Gregorian chant wafted down from above.

Requiem æternam dona eis, Domine,
et lux perpetua luceat eis.

(Grant them eternal rest, O Lord,
and let perpetual light shine upon them.)

The priests, their backs to the congregation, undertook the sacred and serious ritual with intense concentration and military-like precision. As Gallagher watched, he was deeply moved while thinking about his discussion with Father Symanski the night before.

He didn't see Laura in the church but knew she was there, somewhere, among the densely packed and similarly transfixed congregation. After the funeral rite ended, he waited for her. Finally he spotted her walking down the stairs and onto the sidewalk in front of the church. She wore a conservative black dress, a string of pearls around her neck. She clutched a small black handbag and a damp handkerchief.

"Oh, Peter," she said, hugging him and sobbing into his shoulder. "I'm so glad you're here. It was a beautiful service."

Gallagher held her tightly, as he caught Father Thomas's eye him from a distance. He looked at the priest but made no gesture of recognition.

"Come on, Laura. Let me take you home."

"I can't go home yet," she said. "I need to be with my students at the reception. This has been so hard on them."

"I understand. Dinner tonight, then?"

Laura wiped her eyes and nose with a lace handkerchief. "Can't you stay?"

Gallagher was tempted to say yes, but he desperately needed to see Father Symanski again. So many questions had formed in his head the night before, and they were in dire need of some answers. "I need to walk over and see Father Symanski at Georgetown," he told her. "I talked with him last night at length. I can't go into detail now, but I will at dinner."

"Did you discover something?" Laura asked, sniffling.

"I think so, but I'll know more later today. I'll call you when I'm done. We can have dinner and talk."

"Okay, then. I'll see you later. Call me when you can." She kissed Gallagher on the cheek and moved toward the reception at the Parish Center.

Father Edward Sachs's body would be taken back to his home in Massachusetts later that day for burial the next. Gallagher watched as the hearse drove off and Laura disappeared into a crowd that moved in unison toward the reception. He turned toward Ryan Hall on the Georgetown campus. His quest for the "certainty" Father Symanski had spoken about the night before suddenly mixed with a trepidation that he couldn't put his finger on.

Chapter 19

Gallagher was immediately on guard when he noticed that the front door to Ryan Hall was curiously unlocked. The silence in the building was palpable, as was the fear he tasted in his mouth. He drew his gun without thinking and walked up the stairs. He looked right then left. The hallway remained as it had the night before, quiet and void. He approached Father Symanski's door on his toes, his gun at the ready.

The door to the old priest's room was ajar. He pushed it gently open while calling out for the priest. "Father? Peter Gallagher again. Are you okay?"

There was no answer.

Gallagher entered the dimly lit room and holstered his weapon. "Oh, God," he said.

The room had been searched, Gallagher could tell, even through the normal confusion of the mess that was Father Clarence Symanski's personal prison. He walked to the bed and placed his fingers on the pulse of the old priest. It confirmed what he'd suspected when he had walked in. Symanski was dead.

"Ty?" said Gallagher, after dialing his partner. "You need to get over here."

"Where are you? The captain was in a furious mood last night. Some calls came in about your investigation at St. Gabriel. Doesn't sound good."

Gallagher was unmoved. "Forget that for right now. I need you over here now."

"At the parish?"

"No. Georgetown University. That priest I wanted you to locate for me—Father Symanski—I met with him last night. Ryan Hall, room four, second floor."

"Can he help with the case?"

"Not anymore. He's dead. Send over a team."

Gallagher quickly scanned the room. The police would be on the scene in a few minutes. Whoever had been there was looking for something, Gallagher thought. He glanced at Symanski's desk. The jumble of papers that had donned its top was reshuffled, most of it now on the floor.

His eye caught sight of an old leather book open on the desk, *The Mass in the Roman Rite*. Perhaps the old priest had pulled it out the after he had left the night before, Gallagher pondered, looking at the ritual that he had just experienced only an hour before during Sachs's funeral.

He glanced down on the open page, catching the title "Ordinary of the Mass." The words he randomly focused on at that moment, before rushing down the stairs to await his fellow police officers, he found hauntingly curious:

Judica me, Deus, et discerne causam meam de gente non sancta: ab homine iniqo et doloso erue me.

Gallagher read the English translation.

Give Judgment for me, O God, and decide my causes against an unholy people,
from unjust and deceitful men deliver me.

Chapter 20

By eight a.m. Monday morning, Peter Gallagher's career was in tatters. Facing six members of the Washington, DC, police department and representatives from the City of Washington, he sat stiffly in a hard chair, awaiting questions and scrutiny he never could have thought possible a few days before. Along with Captain Drexler, the inquisition compromised two lawyers, a senior member from the mayor's office, and two assistant police commissioners. The questions were sharp and direct and the mood deadly serious.

"Detective Gallagher," stated one of the lawyers, "you are here before this board of inquiry to answer questions regarding your recent conduct relating to the deaths of Fathers Edward Sachs, SJ, and Clarence Symanski, SJ. I must advise you that you are not currently being charged, but your answers here today may be used in a court of law. Do you understand what I have just told you?"

"Yes."

"I must also inform you that this session is being recorded." The lawyer looked over to one of the assistant commissioners.

"Mr. Gallagher," said the assistant commissioner, "according to Captain Drexler here, you and your partner, Detective Johnson, were assigned to look into the death of Father Edward Sachs six days ago. Is that correct?"

"Yes."

"Since that time, Detective, this department has had a formal complaint registered by a member of the DC Bar and member of the parish who, it says in this complaint, contends that you verbally assaulted then threatened with bodily harm. It goes on to say that prior to this altercation, you harassed the wife of a distinguished member of the US Congress and then a senior citizen working as a volunteer for the parish. Can you explain this?"

"I was undertaking an investigation of Father Sachs's death. The lawyer who I assume lodged this complaint was interfering with that investigation. The other claims are simply false," said Gallagher calmly.

The commissioner did not respond but continued with his questioning. "We then have a complaint lodged by the pastor of St. Gabriel Parish, Father Damien Thomas. He contends that, after threatening him with possible charges in the death of Father Sachs, you entered parish property, without proper authority or a warrant, and examined confidential parish records. Would you like to comment?"

"I was given authority by Father Thomas to conduct my assigned duties."

One of the lawyers interjected, "Did you have the express permission of the pastor to enter the parish building?"

"I had an understanding with Father Thomas that I could go about my job. I was trying to solve a murder case, counselor," said Gallagher, losing his composure a bit.

The lawyer shot a defiant toward Gallagher and produced another file. "Murder, Detective?"

Gallagher didn't speak.

"Isn't it true, Detective, that Captain Drexler stated quite clearly, to both you and Detective Johnson, his assessment that there existed absolutely no physical evidence to support any logical conclusion in the case other than an accidental death?"

Again, Gallagher didn't speak, catching Captain Drexler's eyes in the process. Drexler looked away.

"Detective?"

"Yes."

"But you took it upon yourself to treat this case otherwise and with apparent disregard, launching into an aggressive and hostile investigation of this matter?"

"I don't see it that way," said Gallagher. He looked directly at Drexler again and sensed his unease with being part of the spectacle.

The other lawyer took control. "Detective, can you explain to this board your decision to talk with Father Clarence Symanski, SJ, at Georgetown University this Friday last?"

"I thought he might be able to tell me more about who might have a motive to kill Father Sachs."

"And did he?"

Gallagher knew at this point there was little hope that any answer would prevent what he knew was coming. "Not with any specificity."

"Were you drinking at the time you were meeting with Father Symanski?"

This, Gallagher knew, was a question to which they already had the answer. He was sure that his fingerprints had been found in the old priest's room and on the glass he had used that night. "Not while I was on duty."

"But you were at Father Symanski's residence to ask questions on an official matter, were you not?"

"Yes," said Gallagher. The lawyers made notes.

"Detective? Can you explain why the police found no other fingerprints—other than your own and that of the deceased—when searching Father Symanski's room?"

"I was there, as I've already explained to you."

"Yes," said the lawyer. "I'm sure your memory of that evening is very lucid."

Drexler spoke up after a momentary pause in the grilling. "I'd like to point out to this board that Detective Gallagher has been one of the most productive and professional members of my team. His integrity is beyond reproach, and I think this board needs to keep that in mind. Gallagher is a stellar member of this department and his long service to this city a great credit."

Gallagher's eyes brightened, his look thanking Drexler without words.

"Thank you for your thoughts, Captain," said one of the assistant commissioners without looking at Drexler. The assistant commissioner whispered something to his fellow commissioner then summoned one of the attorneys, who moved next to him.

Gallagher stared at Drexler for a moment more while the others huddled together in near silence. Gallagher looked away from Drexler as the group retook their original places behind the table.

"Detective Gallagher," said the senior assistant commissioner, "this board finds there is sufficient evidence to warrant a formal investigation into your conduct. We further find that there is sufficient evidence to consider the filing of formal criminal charges."

Drexler looked toward the board with apparent disapproval. Gallagher remained stoic.

"From this moment, Detective," the senior assistant commissioner continued, "you are hereby suspended indefinitely with pay from your duties as an officer of the Washington, DC, Metropolitan Police Department, pending further investigation into your conduct. You are to surrender your badge and gun at this time. You will then be allowed fifteen minutes to remove your belongings and vacate this building. Captain Drexler, if you could please see to this."

Drexler looked on incredulously as Gallagher rose from his chair and handed over his badge and gun.

"You are dismissed, Detective. Captain, please take charge now."

"Yes, sir," said Drexler.

Fifteen minutes later, Gallagher walked out like a common criminal from the office and job to which he had given more than a decade of faithful service. Ty Johnson escorted him outside, carrying one of the two boxes that contained Gallagher's personal effects.

"Tell the captain I'm sorry, Ty, will you?" said Gallagher.

"I will, but I think he'd like to say the same thing to you."

"I know, and he did. It's not his fault. I got too emotionally wrapped up in this case for some reason."

Johnson loaded the boxes into Gallagher's car then looked at his partner. "You going to be okay?" he asked, reaching for his hand.

Gallagher shook it and gave his partner a rough hug. "I'll be fine."

"What are you going to do now? The investigation into the case is over. Shut and closed."

"Very effectively done, don't you think?"

"What do you mean?"

"Don't you think it's a little curious that what everyone calls a simple 'accidental death' has resulted in this witch hunt?"

"Let it go. Nothing we can do about that," said Johnson. "So what are your plans?"

"I think I'll go home and sleep for a couple of days."

"And then what?"

Gallagher just smiled at Johnson. "Let me know if you hear anything. Okay? I'll be in touch."

"Will do, brother. Hang in there."

Gallagher turned the ignition, looked in his rearview mirror, and drove off. He gave a wave to Johnson, who stood on the curb with a curious expression.

Johnson stood for a moment as Gallagher's car moved into traffic and out of sight, thinking that the drama that had just unfolded was indeed "a little curious." He also knew his old friend and partner, Peter Gallagher, was most certainly not going to just "let it go" until he had discovered the truth.

He only hoped that what Gallagher might find or do in the days ahead would not destroy him—or his career—in the process.

PART II

Chapter 21

The Apostolic Nuncio, Archbishop Pio Lucessi, sat behind his imposing oak desk at the Washington Embassy of the Holy See, sipping the last drops of his morning coffee. He was a large, imposing Italian, heavy set with a Roman nose and puffy eyes. He looked at the diplomatic cable again, wondering what would transpire in the next few minutes. He put down his cup and took a cigarette from the silver case on his desk. A minute later the door to his office sounded.

"Excellency?" said a young priest, opening the door. "Archbishop Dietrich is here."

Lucessi stamped out his cigarette and slid the cable back into the plain manila folder. "Send him in."

Archbishop Hans Dietrich, carrying an expensive black attaché, marched into the office. "*Pax vobiscum*," he said to Lucessi. Dietrich was tall and immaculately groomed. The appearance of a receding hairline was diminished as a result of his short haircut and expensive and stylish rimless eyeglasses.

"*Et cum spiritu tuo*," responded Lucessi. "Please sit down. May I offer you some coffee?"

"Thank you, no." Dietrich sat down, his tall aristocratic features matching those of Lucessi, his stern German bearing evident.

The graceful Italian moved back to his chair and sat down calmly behind the bulwark that was his desk. "How long has it been, Hans? Two years?"

"Three," said Dietrich. "You are looking well."

"I am getting old, my friend. I will be ready to go home when the Holy Father deems it is time."

"The Holy Father is well aware of your diplomatic acumen for Washington and with the Americans, Pio. The Holy See is very proud."

"Thank you. I'm sure the same is said about your work." Lucessi looked at the young German closely, his eyes indicating nothing. He waited, the forced quiet asserting his control. "I take it that is why you are here this morning."

"You received the cable."

"Yes. It was curiously vapid in its content."

Dietrich remained stoic. "There was concern that a more detailed message would have raised suspicions."

"So what do you have to tell me, Hans?"

"The Holy See is concerned over the death of this second Jesuit, Symanski, coming so suddenly after the death of the other. There have been increasing whispers among the Jesuits and their leadership in Rome."

Lucessi reached for the silver cigarette case; offered one to Dietrich, who declined; and lit his own. "The Holy See asked us to undertake this assignment. I did not ask why. I merely followed orders. What do you ask of me now, Hans?"

"The Jesuits remain a painful thorn for the Holy Father. This, we both have known for years, Pio. The assignment here was to obtain the needed documentation to break their intransigence." Dietrich paused. "The Jesuit Father General wages war very carefully, Pio. They are cunning, are they not?"

Lucessi looked directly at the top Vatican intelligence operative. "No more than we are," said Lucessi. "But this effort here in Washington had gone cold of late. Until the death of Sachs, we have heard very little about this matter."

Dietrich unlocked and opened his attaché and pulled a case file from inside. He opened it and glanced at the information it contained. "Your intelligence officer here, Monsignor Sansevarino, has been very capable, yes?"

"Very. If there was something afoot, he would know it."

"Which is why Rome is concerned," responded Dietrich. "We received some new information on this matter yesterday. Information relating to the Washington, DC, police investigation of Father Sachs's death was passed to the Nicaraguan government via diplomatic cable. The cable was sent from the Nicaraguan embassy here in Washington."

"And the contents of the cable?" Smoke from Lucessi's cigarette wafted up in a cloud as he spoke.

"There was an investigator from the police, it said." Dietrich looked down at the file. "Name of Gallagher. This cable expressed interest in which questions this man was asking and what he might be finding."

Lucessi stamped out his second cigarette that morning and pushed a button on his desk.

"*Si*, Excellency?"

"Sansevarino. Summon him to my office," said Lucessi. He looked on as Archbishop Dietrich smiled cryptically.

"You see now, Pio, why I was flown so swiftly from Rome."

"We shall see what Monsignor Sansevarino has to say," said Lucessi.

"Yes." Dietrich waited confidently. "And then we will provide him with his new orders."

Chapter 22

The clock next to Peter Gallagher's bed read 12:04 p.m. He winced and rolled onto his side as he began to awaken more fully. "Another hour," he mumbled and closed his eyes. The phone that had rattled him from his rest continued to ring.

Reluctantly he reached for the phone. "Hello?"

"Peter? It's Laura."

His eyes opened, and he sat up. "Laura? What day is it?"

"It's Tuesday. Are you drinking?"

"No, sleeping," said Gallagher with a yawn. "Best rest I've had in weeks."

"I need to see you."

Gallagher sensed something was wrong. "What is it? Are you okay?"

"I'm fine, but I need to talk to you about the pictures from the parish archives."

"I know. We need to get those back to their boxes someway. With me out of a job for the foreseeable future and you *persona non grata* at the parish, it may be a little difficult, but we can probably figure out something."

"Forget all of that right now." Her voice sounded panicked. "They're gone."

"What do you mean, 'They're gone'?"

"They're gone. After you dropped me off Friday afternoon, I put the photos in a big envelope and shoved it under the mattress in the spare bedroom. With the funeral the next day, then your call about missing dinner because of Father Symanski, my suspension, then your suspension yesterday, I didn't think about them at all. After everything that happened, they didn't cross my mind until a few minutes ago. When I went to get them, they were gone." Laura's voice sounded even more distraught. "What are we going to do, Peter? I'm scared."

"Okay, calm down." Gallagher slipped out of bed, walked over to his bag, and looked in it. His portion of material from the Friday reconnaissance was still there. "I'll be at your place soon. Don't touch anything, and lock the door."

"Should we call the police?"

Gallagher's mind was working. "Not yet. I'll be there soon."

"Okay. Please hurry."

"Lock the door, and keep your phone in your hand. Take a look around at the rest of the apartment and see if you notice anything else unusual or out of place. But don't touch anything."

"Okay," said Laura. "But hurry."

"I'm on my way."

Gallagher put down his phone and tried to collect his thoughts as he quickly shaved, showered, and dressed.

For the next few concentrated minutes, he gathered all of the materials from his recent investigation that he still had with him. The day before, he had turned over to Ty Johnson Sachs's daily planner and the files he had taken that first day at the rectory. Likely, the materials were now on their way back to the parish or being sent with the rest of Father Sachs's personal effects to his next of kin.

Gallagher took an inventory. He had retained the material he'd taken Thursday from the Center for Liturgy, including the Symanski books and the Easter Mass DVD. He also had a fair number of pictures that he and Laura had shoved into his bag seconds before Father Thomas had arrived in the archives on Friday. With those in mind, he grabbed the missal that Symanski had given him Friday night. Ensuring there was nothing else left in his apartment relating to the Sachs and Symanski cases, he gathered what he had and placed it into his attaché.

Gallagher grabbed his cell phone and walked to his desk, finding his investigator's notepad. He took a pen and wrote a note on the pad then shoved the pad into his bag pocket. He stood still, thinking.

The black plastic case was on the top shelf of his bedroom closet. "I hope we don't need you, old girl," he said. He unlocked the case, revealing the well-kept 9mm pistol. He loaded it and stuck it in the back of his pants, his polo shirt hanging over the protruding handle.

Gallagher looked around his apartment, left the lights on, and made for his car. Laura Miller's apartment was only a few minutes away.

* * *

In a mid-size, American SUV, the giant sat two blocks away on the street and watched as Gallagher got into his own car and drove off. He waited a second then dialed.

"Yes?" said the well-dressed man behind the desk.

"The detective has just left for the woman's house."

"How much time do you have?"

"Thirty minutes at least."

"Good. You have the other items?"

"Yes," said the giant.

"Then do it. And do it quickly."

"Yes."

"And then you return here. Do you understand?" said the well-dressed man on the other end of the phone.

"Yes."

"Good. You have done well." The man hung up the phone.

The giant didn't register the comment. He hung up the phone, moved his listening device under the front seat of his car, and got out. He looked around at his surroundings, checked his watch, and began to walk.

Chapter 23

The knock at the door shocked Laura. She took a deep breath, peered through the peephole, unbolted the door, and removed the chain. "Thank God, Peter…" she said as Gallagher stepped in and placed his finger to his lips. He pulled out a pair of latex gloves and quickly slipped them on.

He walked over to the stereo and tuned it to a classical music station then turned up the volume.

Giving Gallagher a puzzled look, Laura closed and locked the door, "Don't talk. The apartment may be bugged," read the message on Gallagher's notepad.

"What?" said Laura out loud and then again in a hush as Gallagher looked at her sternly and placed his finger to his lips again. He pointed toward the back bedroom and moved off. Laura followed him.

After pointing to the bed, Gallagher silently mimicked the taking of a photograph, asking without words if this was the place where she had stashed the photos. Without making a sound, Laura pulled back the sheet and lifted the mattress corner.

Gallagher looked around the room then proceeded to check behind the pictures and in the lamps. He found nothing. Laura looked on quietly.

After twenty-five minutes, Gallagher still had found no sign to justify the paranoia that suddenly had overtaken him in the last hour.

He looked at Laura, who was growing increasingly impatient. She breathed a heavy sigh and moved over to the couch and sat down, her arms folded and her foot tapping the floor. She watched as Gallagher continued to scour the place, looking for whatever it was he had so far failed to find.

Standing in the middle of the living room, Gallagher scanned the place, taking notice of the sleek modern desk that he imagined Laura used to sort the mail and review student homework. He walked over to it. A landline phone sat on one side. He stood in front of the desk as Laura looked on disapprovingly. He bent down and looked under the tabletop. He wasn't sure at first, but after pulling down the lamp from the desktop, he was more than confident. He snapped his fingers toward Laura, who stood up and walked over and peered under the desk with him.

Laura gasped as Gallagher pointed to the small black listening device that was no larger than a thumbtack. She remained stunned as he stood back up and jotted something on his notepad.

"Did you call me on this phone?" read the second message. Laura nodded.

Gallagher looked closely at the phone and turned it over. The screws to the back had been removed and replaced. He indicated to Laura with his hand that he needed a screwdriver.

Laura returned from the kitchen moments later carrying a variety of screwdrivers and a pair of pliers. Gallagher grabbed a small Phillips head and opened the back of the phone. Inside they saw the second listening device.

Gallagher wrote down his last note that afternoon, showed it to Laura, then carefully reassembled the phone.

Twenty minutes later, Laura came out of her bedroom carrying a small bag of clothes. She grabbed her phone, her laptop computer, and some documents Gallagher had told her to collect. He was waiting for her, after having continued his search while she was packing. He had found no further evidence of surveillance.

They walked out of the apartment a little more than an hour after Gallagher had first arrived, walking quietly a few feet from the apartment door and into the elevator, before Laura broke the code of silence. "My God, Peter! We need to go to the police."

"We can't."

"What do you mean? What's going on?"

The elevator stopped at the next floor down, and an old woman got on. Gallagher and Laura stopped talking. The woman looked at them curiously, clearly sensing something was amiss, then puttered along on her way when the elevator reached the lobby.

Gallagher pulled Laura over to a seating area and sat her down. "I don't know what's going on. All I do know is that someone is interested in what we were looking for over the last few days."

"But, Peter, we can go to the police. You're a police officer for Christ's sake!" The apartment-building manager on duty looked over then buried his head back into his paperback book.

"Keep cool now." Gallagher looked intently at Laura, who was now clutching her duffel bag and other possessions like a refugee. "Think about this for a minute, will you? I've just been suspended from the force. There are possible criminal charges pending. We're in possession of stolen documents from a likely crime scene. Two people involved in this have died under suspicious circumstances—Sachs and Symanski. Whoever bugged your apartment and removed those photos—do you think calling the police now is going to help with that?"

Laura said nothing. Her eyes revealed a deep fear that Gallagher also was beginning to feel.

"How much cash did you bring?"

"About a thousand in travelers checks and cash. But that was for my vacation. Why?" asked Laura.

"Good." Gallagher looked at her and tried to reassure her with his eyes that things would be okay. He made little impact, though. "We need to make some stops this afternoon."

"What are you talking about? We should call my father. He'll know what to do."

"No, Laura. We can't do that either." For the moment, Gallagher didn't elaborate on why. "Do you trust me?"

"Peter, I..."

"Do you trust me?"

"Yes," she said.

"Because I trust you. You're just about the only one I do trust. Do you remember what you told me the other day after we went to the archives? We have to do this together, okay?"

"Okay, Peter."

He reached over and gently stroked Laura's face, wiping away the forming tears from her eyes. She summoned a small smile and a sniffle.

They sat for another minute together holding hands.

And then they were gone.

Chapter 24

"Forgive me, Father, for I have sinned."

Monsignor Marcello Sansevarino couldn't see the man's face through the confessional screen but knew his identity. While the use of the confessional as a method for communication was old hat in the game of espionage, Sansevarino found it markedly convenient and very private. In the months before, he personally had overseen the installation of state-of-the-art technology that assured him that no listening device would work within a radius of twenty feet from where he sat inside St. Matthew's Cathedral—except perhaps his own. The use of a confessional also assured him of not being seen in public with an agent of the Central Intelligence Agency.

"Are your sins great, my son?"

"I do not know, Father. Perhaps you will tell me what I need to reflect upon," said the man back to the Vatican operative whom the CIA had codenamed "the Hawk."

Sansevarino accepted the authentication and looked down at the encrypted device in his hand. The light still showed a strong green, indicating that neither any electronic surveillance was active nor was a human agent lurking in the pews. A young priest, holding a similar device in his hands, watched carefully from above on an upper chapel kneeler. "It has been a while, Simon? Have you lost your faith in the Church?"

"I don't know, Monsignor. You tell me. We haven't heard from your office for many weeks. Has the Church lost faith in us? Why the sudden need for a meeting after so long a pause?"

"Have you heard about the priests?"

"Yes."

"How much do you know?" asked Sansevarino deftly, beginning the cat-and-mouse game of reestablishing bona fides.

The CIA agent, known only as "Simon," grew stern. "We know that it wasn't us, Monsignor. I'm surprised that you would question me on that."

"That is my job. I apologize for asking, but when I am denied information, my curiosity is sometimes piqued. I thought there were no secrets in the confessional, Simon."

"We only found out about the Nicaraguan cable yesterday," Simon said, knowing the information to which Sansevarino was referring.

"Then we will let that sin be forgiven—this time. What other sins do you have to confess? I remind you now that the Vatican's relationship with American intelligence has been very good thus far, and we want to keep it that way. Both of our interests have been very well served over the years because of it."

"Yes, Monsignor. That's true."

"Then tell me what you know."

Simon adjusted his knees on the kneeler, his legs starting to go numb. "We suspect the parish housekeeper, a woman known as Maria Rosario, may be an asset of the Nicaraguan intelligence service. Her real name isn't Rosario, but her papers are genuine. We suspect she's been planted with the parish under deep cover for many years."

"Does she suspect your watchful eye, then, Simon?"

"We have no reason to believe she knows anything about our involvement in this matter. What do you have on her?"

"Nothing. This is new information for us." There was silence in the confessional.

"*Quid pro quo*, Monsignor."

Sansevarino glanced at his handheld device again—still green. "Father Sachs must have discovered something new. But I did not have a chance to debrief with him before his untimely demise. We do not know who killed him…if he was killed at all."

"I think we're both smarter than that, Monsignor. What about the dead Jesuit at Georgetown? Is that also just a coincidence?"

"You tell me."

"We didn't have involvement there either, Monsignor. Perhaps I should ask you the same question."

"*Touché*. But, no, we did not. Symanski was working for Sachs."

Simon's eyes opened wider when he heard this. "Working on what?"

"Mostly matters of theology, matters that concern only the Church."

"Mostly?"

"Sachs had been probing Symanski gently about the issue at hand, although he was removed before he could learn more."

"That's unfortunate," said Simon. "What about this detective and the police investigation?" He waited to see what response would come from the loaded question.

"We know what you know from the cable. I was hoping you could shed some light on that issue."

The CIA agent was silent and thought quickly before answering, the tests of truthfulness continuing to go back and forth. "His name is Peter Gallagher. He was leading the investigation into the death of Father Sachs. He did indeed meet with Symanski the day before he died. We don't know what they discussed specifically, but if what you say is true—that he was talking about the issue at hand—it would tend to indicate there may be someone else on the scent."

"That is an interesting theory. Perhaps the Nicaraguans, then?"

"We've considered that as a possibility, but we're not sure."

Sansevarino waited quietly, he too thinking before redirecting. "We understand that the police investigation has been closed."

Simon grew defensive and was careful now with where the Vatican operative was taking the line of questioning. "That's true. The death of Sachs officially has been ruled an accident."

"And Symanski?" asked Sansevarino, again knowing the answer to the question.

"Natural causes. Pulmonary edema. A heart attack."

"What else do you know about this investigator, Gallagher?"

"We know that, as of yesterday, Gallagher was relieved of his duties, following an internal preliminary disciplinary hearing. He's on paid leave."

Monsignor Sansevarino was intrigued by this new information. "Why was the investigation of the Sachs case so controversial?"

The CIA agent grew noticeably quiet behind the confessional screen. Sansevarino took notice of the heavy breathing and waited patiently.

"We don't know, Monsignor." Simon waited to see whether his answer would be sufficient.

Sansevarino noted the answer with suspicion. "I see."

There was quiet between the penitent and priest. The CIA agent wondered what was running through the mind of Monsignor Sansevarino.

"Are those all of your sins, my son?"

"For today, Father, yes. But I may need to confess again soon."

"There is great joy that the Lord finds in the sacrament, Simon."

"As there must be satisfaction in absolving the penitent, Father, so too does the penitent find comfort through absolution."

Sansevarino smiled behind the confessional screen, knowing that the CIA man across it was smirking no doubt as well. They both enjoyed the game they were well trained to play.

"Then I shall grant you absolution, my son. You may go in peace to do the Lord's work."

"For there is much work to do, Father, don't you think?" said Simon.

"There is indeed, my son," said the Hawk sardonically.

Chapter 25

There were subtle things that confirmed what Peter Gallagher had expected when walking into his apartment after a hurried afternoon and evening—a piece of paper moved from one side of his desk to another, a sofa cushion a bit too neatly in place. Someone had visited. Who it was he didn't know, and he was getting too tired and increasingly angry to care for the moment.

Laura waited in the lobby as Gallagher packed a bag. She was tired too, drained from the reality of how her life had suddenly and unwantedly changed over the last couple of days. She only hoped that Gallagher knew what he was doing.

After leaving Laura's building earlier that afternoon, they had rented a car, driven through the city, and visited a number of automatic teller machines and a couple of banks. Between them, they had withdrawn more than ten thousand dollars in cash. Now, with a couple of lightly packed bags and the material and photos of the investigation, they were on their own.

"Did you get everything?" asked Laura, her eyes beginning to show signs of her fatigue.

"Yes. I got what I needed," said Gallagher, holding a canvas backpack. Laura handed over the mailbag attaché that Gallagher had left with her when he had gone up to his apartment. "Looks like I had a visitor too," he said.

Laura's eyes opened widely. "We can still go to the police. It's not too late."

"No," insisted Gallagher. Laura looked at the floor. "Let's get you to bed," he told her. "And then I have one more stop to make tonight."

After ensuring they weren't being followed, Gallagher and Laura checked into a small but comfortable DC hotel that evening under the name of Mr. and Mrs. Martin Jones. Laura had showered and was asleep in her bed before Gallagher finished his cigarette on the hotel-room balcony. He walked in, kissed her gently on the forehead, and slipped out of the room, his mailbag and gun with him.

Thirty minutes later, Gallagher found himself driving through a rough patch of DC's Anacostia neighborhood. The streets were alive with people as the heat of Washington summer drove them from hot and cramped housing.

Turning a corner, Gallagher approached Ty Johnson's house. The lights were on, and he saw movement inside. He parked around the corner, got out, and walked, all the while garnering the curious looks of a few black residents who rarely saw a white face in their part of town.

The sound of a large dog barking, a breaking bottle, and loud rap music filled Gallagher's ears as he walked up the front steps to the brick row house and knocked gently. Johnson glanced out his window, reassured his wife that everything was okay, and opened the door.

"Pete, what the hell are you doing here? Are you nuts? This neighborhood is not used to white faces around here, unless they're cops and then the welcome is not usually a warm one. Not to mention that I'm not supposed to be talking to you. You're suspended, remember?"

"Hello to you too, partner," said Gallagher. "Can we talk?"

"I suppose, but we'd better make it quick," responded Johnson hesitantly, not sure of what to make of the unexpected visit. "Come on in."

"Not here. Can we walk for a minute?"

Johnson crinkled his eyebrows then caught Gallagher's serious look. "Okay." Johnson turned and yelled back to his wife that he had to talk to his partner and would be back in a few.

"Hi, Peter," said Johnson's wife, Candice, from a distance. She was slim and pretty with sultry dark eyes, her jet-black hair straight and short. She came to the door holding an infant and looked over her husband's shoulder. "What are you doing here? Are you okay? Ty told me what happened. I'm so sorry."

"I'm fine. Just need to borrow your husband for a second."

"All right. You be good now. We'll have you over for dinner soon, okay?"

"Sounds great."

"Honey, lock the door. I'll be back in a minute," Johnson told his wife. The door closed and locked. She looked curiously out the window as her husband and Gallagher sauntered down the sidewalk together.

"You okay?" asked Johnson. "What the hell are you doing here at this time of night? Shit, I don't even go out after dark around this place, if I can help it."

"No, I'm not all right." Gallagher stopped and looked at his partner. "What did they find out about Symanski?"

"Come on. You're suspended. I could get in a lot of trouble now, partner."

Gallagher's appearance of calm broke. "Goddamn it, Ty! What did you find out?"

Johnson looked shocked and stood quietly then finally said, "Heart attack. The old man died in his sleep."

"And you believe that?" Gallagher looked around at no one in particular.

"What's going on? This isn't you. I know this whole suspension thing has been hard and all but—"

Gallagher cut him off abruptly. "The priest was murdered."

"Symanski too now?"

"Both of them."

"Come on. This has gotten way out of control. I think you need to talk to someone."

"Don't give me that departmental crackpot-cop bullshit! I know what I'm talking about."

Johnson took Gallagher by the arm and got them moving again down the sidewalk and out of sight of his wife, whom he correctly assumed was watching them through the window. "Let's keep walking," Johnson said. "What's this all about?"

A half-block later, Gallagher stopped again. "Someone is watching me. The girl I told you about—Laura Miller—that teacher from St. Gabriel's?"

"What about her?"

"Someone broke into her apartment."

"How do you know?"

"I'll tell you."

Over the next few minutes, Gallagher gave Johnson a rough summary of what had transpired over the last few days, including the events he had failed to already share with his partner as part of the official police work they had been tasked to perform.

"This is serious," Johnson said. "You need to come in. The department will be able to protect you."

"From whom? Drexler was right the other day. You think anyone will believe any of this? I'm under suspension. The two death investigations are closed. I'm pending possible formal charges." Gallagher looked at the lingering doubt in his partner's eyes. "Even you don't believe me!"

"Pete? Look, partner. Even if I do, if you don't come in and make this formal, you'll just make this worse." Johnson looked at Gallagher and could see from his eyes that his partner wasn't going to change course. "What do you want me do with all this crap you just dumped on me, Pete?"

"I need your help."

Johnson said nothing then let out a sigh. "Shit, Pete. I guess we can share a room in the psych ward. Okay. Now what?" Johnson put his right hand out, his thumb facing up, to Gallagher.

Gallagher smiled for the first time that day and grabbed his partner's hand. "Here's what I need you to do, Ty."

Chapter 26

"They boarded flight eleven sixty from Dulles this morning at oh-nine-thirty. Arrives Mexico City today at fifteen hundred EDT. They paid cash for the tickets."

The CIA officer sitting in his Langley, Virginia, office glanced at the agent known as Simon. "Do we know where they're going from there?"

"No."

"Call the station chief in Mexico City. Tell him to find out."

"Yes, sir."

"Do the DC police know their man has left the country?" asked the CIA officer.

"We don't think so. They likely would have issued an arrest warrant for attempting to evade a police investigation," said Simon.

"Keep it that way. If this Gallagher is on the trail of something, then it's in our best interests to keep his search unimpeded for the time being." The CIA officer looked at the notes on his desk. "What about your meeting with the Hawk?"

"Nothing much. There was suspicion on both our parts yesterday. I needed to provide enough information to reestablish some trust." Simon waited. "He did tell me that Sachs had been working with Symanski. He didn't know how far the two priests had gotten before Sachs died."

"Do you believe him?"

"I tend to. The fact that the Hawk didn't know about the Nicaraguan cable until Hans Dietrich arrived unexpectedly from Rome seems to indicate that he may have been sloppy in handling the Sachs effort over the last couple of weeks."

The CIA officer smirked. "You think that could have been a ruse?"

"Perhaps. But the Vatican wants the information as much as we do. If the Hawk had known more, why signal for the meeting? They'd be on the trail themselves, without our help, if they knew where the trail was going."

"This is true." The CIA officer sat back in his chair. "There's little doubt that if the Vatican obtains the information before we do, they won't share it with us. It isn't in their interest."

Simon said nothing for a few moments. "Probably. We've been operating under that assumption for some time now."

"Then this police detective, Gallagher, may be the perfect unwitting asset for us right now."

"Don't you think the Hawk and the Vatican are aware of that as well?" asked Simon.

"Perhaps. The question is whether they know Gallagher has left the country and whether they think he knows something they don't."

"If they do know, I can't pretend otherwise during my next meeting with the Hawk."

"True," the CIA officer said. "That wouldn't be in our interests either. We can't burn our vital bridge with the Vatican."

"No. We can't."

The CIA officer paused then looked at Simon with a mischievous grin. "But we can certainly try and throw them a few wrong turns along the way."

Chapter 27

Somewhere over the continental United States, Peter Gallagher opened one of the books he had purchased after their last bank visit the day before. Laura was sound asleep next to him on the plane, still dealing with the exhaustion that had taken a deep toll on her. He looked toward her for a second then focused on the book in his hands. The book was an eye-opener for Gallagher: providing insights into a modern Jesuit order that—and even as a student under Jesuit tutelage—he had curiously not been privy to.

In 1973, with the publication of his book *A Theology of Liberation*, a Peruvian Jesuit by the name of Father Gustavo Gutierrez formally put forward the concept of liberation theology. A concept fundamentally rooted in the spirit of political and economic liberation of the masses, liberation theology was eagerly embraced by a number of Marxist revolutionary political movements, particularly in South and Central America. At a time when the Society of Jesus was revolting from its own theological foundations, liberation theology found fertile ground for active Jesuit support.

Under the leadership of the Jesuit Father General Pedro Arrupe, the Jesuits were quickly shedding the spiritual ideals of their founder, St. Ignatius Loyola, and a new mission was replacing it—the liberation of the poor from the "perils" of capitalism. For the Jesuits, the ongoing battle between themselves and the Vatican for the soul of their society and the political battles occurring in Central America were one and the same. Jesuits such as Francis Carney, SJ, who took up arms with commandos in the jungles, or Arthur F. McGovern, SJ, who authored *Marxism: An American Christian Perspective*, typified the Jesuit zeal for the sociopolitical struggle that had replaced time-tested Jesuit theological adherence and epitomized the bold and defiant nature of Jesuitism in the late twentieth century.

In Nicaragua, the revolution undertaken by the Sandinista National Liberation Front (FSLN) became a rallying cry for Jesuits who saw in Nicaragua the perfect venue to express their new philosophical, theological, and sociopolitical ethos. Among the supporters of the FSLN came men such as Jesuit Father Fernando Cardenal, who would become a prominent member of the Sandinista government, along with dozens of other Jesuits. The Sandinistas were quick to see in these Jesuits the value of their sharp minds and the legitimacy they provided among the people as Roman Catholic priests, especially at a time when the Roman Catholic hierarchy in that country continued to oppose their aims.

The Nicaraguan war against capitalism and American imperialism was a powerful motivation for many Jesuits from the United States, resulting in active American Jesuit support that included fundraising, prolific written advocacy, domestic political involvement, and even direct armed intervention into the fray. Jesuit supporters of the Marxist government were often involved in the formation in-country of so-called "base communities" that further conflated the line between religious faith and sociopolitical indoctrination. The arrangement became a convenient and natural axis; both Marxist and Jesuit revolutionaries found comfort and legitimacy in moving forward together to promote a "vision" for the modern world in which the capitalists, imperialists, and the anachronistic hierarchy of the Roman Catholic Church were openly declared as enemies to be destroyed.

How the work of the Society of Jesus could so easily find itself wrapped up in Marxist revolutionaries, insurgencies, and armed conflict, Peter Gallagher could only at first speculate. But then, with his experiences over the last few days, and reflection upon the years before, the picture that was being painted in his mind began to include a connection of threads.

Perhaps, Gallagher thought, the second half of the twentieth century was a perfect storm of sorts: the decision by the Roman Catholic Church to call the Second Vatican Council, the end of colonialism and European governance of the third world, the Cold War struggle between East and West, the feminist and civil rights movements, the sexual revolution. The list went on. Among this tangle of politics, religion, and social experimentation, the Roman Catholic Church found itself under siege. The Society of Jesus, once the vanguard of the Church, was revolting from within like a Trojan horse to attack the very institution it originally had been formed to defend with absolute obedience in similar times of crisis and theological doubt.

The picture in Gallagher's mind gained more focus and clarity as he read on and amalgamated the facts and figures in his book with the very personal experience that he had longed to ignore. It wasn't until his discussion with Father Symanski, in what now seemed like another century, that he had begun to ask more questions about his own faith in God and the Church.

Now Gallagher was most assuredly asking those questions, and he was risking his own life for some of the answers.

There was an irony in all of it, he thought. His current search for spiritual and temporal meaning was no different from those of Cardenal or Carney or all the others who had fomented revolution against the Church, the old Jesuit guard, and a geopolitical order they had deemed unsuitable for the "modern" man.

Except now it was those like Edward Sachs who were the insurgents. The former revolutionaries of the late twentieth century—atop the modernist citadels of power and ideals—were now the ones coming under hostile fire. The tables had been turned, over time and space. The hunter had become the hunted.

Perhaps it was just as Father Symanski had said when they had talked; there was a war of ideas underway for the heart and soul of man as well as the Roman Catholic Church. And in this new war, men like Edward Sachs—and even Clarence Symanski—would fall as casualties. That was clear to Gallagher now. Good men, who had the gifts to shape institutions and the integrity to challenge entrenched ideas—and even challenge themselves if necessary with both facts and faith—would fall like soldiers in this war.

The old revolutionaries had too much to lose not to take them down or die trying. Gallagher already had seen that himself, firsthand. But how would he fare on the battlefield? He could only speculate. At least he had taken the first steps in finding out.

Gallagher's mind came back to a needed pragmatism as he tried to stretch his legs from his cramped economy seat. Someone had killed Edward Sachs for a reason. At that moment, he reaffirmed to himself that he would find out who and how. But, most important, he needed to know why.

Once Gallagher had the last answer before him, his greatest challenge would present itself, to deal with as best he could.

Chapter 28

"Purpose of your visit, Mr. Gallagher?"

"Here on vacation," answered Gallagher to the pretty, young Mexican customs and immigration agent. He smiled then watched from a distance as Laura glided through and into the reception area for arriving passengers.

"How many days will you be staying in Mexico?"

"A week."

The immigration agent looked at Gallagher closely then again at his passport, before finally stamping it. "Welcome to Mexico. We hope you enjoy your stay with us."

"*Gracias.* I'm sure we'll have a wonderful time."

"*De nada,*" said the agent before waving the next person in line to her station.

Gallagher picked up his bag and walked through to join Laura, who looked rested and calm as she stood alone with her bags. "You seem at ease," he said. "You swept through customs without a problem."

"First time I've felt this way in a few days. It also helps that I speak fluent Spanish." Laura smiled. "This suddenly has become exciting again."

"Okay, good. Then you can navigate, *Señorita* Miller."

"*Si, si, Señor* Gallagher. Let's go."

* * *

The young CIA officer assigned to the job of welcoming Peter Gallagher and Laura Miller to Mexican soil did not bring flowers. Instead he watched surreptitiously from a kiosk at a safe distance as the two made their way toward the airport cabstand. The officer slipped into the passenger seat of a waiting car and followed Gallagher and Miller as they arrived at the Marriott.

"They're tucked in," said the CIA officer into his phone.

"Tell our man on the inside to watch the package. If it moves, we need to know where," replied the station chief from his office at the American Embassy.

"Yes, sir. We won't lose them."

Chapter 29

Monsignor Sansevarino went down on one knee and kissed the ring of Archbishop Lucessi before taking a seat in front of Lucessi's desk.

"What have you heard, Marcello?" asked Lucessi, as he sat back in his heavy leather chair.

"The police detective has left the country."

"Where?"

"We do not know, Excellency."

"But our American friends would know, yes?"

"Yes," said Sansevarino. "We assume he is traveling on an American passport, so they should be able to learn his location relatively easily."

Lucessi rubbed his chin and examined Sansevarino closely. "Then what do we know? I am a patient man, but I too am growing concerned that we are not approaching this situation with enough initiative. It bothers me that we remain so reliant on the Americans for our intelligence."

In a placating tone, Sansevarino responded, "I as well, Excellency. It has been frustrating to find ourselves so reliant upon American intelligence for progress on this assignment. If the Americans get a hold of any evidence, I am certain they will not share it, regardless of what the original arrangement was to have been. Moreover, from what Father Sachs and I discussed before he died, if there *is* information, it could be damning to the Americans."

Lucessi stood and offered Sansevarino one of his cigarettes. The Monsignor took one and lit it. Lucessi took his own and sat back down in his chair. "Well then," he said. "Tell me what we do know."

"As we discussed with Archbishop Dietrich, the cable the other day was sent by the Nicaraguans. We also know that this housekeeper, who has been masquerading as Maria Rosario, could be a Nicaraguan agent; that Sachs was close to finding something; and that the detective, Gallagher, has left the country."

"To Nicaragua, then?" asked Lucessi, exhaling more smoke.

"Perhaps. If he knew of that connection, and if he was interested in conducting an investigation without the approval of his superiors…and if he was willing to risk his job."

"Or his life?" asked Lucessi.

"Perhaps."

"Or perhaps he is on holiday? This time of year is the time of holiday travel, no? If I were a man who had been given a forced sabbatical, why not take a holiday?" Lucessi looked at Monsignor Sansevarino for his response.

"We can find out where this Gallagher has gone and what he may be doing. If he is on the trail, we would need to help him."

"And why help him, Marcello?" Lucessi asked, more curious of the response than an answer he already knew.

"We still do not know who killed the two Jesuits. Even if the information about the Rosario woman is a red herring, the cable is not. We know the Nicaraguan government is interested in this matter. For all we know, they are responsible for the two deaths. If this Gallagher goes down there, he might be the third."

"Do you think the Nicaraguans are culpable?" said Lucessi.

"I do not rule it out. But if they had an agent in place for so long, why engage in assassination? Why not let the event play out, get the evidence, and quietly fade away from involvement? There would be no need to resort to murder."

Lucessi thought for a moment. "What you say may be very true. If so, then the evidence has not been obtained, and someone else is responsible. But who, Marcello? Who?"

"I do not know, Excellency. Perhaps, there is something we are not seeing about this matter—something the Americans are missing as well," answered Sansevarino.

"If that is true, then this Gallagher may be the key to our uncertainty." Lucessi took a final drag on his cigarette and stamped it out in a fine crystal ashtray. "Find where he is. Go back to Simon. Find out what they know, but do not make them aware that we know of Mr. Gallagher's travels."

"Yes, Excellency."

Archbishop Lucessi rose and walked to the large framed map of the world that hung on one side of his office. He drew his finger around the small portion of Central America then turned back to look at Sansevarino. "And then, Marcello, we may very well need to help Mr. Gallagher on the rest of his journey."

Chapter 30

Gallagher and Laura were nicely tanned and relaxed after spending three days at the Mexico City Marriott, enjoying the pool and other amenities the hotel offered. That morning they had risen early and found themselves at the same breakfast table once again.

"*Buenos días, señorita y señor.* Another beautiful day today, no?"

"*Buenos dias,* Miguel," responded Laura in her perfect Spanish to the Mexican waiter who had served them breakfast the two previous mornings. "How are you?"

"Wonderful, *señorita.* You both look well rested. You are enjoying Mexico?"

"We're having a wonderful rest, Miguel," chimed in Gallagher, now that the conversation had lapsed into English.

"Fresh coffee and orange juice is on the way. Here are your menus. I'll be back in a moment," said Miguel.

"*Gracias*, Miguel," said Gallagher.

The waiter smiled and walked away. Laura took a sip of her water, waited for the silence to take hold, then looked at Gallagher. "Peter, how long are we going to stay here? I've enjoyed the vacation, but I thought we were just going to fly in here and then move on."

"I don't know. I'm not sure we're going to be able to move on."

"Why don't we take that flight we found yesterday, that charter plane? Or the boat that'll take us out of Acapulco and then into Panama?"

"I'm not sure it matters," said Gallagher, as Laura's eyes grew increasingly curious. The two sat back as a busboy placed coffee and orange juice on the table.

"I was thinking last night, trying to fall asleep," said Gallagher as the busboy moved off to another table. "This whole liberation theology thing has been weighing on me since we left Washington. What if Sachs was working on something political and not religious?"

"Come on, Peter. The man was a priest—and a good priest. We've gone over this, haven't we? More than likely, Sachs was killed because of his theological stance."

Gallagher sat forward. "But what if he wasn't? Hear me out for a second. If there is something that connects St. Gabriel's to something political, wouldn't that be a reason to silence Sachs? And Symanski? What if all the theological battles Sachs was waging were the tip of a larger iceberg?"

"Like what, for instance?"

"I don't know. But let's just say for the moment that it was political."

"Well, so what? How does that factor into how we get out of Mexico?"

Gallagher took a sip of his strong Mexican coffee, relishing in the bold flavor. "We both traveled into Mexico on American passports, right? We used our real names, booked the hotel in our names, right?"

"So? Did we really have a choice?" asked Laura.

"Well, then, conceivably we're on someone's radar." Gallagher paused for a few long moments. "If someone wanted to find out where we are, they could do it without breaking a sweat. And they could follow us right around the world for that matter too." He changed track. "Look, Laura, I know I've been a bit paranoid since we got here—setting up these rules where we don't talk about the issue in the room for fear of more listening devices and carrying around these bags with our computers and the materials from the investigation everywhere we go. But I thought after what happened in DC, we should be careful."

Laura smiled, her white teeth highlighting the pretty face that had become deeply tanned during a few short days in the sun. "I think we were smart to do that," she said, "but have you seen anyone here who's given you any indication that we're being watched? We're on vacation. No one cares what we're doing here, and if they do, they'd find two people doing nothing out of the ordinary other than having a good time and getting some much deserved rest."

Gallagher was growing agitated. "If someone were watching or listening, we wouldn't know it. That's what I'm telling you. And if we're really onto something that touches the 'spooky world' as spies call it, we could be in real danger if we continue to travel under our American passports. Do I need to remind you about the two dead priests or what happened to our apartments? For Christ's sake, something is going on out there, and we're involved whether we like it or not."

"Okay, okay. Calm down." Laura clasped Gallagher's hand from across the table.

"I think you should fly back to the States after another couple of days and let me travel on alone," he told her.

Laura frowned. "And do what? Go back to my bugged apartment and pretend everything is normal? I've felt a lot safer over the last three days knowing that I'm with you."

"I don't want anything to happen to you, Laura. I think you know our relationship is past pure friendship."

Laura blushed, her eyes glazing over. "I know. The separate bedrooms and limited displays of affection aside, I know."

Gallagher grew self-conscious about his puritanical approach in his feelings for Laura as he looked into her eyes. "I just didn't want to rush—"

"No need for explanations. I know, and I think I'm coming to understand and appreciate you all the more because of it." Laura smiled. "So what's the plan, Detective? Do we run back to DC and get married or do it here on a beach in ole Mexico?"

Gallagher laughed. "I hadn't thought about that. One step at a time."

"Okay, so how do we get out of Mexico?"

"We need to find a way out quietly. If this thing that Sachs was onto about Latin America does involve political elements, we have to 'slip the tail,' as we say in police lingo. We have to make sure we're free to go on searching without someone watching us as we do it."

"How?"

"I'm not sure." He watched as Miguel returned to their table to take their breakfast order.

The waiter smiled widely. "My favorite Americans. Are we ready for breakfast?"

Gallagher watched as Laura engaged in a discussion with Miguel regarding the breakfast specials. His eye caught the black, close-fitting bracelet on Miguel's right arm. He noticed pieces of a blanched tattoo under it when Miguel turned to him and asked for his order.

"Eggs and bacon, Miguel, with fresh fruit."

"Very good, *señor*. You are the same, every day. You are a man of routine, I can tell."

Gallagher looked up and smiled. "Yes, Miguel, but we contain unexpected surprises inside. Wouldn't you say?"

The waiter's expression turned deadly serious, but he quickly covered it up with his usual smile and lighthearted demeanor as Laura looked on nervously.

"*Si, señor,*" stated Miguel, meeting Gallagher's eyes. "I would say that is true."

Chapter 31

"What was that all about?" asked Laura, not sure what to make of the exchange between Gallagher and the waiter.

Gallagher looked over as Miguel walked toward the kitchen. He was surprised when Miguel turned around cautiously and looked at him ever so briefly before continuing on.

"Wait here," Gallagher told Laura. "I'll be back."

Laura grew anxious, but supplanted her concern, as Gallagher got up from the table.

He walked toward the kitchen and back into the alcove, where the busboys minded pots of hot coffee and jugs of filtered ice water for the guests. He peered through the swinging doors of the kitchen but couldn't see Miguel. Glancing to his right, he quietly walked down a service passageway that was dimly lit and empty. Nothing. He turned back and sauntered back toward the table. Suddenly a door off the service hall opened, and Gallagher was pulled inside a dark room so forcibly that he didn't have time to react or yell out. The door slammed closed.

Inside the dark, cold room, Gallagher could see nothing. He felt the blade of a sharp knife at his throat and a strong hand covering his mouth.

"One sound or move, *señor*, and it will be your last," said a voice Gallagher instantly recognized. The hand lowered from his mouth.

"We need your help, Miguel. I am not with the Mexican police or the army. Put the knife down, please," said Gallagher quietly, trying to muster his senses. "I am a friend."

A moment of strong silence filled the tiny, dark room. Gallagher felt the knife at his throat carefully lower. The hand that had just covered his mouth reached for something a foot away.

The room was suddenly a pale yellow with the pull of a string to an old light bulb that hung from the low ceiling. Gallagher adjusted his eyes, seeing Miguel before him. The eyes of the waiter appeared fierce and defiant—the cold lenses of a professional soldier ready to kill if Gallagher made one wrong twitch.

"What do you want, *señor*? You are American intelligence or the drugs squad?"

"No."

"Then what do you want with me?" Miguel remained ready to cut Gallagher's throat if he made a sudden move.

"*Las Arañas*," said Gallagher. "Your tattoo."

Miguel looked at his right hand and the close-fitting bracelet that covered the scarred remnants of his former affiliation with the notorious cartel mercenary organization. "I am not a member of *Las Arañas*. Is that clear? It has taken many years of pain and suffering for me and my family to put those days behind. Now you come along and dredge up my past. Why?"

Gallagher had learned about the Las Arañas—"The Spiders"—while working DC homicide. The uptick in drug-related violence in Washington and the surrounding suburbs had grown increasingly connected to members of the infamous drug cartels from Mexico. The Spiders were one of the most ruthless and formidable of these groups. Established to provide the Mexican drug barons with professional muscle, Las Arañas was one of several enforcer groups within the Mexican drug underworld. Its ranks overflowed with former army and special-forces soldiers from across Latin America, their skills and training providing the underworld with a professional corps of soldiers that could counter the best that the Mexican Army—or even US special agents—could bring to bear in the war on narcoterrorism. Their call sign was the tattoo of a black widow spider, branded into the right arms of its members. Once branded, a member was considered tied for life to the gang. He would have nowhere to go and nowhere to hide; the badge tied the individual's membership to a life of loyal criminal service or a painful death.

Gallagher gathered his wits and spoke carefully. "Laura and I need to leave Mexico. We're being watched."

Miguel dropped his hand that held the knife and relaxed. "So it is you then, hey, *señor*?"

"What does that mean?"

"This hotel has many agents inside it, *señor*: Mexican police, American drug enforcement, members of the drug cartels. Few here do not have a past history or current agenda." Miguel sat down on a crate. "There are many open secrets here within the staff. There is an understanding as well. We do our jobs, whatever those may be, and everyone looks the other way." Miguel laughed sardonically. "If that was not the case, there would be very few to do the work here."

Gallagher slowly lowered himself and sat across from Miguel on a crate of tin cans. "I'm sorry for being so obvious," he said. "Please, you must believe that I'm not interested in doing you or anyone harm. I'm not here to arrest anyone."

"I know you are not. If you were, you and the *señorita* would be dead by now."

"What did you mean when you said, 'So it is you then?' a few moments ago?"

"We catch whispers and hear things. It goes with the territory." Miguel looked closely at Gallagher. "I overheard one member of our staff here talking to a *yanqui* about two Americans." He waited for a while then continued. "This man is a paid agent of your government. You must be in some trouble, hey?"

"I—" began Gallagher before Miguel interrupted.

"I do not need to know the details, *señor*. It is often better not to know about these things, yes?"

"Perhaps."

Miguel was quiet again as Gallagher searched for what to say next. "Your room is likely bugged," the waiter finally said. "Most rooms here are, you know."

"I suspected as much. Can you help us, then?"

"Oh, of course, *señor*. For a price, anything can be obtained." He smiled at Gallagher. "But I like you and the lovely *señorita* very much. I feel you are good people."

"Thank you, Miguel," said Gallagher. "We're fond of you, as well."

"It is good to have friends. I can arrange for whatever you need."

"*Gracias*, Miguel." Gallagher spoke to him with a sense of urgency now. "We need passports, travel documents, and transport out of Mexico. Eventually we'll need to get into Nicaragua, but anywhere close will be good. No one must know we've left the country, but we must take our belongings with us."

Miguel nodded. "It may take a couple of days to arrange this. I also will need money."

"We understand," said Gallagher.

"Go back to the table. Say nothing about this to the *señorita* until you have finished breakfast. I will contact you in the next twenty-four hours. In the meantime you need to get as much cash as you can while you are still here in Mexico. After you are out of the country, you will not want to use anything that can be used to track your movements. No credit cards. You understand, *señor*?"

"Yes."

"Spend the day in the city. Do some sightseeing, anything that would seem normal for a young couple on holiday. Do not speak of this in the hotel room or in public. You are being watched, *señor*."

"We will be careful," said Gallagher.

"Okay, then. You need to go back to the table now. The *señorita* will be worried. I will go out first and see if it is clear, then you go back to the table."

Miguel turned off the light inside the room, opened the door, and peered into the hall. "It is clear. Twenty-four hours."

Gallagher shook Miguel's hand and slipped into the hallway. Suddenly he turned back to Miguel. "You said '*yanqui*' before. For whom is that staff member working?"

"Like I said, *señor*, you must be in much trouble. The member of staff I mentioned was an American informer."

"For whom?"

"For your intelligence, *señor*." Miguel raised his eyebrows. "CIA."

Chapter 32

The streets of Mexico City bustled with activity. It was hot too. Very hot. As Gallagher and Laura walked leisurely along the streets, they tried, under canvas hats and sunglasses, to remain cool. Over the last three hours, they had taken in the sites while keeping an eye on anything that would seem to corroborate what Miguel had told Gallagher earlier that day in the hotel storeroom.

Laura hadn't received the news well. Her previous sense of relaxation was now gone. Remaining very quiet, she clung tightly to Gallagher's arm as they walked.

"Are you okay?" asked Gallagher.

"No."

"We have to remain calm."

"I can't anymore. We're in a town filled with drug dealers and spies. Our hotel isn't even a refuge. I want to go home."

Gallagher said nothing but knew that going home wasn't an option. "Come on," he consoled her. "Let's get you something cool to drink."

They walked into a street-side café and sat at an outside table in the shade under a green-and-red awning. "*Dos cervezas, por favor*," said Gallagher to a heavyset Mexican waitress. She smiled and went inside to get their order.

Gallagher pulled off his hat and wiped his brow with a handkerchief. Laura looked down at a tourist guide and said nothing as a cold beer was placed before her.

"*Gracias*," said Gallagher to the waitress. He picked up his beer and drank it eagerly. Sitting forward, he looked out at the busy street—the cars and pedestrians making their way through the city. He looked on without thinking and took another sip of his beer, catching sight of a car a block away with two men suspiciously sitting inside it. He looked down at the table and put his hat back on.

"Let's finish these and move on," he said. "We can go back to the hotel now."

"I don't want to go back to the hotel…back to that listening post of bandits and thugs."

Gallagher shot another protected glance under the cover of his hat and sunglasses at the car and the two men sitting inside it. He could tell they weren't Mexican nationals. He couldn't see the license plate.

"Have a sip of beer and you'll feel much better. Then we can go back and cool off in the pool." Laura didn't respond but fingered her beer bottle without drinking it.

They sat for another few moments in silence, Gallagher watching the car and a young boy passing out leaflets for a souvenir shop to the tourists sitting at the café.

"Good souvenirs. Good prices. Real Aztec and Mexican pottery. Come now. Only two blocks away," said the boy.

Gallagher watched as the boy dropped the leaflets onto tables with great agility.

He walked over to where Gallagher and Laura sat. "Pretty lady, real souvenirs. You come." He dropped a folded leaflet on the table and looked at Gallagher. "You come, mister. Miguel say to come."

Upon hearing the name, Laura looked up, the shock on her face hidden under her hat and sunglasses. The boy moved to the next table and continued to drop his leaflets.

"Look normal, Laura," said Gallagher quickly. "Don't do anything yet." She attempted to speak, but Gallagher cut her off. "There's a car a block or so away. I think they're watching us. Two Caucasians. Just smile and drink your beer."

"Oh, lovely. Fine mess we're in now. I'm so sick of this."

"Calm down. Smile and drink your beer. I'm going to not look at this leaflet for a minute. I'll let our friends think it's nothing." He sipped his beer and glanced at his watch without moving his arm from the table. 2:12 p.m.

Laura drank her beer and watched carefully as Gallagher opened the leaflet. It read, "*Catedral Metropolitana de la Asunción de María:* crypts, 1530."

"What does it say?" asked Laura.

"Cathedral of the Assumption of Mary: crypts, three thirty p.m."

"That was fast."

"Yeah. It makes me nervous how fast."

"You think it's a trap or something?" Laura asked.

"I don't know. I don't think so." Gallagher sucked down the rest of his beer and looked over again at the car down the street. "It's about quarter past two now. We'll stay here another ten minutes, then we'll walk leisurely around again. We need to gather some more cash too. Then we'll go over to the cathedral, take some pictures, and play tourist." He folded the leaflet inconspicuously into a small square and stuck it in the palm of his hand. "I'm going to the bathroom. I need to get rid of this. Order a couple of Cokes for the road and pay the check. I'll be back in a minute."

Gallagher walked into the toilet stall and ripped the leaflet into shreds, did his business, and flushed the leaflet down the drain. He walked back out and found Laura chatting with the waitress, thanking her for the service.

"Ready?" he asked.

"Do I have a choice?" said Laura, her demeanor now revived with the effects of the beer and the pleasant banter with the waitress.

"I'm afraid not. Not yet at least." Gallagher peered down the block and noticed the car was no longer there.

"Wonderful," Laura said. "Perhaps God will have some answers for us at the cathedral."

"As they say, the Lord works in mysterious ways," said Gallagher.

"Well let's just hope to hell he finds us a way out of here."

Chapter 33

"The client is not pleased." The giant sat and said nothing as the well-dressed man looked over the desk at him. No question had been asked nor any order given. The well-dressed man continued, "And there is still no sign of them?"

"No," answered the giant.

The well-dressed man stood and paced in the office. "So they slipped our net, and now they have simply vanished?"

"Yes, sir. It would seem to be the case. We've checked the woman's phone and her likely places of refuge in DC. Same for the detective. Nothing."

The well-dressed man continued to pace. "Then they must have left the country." He was silent for a minute and then continued. "We'll go through the materials you took from the woman's apartment again."

"Yes, sir."

"And then we may need to have the client assist us directly. This isn't what we envisioned, but it was always a possibility." The client had given the strictest of orders not to be contacted, but there was little more they could do now. "If they're on the trail, they may find it. We can't have that happen. And find it or not, we may have no choice but to terminate their involvement once and for all."

Chapter 34

The taxicab driver was more than a little curious that Gallagher asked him to drive in and out of the streets of Mexico City for twenty minutes in no particular order before finally dropping off the couple on Madero Street. While trying to keep his eyes on the hectic city traffic, the driver realized his passengers were afraid of being followed, and he assured them when coming to a final stop that there was little chance of anyone having tailed them. He said he had made sure of this himself.

Gallagher and Laura paid and thanked the driver then quickly walked the remaining distance from the street into the massive Baroque Metropolitan Cathedral of the Assumption of Mary of Mexico City. Gallagher removed his hat as they quickly mingled with the hundreds of other tourists who snapped photographs and admired the more than two hundred years of detailed construction. For a moment the two stood in awe and forgot about their troubles as the sight of the magnificent architecture and rich Catholic history took hold.

"It's wonderful," said Laura, her eyes cast toward the ceiling.

"All of this history," responded Gallagher.

Laura walked toward the Altar of Forgiveness. She genuflected, slipped into a pew, knelt, and prayed quietly. Gallagher left her alone and sought out a map of the cathedral and the location of the crypts. He looked at his watch. It was just after three twenty p.m.

As Gallagher examined a small paper map of the cathedral, a man slipped from a pew and approached him. "Excuse me, *señor*, can you tell me where the Altar of the Kings is located?"

Gallagher looked up from his map. A well-groomed man about his own age and height stood before him. His hair and eyes were dark brown set among a European-like skin tone. "I'm sorry. I'm trying to find that myself. Let me see here," he said, looking back at the map.

"Mr. Gallagher," began the man, "do not look up from your map. There is a tour group just up ahead approaching the Altar of Forgiveness. You and the *señorita* need to join it now."

Gallagher could not resist disobeying the previous order and slowly looked up from his map and gazed directly at the man. He said nothing.

The man looked back at him, understanding Gallagher's curiosity. "There is no need for alarm, Mr. Gallagher. I am a friend of Miguel. Do as I say." The man turned and headed around a corner and out of sight.

Without haste, Gallagher moved toward where Laura was quietly praying. He genuflected next to where she knelt. "Laura, we need to go. Get up quietly and follow me."

Laura made a sign of the cross and got up. Gallagher gently grabbed her hand, told her quietly about the message, then walked with her toward the tour group, which now stood in front of the main altar. The two reached the back of a pack of tourists, just catching the end of the guides' information on the tour stop.

Gallagher and Laura tagged along nervously. After seeing the Altar of the Kings, the tour guide noted the next stop as the underground crypts. Anxiously, Gallagher and Laura stepped off through a large wooden door, following the other tourists down a winding yellow staircase. The tour continued below ground, as the guide highlighted some of the many plaques, markers, and resting places. Ten minutes later the visitors ascended the yellow staircase. Gallagher and Laura remained at the tail end of the group.

"Quickly. This way," said the same well-groomed man Gallagher had met only so briefly before, reappearing from nowhere. Laura said nothing as she squeezed Gallagher's hand.

The man pulled Gallagher and Laura back from the winding line of tourists making their way back up into the cathedral. Ensuring that none of the other tourists noticed Laura and Gallagher's absence, the man opened an iron gate and ushered the couple into a dark, damp passageway. He looked out toward the public area of the crypts, made sure that no one had been left behind, and closed and locked the gate. "This way, please." The man pulled a flashlight from his pocket and moved ahead of Gallagher and Laura down the low-ceilinged passageway.

"This seems eerily familiar," Gallagher told Laura, thinking of a somewhat similar, yet less dramatic, tunnel at the St. Gabriel parish. Laura was able to smile briefly to herself.

"No talking. We must remain silent," said the man as he continued with great focus in leading them down the cool, humid corridor.

After another hundred feet, the man stopped and listened. Gallagher and Laura were dead quiet, the seriousness and uncertainty having garnered their respect. After thirty seconds, the man pulled a heavy key ring from his pants and opened the heavy steel door that neither Gallagher nor Laura had noticed. "This way."

Gallagher and Laura waited in the near pitch darkness as the man followed them through the door then closed and locked it when he was inside. He retook his position as guide and led them another twenty feet to where yet another door—this one heavy oak—awaited another key. They entered, and the door was again closed behind them. Seconds later a light switch was flipped, revealing a small but tidy room that housed a large wooden table and four heavy chairs.

"Mr. Gallagher, Ms. Miller, my name is Father Luis Avino. I apologize for my being incognito and for all of the walking, but this is how it must be done. We had to be sure you weren't being followed." Father Avino offered his hand to Gallagher then shook Laura's hand when she offered it. "Please sit down."

Gallagher and Laura each took a chair, as Father Avino remained standing, propping his rear end on one edge of the heavy table. "You are friends of Miguel."

"Yes," said Gallagher. "He told us he could help. You're a friend of his as well, we take it?"

The young priest pulled the sleeve of his white button-down shirt up to the elbow. He pointed to a scar on his right arm. *"Las Arañas."*

"But you said you were a priest," said Laura, another blow to her youthful idealism forcing the question from her lips without thought.

Father Avino smiled softly as he looked at Laura with priestly compassion. "I am, Ms. Miller. God has shown himself to me. Like Miguel, I have tried to escape my past—a past for which I have nothing but disgrace in having behind me."

"I'm not sure we understand, Father: all of these hidden secrets from men of the cloth. Where we come from, this is not something that we are used to," Gallagher said. "But we've experienced a rather rude awakening over the last few days."

The priest pulled out a chair and sat down to eye level with Gallagher and Laura. He placed his hands on the table, his fingers intertwined as if in prayer. "As I said, my name is Luis Avino. I am a priest of the Mexico City Archdiocese. I've been a priest for a little more than five years. I was born in El Salvador to a family of high stature. I was sent to Catholic boarding schools until I was about eighteen, the last of which I was expelled from. With my father's connections, I was able to get a commission in the army. Then I moved into its special forces and attended your School of the Americas just before it closed." He looked at the table. "Then my life slowly fell apart—the drugs, the women. I was asked to resign from the army. I was angry and young and stupid and wholly unsettled. I was recruited into *Las Arañas* when I was thirty while wandering aimlessly through Mexico and then finding myself in jail." As Father Avino rubbed his eyes, Gallagher and Laura sensed the pain that still resided with the priest. "I won't provide you the details of that time in my life, but my sins were great.

"It is ironic that a young boy from a good family, raised as a Catholic, would see a life so drastically taken off course, but it happens," Father Avino said. "Of course, the frequency of this occurring seems to be much greater in today's modern world."

Gallagher spoke first, breaking the man's soliloquy. "Why is that, Father?" he asked, thinking back to his time with Father Symanski and a discussion that seemed eerily familiar.

Father Avino looked at Gallagher first, then Laura. "You are both Catholic? Educated by the Church?"

"Yes," answered Laura, she too intrigued.

"Then you must also sense that the Church that educated us was much different from the one my parents, and assumedly yours, were shaped by. The world, mind you, has become coarser and unsettled as well. But, over the last half century, had the Church remained focused on the fundamental mission of propagating the faith and reinforcing its primacy in the battle of good and evil, the Church and the world would have been much better places."

"Liberation theology?" Gallagher asked, the non sequitur jolting Laura.

Father Avino's eyes appeared stern and angry, his hands tense and uneasy. "Why do you mention that, Mr. Gallagher?"

"Do you feel the Church became too politically involved?"

The priest's curiosity was markedly piqued, and he looked at Gallagher carefully. "In my opinion, the Church betrayed itself with politics. As a Catholic student in El Salvador, I witnessed a movement in Church circles to focus on politics, liberating the poor with Marxism. As a soldier, I saw the horrors that the conflict produced." He got up from his seat and began to pace the room. "For many years I believed the Church had betrayed me, failing to provide me with the guidance and spiritual grounding I needed to make better choices. Too busy, it was, encouraging revolution and engaging in political priorities."

"But you're a priest now," said Laura, trying to ease the man from the place that their impromptu discussion had taken him.

Father Avino took a breath to calm himself. "I'm sorry. No matter how much I ask God for temperance and peace and forgiveness, sometimes the old bitterness creeps back into me. Yes, I am a priest, having found my own way through a wilderness of doubt by a reexamination of the Church and my own failings. I am coming to see myself, through my own sins, as someone who could, perhaps, right the ship and save others from the course I took by ministering in a way I wish I had been ministered to—from a position of confidence in Catholicism's faith and traditions. I have come to realize that spiritual doubt, theological distractions, and moral relativism are true evils. They lead the sheep to the slaughter."

Gallagher said nothing but found the comments made by a priest his own age hauntingly similar to what he imagined Father Edward Sachs had been saying and thinking in the days, weeks, and years before his untimely death.

The room remained deafly quiet before Father Avino finally said, "We should turn to the work at hand." He got up and walked over to a small locked closet. He inserted a key, unlocked the door, and pulled out an expensive-looking camera on a tripod. He set it up to face one of the room's heavy rock walls. Then he retrieved a small stool and assembled a plain black screen behind it, as Gallagher and Laura watched in silence.

"The services you provide here—are those for the good of the Church?" asked Gallagher.

"You sound unsure, Mr. Gallagher, of my motives," Father Avino said with a smile. "My role here is to provide others like Miguel a chance to start over—to free themselves from lives of sin and to find redemption in Christ and in the Church. You're looking for that as well, Mr. Gallagher, or you would not be here, yes?"

Gallagher swallowed his embarrassment. "Yes, Father, that is true."

"Ms. Miller, please sit on the stool," requested Father Avino.

Laura rose from her chair and sat in front of the camera. Gallagher could tell she felt troubled, that she was desperate for anything that would pull her out of her current emotional state. But they had to go on.

Laura sat as Father Avino took a series of photos, her face serious and sad in all of them. "Now I need a smile, Ms. Miller," said the priest. "We must have this. Do the best you can." The priest, too, could sense Laura's internal conflict.

She mustered enough false smiles to satisfy Father Avino. He was checking the shots he'd taken when Laura bent over in her seat, placed her hands across her face, and completely broke down.

"I can't do this," she cried, the sobs uncontrolled. "I can't keep going on like this."

The priest stood in compassionate surprise.

Gallagher moved over to comfort Laura, squatting before the stool on which she sat and placing his arms around her.

Laura threw herself into Gallagher and wedged her tear-covered face into the crook of his neck. Gallagher allowed her to cry; he waited nearly two minutes as she released what he knew had been building all day. "You must tell Father Avino," she said to Gallagher. "You must tell him about all of this. We're all alone. We have to tell someone."

With Laura still in his arms, Gallagher looked at Father Avino, who remained respectfully distant as he allowed Laura to regain her composure. They didn't speak, nor did they have to.

Gallagher stood with Laura and sat her back down in a chair then handed her his handkerchief. He looked at Laura, who now waited to see what he would do.

"Father," began Gallagher, looking at Father Avino with a blind sense of trust, "there are some things we must tell you now."

Chapter 35

The small room deep under the Cathedral of the Assumption had become hot and the air stale over the three hours during which Gallagher, Laura, and Father Avino sat in intense discussion. Gallagher himself, at first reluctant to tell the young priest what had transpired in Washington and then after, had felt as if an enormous burden had been lifted from his shoulders. Having done so, Gallagher now fully came to appreciate and understand the pressure that had seen Laura break down hours before.

Father Avino had remained calm and seemingly impassionate, as he had listened to what the two Americans had trusted in sharing with him. His own background in El Salvador, and as a mercenary of the Mexican drug cartels, had contributed to his even keel, for the young priest wasn't ignorant or naïve to such matters and the risks the young Americans now faced.

"I don't need to tell you that you're both in great danger if what you say is true," said Father Avino, pouring more of the wine that he had brought out of the closet an hour before. Gallagher and Laura sipped at their glasses, enjoying the relaxation that both the confession and sure protection of the cathedral provided them for the time being.

"But as I said," began Gallagher again, "what is it that is of such interest? All we suspect is that there may be some connection between the Washington parish and the Nicaraguan revolution."

The priest sipped his wine then stood. "It's clear that you're on the trail of something, Peter. If the two Jesuits had found something that could connect the parish to active support for a communist revolutionary government, that would be of interest to many people."

"Whom exactly?" asked Laura, her sharp mind having clicked back to normal over the past few hours.

"Well, it's clear that American intelligence is interested. We can assume this from what Miguel told us, as well as the presence of the car and the people in it this afternoon. The American government wouldn't want such information in the hands of a foreign power who could use it to wield enormous political leverage."

"Could the CIA have been the source of the break-ins at our apartments in Washington and responsible for the audio surveillance devices?" inquired Gallagher.

"Perhaps. But why would they continue to trail your movements down to Mexico?" said Father Avino. "I suspect they don't know what they're looking for either."

"What do you mean?" asked Laura.

The priest looked at Laura. "My guess is that you and Peter, through your investigations, have led the Americans into believing they can use you to get whatever it is they're looking for. They now merely watch where you're going. Eventually you'll lead them to the discovery. If they were responsible for the break-ins at your homes, they most surely didn't find anything conclusive."

"But what about Father Sachs? Was he also working for the American government?" asked Gallagher.

"It's possible. The Church isn't immune to this sort of thing." The priest chuckled. "You now sit under the Cathedral of the Assumption of Mary with a former mercenary-turned-priest discussing this matter."

Laura put out her glass to Father Avino, who poured a healthy splash of red wine into it.

"Yes, Laura, the world is a complex place, no?" the priest said. Laura smiled sardonically. "The other consideration is that other parties are interested in what you two are searching for."

"Who?" Gallagher asked.

"Perhaps Sachs was working for the Church. Your discussion tonight, Peter, on the Jesuits leads one to that possible conclusion. The comment you made earlier about what the Georgetown priest said regarding a 'war' for the heart and soul of the Church and the Jesuit Order is accurate." Avino put down his glass. "The Jesuits are a powerful order—not as powerful as they once were but just as smart and cunning as they've always been. Had it not been for the Jesuits, the Church wouldn't have obtained for itself the majority of the souls of Central and South America. That said, for the last half-century they've been a problem for the Church, a defiant and almost insurgent order, if you will. If what Sachs found—and what you're now looking for as well—could provide the Church something that could gain them advantage in this war against the Jesuits, then it would support the theory that Sachs was an agent of the Church."

"You mean that Sachs was a spy, Father?" asked Laura incredulously. "I can't fathom that. Frankly, most of this seems too much to believe."

"Believe it," said Father Avino, his eyes serious. "I must also be very honest with you tonight. The secret work I do here is monitored by my superiors. As I've said, my efforts usually are focused on providing men a chance to begin again, to free themselves from lives of sin, to have an opportunity to use the rest of their lives to redeem themselves in the eyes of God. These efforts typically are of little interest to my superiors." Father Avino paused again. "But this situation with you may be different."

The hair on the back of Gallagher's neck stood up. The priest sensed his alarm and worked to calm him. "I see your concern, Peter. If what I said about the Church being involved is true, you have every reason to question my loyalty and my trust." Father Avino waited and watched as Gallagher and Laura looked at each other for a sharp second. "Do not fear. I'm your friend and your priest tonight. What we say is said in confidence."

"But how can we be sure?" asked Gallagher.

"Because I give you my word. However, if I'm questioned specifically by my superiors, I'm bound by my loyalty to the Church to provide them honest answers. I apologize for not having mentioned this earlier."

"What does that mean?" asked Laura, her nerve now up.

"It means that what I said is true. What we discuss tonight and the plans I will assist you with will be kept quiet in so far as I can keep them quiet. But I also promise you this—if the Church is involved, there are bound to be questions that I will be asked. But the Church will also do whatever it can to protect and help you. This too you must have faith in believing."

"Just as Father Sachs believed? Just as Father Symanski believed?" asked Gallagher, trying to control his rising anger.

"And what makes you think those two men were victims of the Church? They gave their lives for it. They died as martyrs for it." Father Avino was rising to Gallagher's hostility but then settled back into a more sober tone. "You know that, Peter, and so do you, Laura, or we wouldn't be having this conversation in the catacombs beneath a four-centuries-old cathedral in the heart of Mexico City. You both undertook this crusade to find the truth…and why?" Father Avino paused before answering his own question. "Because you believe. Because you have faith. Because you're seeing things for the first time and also seeing them all over again. That is the mystery of faith—the journey we are all here on Earth to undertake. You should be grateful that God has given you that gift."

Gallagher was lost in deep thought, the tiredness now taking hold. Father Avino poured the remaining wine for himself and a contemplative Laura. The room was peacefully quiet as Gallagher thought of the words he had read in Latin the night of Father Symanski's death. As if in a trance, he spoke quietly aloud without realizing it. *"Judica me, Deus, et discerne causam meam de gente non sancta: ab homine iniquo et doloso erue me."*

Laura turned her head, her face one of bewildered interest.

Father Avino quietly walked over to Gallagher and placed a hand on his shoulder. "You need not worry, Peter. I have a plan to help deliver you both from those unjust and deceitful men."

Chapter 36

Deeply tired, and while still trying to wrap their heads around the surreal course their lives had taken over the last few days, Gallagher and Laura managed to do what Father Luis Avino had instructed the night before and replicated their daily holiday routine, as if nothing were wrong. They had breakfasted as usual with few words passing between them and Miguel, who had appeared cold and distant yet remarkably calm.

"Tonight, *señor*," Miguel had said. "I wish you the best of luck."

They had thanked him quietly and without fanfare, slipping unnoticed back to their room and then out to the pool deck where they both fell asleep soundly for what must have been an hour or more. Sunburned, they had returned to their room and, without a word spoken between them, packed their bags.

Gallagher and Laura spent the remainder of the day walking in Mexico City, pulling the final dollars they had out of ATMs to augment their cash reserves and trying to prepare themselves for more of the unknown. At three p.m. they found the small café that Father Avino had mentioned. They took a table inside and ordered drinks, Gallagher catching the eye of the barman, who met, to a tee, the description of the burly, bald man with a moustache, given by Father Avino. Gallagher rose from his seat and headed to the bar. The barman sauntered causally toward him.

"You are from the cathedral?" asked the barman.

"Yes," answered Gallagher. "You have a phone I can use?"

"*Si, señor.* Around the corner you will find a door to a small office. The phone is safe. Take as long as you need."

"*Gracias*," said Gallagher.

The barman nodded gently but said nothing as he turned and scanned the café as if looking for possible trouble.

Laura watched as Gallagher turned the corner and disappeared.

Inside the office, Gallagher dialed the number he had memorized shortly after Ty Johnson had given it to him that night in DC. The phone rang twice, and Gallagher hung up. He waited thirty seconds and dialed again. The phone was picked up on the third ring.

"Jefferson's Crab Shack," said the man on the other end of the phone in southern Maryland.

"Hello. I need to speak with Uncle Larry," said Gallagher, using the prearranged name Johnson had given him.

"Speaking."

"Do you know who this is?" asked Gallagher.

"Yes."

"Are there any updates?"

"The boats are still out, although I think they may be called in at any moment."

"How is the captain?" asked Gallagher, using the prearranged dialogue.

"Still searching for the best waters. Odds are that he'll find them. He's doing his best."

"Any special guests out on the water today?"

"The mayor may come out at some point," said the man. "He does love his crabs. I'm told he's very interested in this year's catch. The captain thinks he knows when the mayor might come out with him, but he's still trying to get a firm date with his office."

"Anything else?" asked Gallagher.

"The captain picked up some new gear for the boat the other day. He's got it safely installed now. It should make the boat safer."

"Well, that's good to hear. We're looking forward to getting up there to see you soon. Not sure when, but looking forward to it."

"You're welcome at any time. Check back in soon and we can get you scheduled for a trip out with the captain. He's anxious to see you again."

"Will do. Thanks again." Gallagher hung up the phone, walked out of the office, closed the door, and headed back to where Laura sat.

"What did Uncle Larry have to say?" asked Laura with a slight smile, knowing that Uncle Larry was the codename for Ty Johnson's father-in-law in Maryland who owned a business of the same name. The arrangement had been put into place between Gallagher and Ty Johnson as way for the two to stay in contact without compromising their whereabouts. She sipped at a cold soda.

Gallagher sipped at his drink, caught a nod from the barman indicating that all was well, then answered Laura's question. "Looks like Ty picked up my gun and the other items we left in the Dulles Airport locker without a problem. He's got them tucked up somewhere safe."

"Did he say anything about the department investigation?" asked Laura.

"Nothing new, other than they may want me back at some point soon to either answer more questions or sit through a formal hearing on my future with the department."

"What if they do call you back? Do we fly back then?"

"We'll have to see. We have a bit more time, so I think it wise that we press on with the plan. If they call me back, we can get a flight out and go home to face the music, whatever that may be."

"Did he say anything else?" asked Laura, finishing her soda.

"Ty is still looking for that priest in Uganda, and he may have information on who the source was for the mayor's call to Captain Drexler in those first days of the Sachs investigation."

"Did you get a name?" said Laura.

"No. I can't do that. It's part of the system we set up. If Ty gets more information, then the next time I check in, I'll ask him. But in reality, even if we knew the name, there isn't much we could do about it from here."

"I suppose that's true. When will you check back in?"

"Once we get out of Mexico and settled. Right now let's just follow the plan." He checked his watch. "Come on. Let's get back to the hotel and get something to eat. It may be the last good meal we'll have for a day or so."

Laura flashed another of her patented smiles, which Gallagher never would grow tired of seeing. "Come on then, Mr. Detective."

They stood, and Gallagher put his arm around her. "Come on then, Watson." Laura let out a flirtatious laugh and wrapped her arm around him.

"*Gracias*," Gallagher told the barman, who smiled back.

"Good hunting," said the barman with a wink.

Gallagher nodded back with a smile, feeling as if, for the first time, there was new hope that the hunting would indeed be good, and that he and Laura might find themselves out of the jungle and back home.

But feelings often aren't what they seem.

Chapter 37

The young priest was under the employ of Monsignor Sansevarino, working the phones between the Washington Embassy of the Holy See and those located south of the American border. He had thought himself at a dead end before his connection to his counterpart in Mexico City had provided him the lead he'd been seeking.

"Are you sure, Father?" asked the young priest in perfect Spanish as he stamped out a cigarette.

"Yes. Two Americans were here last night. One of our priests met with them."

"What was the nature of the visit, Father?"

"We don't know. We haven't questioned Father Avino about this. His work here is sensitive, as you may imagine. We have an understanding."

The young priest in Washington was careful now. He understood what was being conveyed. "We understand. Can you confirm the names of the Americans?"

"I may be able to do that, although I must be careful."

"I understand," said the priest in DC. "However, this matter is of particular importance. We wouldn't ask otherwise."

The young priest on the phone at the Mexican Embassy of the Holy See was silent before finally saying, "I'll check. Give me a day. Father Avino is out of the city today. He'll be back tomorrow. I don't wish to signal any alarms, if we can avoid it."

"We're very grateful, Father, for your attention to this matter. I don't need to remind you of the secrecy with which this must be handled."

"We understand and will act accordingly. I will contact you directly as soon as I learn more."

"Thank you. *Pax vobiscum.*"

"*Et cum spiritu tuo.*"

Chapter 38

At nine that evening, Gallagher and Laura watched as two large service trolleys rolled into their hotel room, carrying the five-star cuisine they were told they should expect. The trolleys were covered in fine white linen that hung down nearly to the floor and carried a veritable feast of shrimp cocktail, Chateaubriand, and fresh berries with cream. One of the two liveried waiters raised the folded ends of one trolley up and placed two chairs on either side.

"*Señorita*," said one of the waiters, holding out a chair. Laura smiled and sat down. The waiter pushed in her chair and placed a white linen napkin on her lap.

The other waiter turned to Gallagher and seated him as well before popping a chilled bottle of fine Champagne and pouring two glasses. The first waiter tended to the food tray, opened bottles of red and white wine, and moved the shrimp cocktails in front of the guests. "*Bon appetit*," he said, before the two waiters lit some table candles, dimmed the lights, and walked slowly away without turning their backs toward their important hotel guests.

The door gently closed, leaving Gallagher and Laura looking at each other across the candlelit table. They met each other's eyes, their mutual desire evident.

"This is quite a meal," said Laura, remembering not to mention the word "send-off," which she was tempted to use, lest their conversation was monitored. She smiled widely, her face radiant in the low light.

Gallagher's stomach registered nervous euphoria as he looked at her, the same as it had that day they had first met in Washington over a much less sumptuous cup of coffee. "Here's to us, then," he said, raising his glass of Champagne.

Laura raised her glass with a smile and tapped it gently against his. "Cheers." She took a sip and watched as Gallagher did the same.

"Excellent," he said, admiring the choice of Champagne that he imagined Miguel had selected for the evening, then watching curiously as Laura slipped from her seat and moved to the other side of the table, plopping herself down on his lap.

Gallagher said nothing as Laura nuzzled his neck and kissed him passionately. He responded fully, the heat of the moment rising unexpectedly.

"This is the first time we've had a romantic dinner," Laura whispered in his ear. "We don't know when we'll have another moment like this, do we?"

He could feel Laura's tight, toned body through her clothes and kissed her passionately on the neck. "No," he said. "But we don't want to make too much noise. Big Brother is listening."

Laura cradled Gallagher's head in her hands, her fingers running through his hair. "Yeah, we'll I don't give a shit, Mr. Detective. Tonight is all ours."

"Laura…" said Gallagher, trying to subdue his emotions and remain pragmatic about what the next few hours would hold for them.

"Shut up," whispered Laura, her passion at its fullest, Gallagher broken by her spell. "Big Brother is listening."

* * *

They awoke six hours later, a little after five o'clock, to the sound of the unwelcomed room phone, which signaled their prearranged wake-up call. Laura rolled over and picked up the phone, her head slightly throbbing with the wine and rich food of the previous evening. She reached over to Gallagher, who was already awake, and kissed him on his neck. "Wake up, Mr. Detective," she said.

"I'm up," Gallagher responded. He turned and kissed her passionately, wishing desperately that the night before had gone on forever.

"Me too," said Laura, answering the question she knew was in Gallagher's head. "We need to get going."

Thirty minutes later, having showered, shaved, and dressed, Gallagher had snapped back into the stark reality of their situation, still buoyed by the evening before and Laura's ever presence with him.

Quietly, they packed their bags and moved them near the door to their room. They would carry one bag apiece when they left—the rest transported by and in the hands of others—and Gallagher was extra attentive that the most important items relating to their seemingly never-ending investigation were properly secured in the bags they could not lose track of for whatever reason.

The room packed and ready, Gallagher and Laura made some instant coffee and waited on the couch, their eyes peeled to the ticking minutes of their watches.

At exactly six a.m., Gallagher, looking through the peephole of the room door, saw a man waiting nervously. Gallagher opened the door without making a sound.

Laura was already on her feet when what appeared to be a hotel porter rolled in a laundry cart and nodded to the room's occupants.

Gallagher pointed to the bags on the floor then watched as the porter removed some linens and towels from the cart, dropped in their bags, and covered them back up. The porter nodded again, held up his hand as if indicating five minutes, then slipped from the room with the cart in tow. The entire exchange took less than a minute and without any noticeable sound.

Gallagher closed the door, the transaction having brought back the graveness of what their plan would entail. He looked at Laura, who remained calm, although Gallagher could sense the trepidation that he too felt.

He walked over to Laura, hugged her tightly, and kissed her. "I love you," he whispered, his breath tingling Laura lips as she closed her eyes to his touch.

"I love you too, Peter."

Gallagher looked at his watch then back out the peephole. The two waiters from the previous evening were in the hallway. Gallagher again opened the door.

The men were larger and more powerfully built than Gallagher had remembered from the night before. He sensed they too must have been *Las Arañas* or from some similar ignoble background that Gallagher was content not knowing about at that moment.

The men moved the trolleys to the middle of the room, removed most of the used dishes and glasses from on top, then lifted the sides of the long tablecloths that had nearly touched the floor. Gallagher and Laura looked on as they noticed the reinforced shelves under each trolley. There was plenty of room for a man or woman to sit without fear of collapse.

The men glanced at their watches then nodded to Gallagher, signaling that time was of the essence in a plan that seemed to be run with an impressive military-like efficiency. The men pointed to the shelves.

Laura was first, her small body slipping easily into the shelf of the first trolley. She watched as Gallagher struggled to do the same, his larger frame and the previous evening's rich food adding to his discomfort.

Gallagher smiled to Laura nervously before the curtains of table linen were thrown back down over the sides of the trolleys. The men worked quickly to transport the trolleys across the room door threshold and out into the hallway.

The waiters rolled the trolleys carrying the two Americans down the hall, abruptly stopping at what Gallagher assumed was an elevator. He grew nervous when he overheard a senior porter asking the two waiters questions in a confrontational tone. Later, Laura would tell him that the porter had reprimanded them for not having picked up the trays the evening prior.

Five minutes later, the two trolleys came to a stop. Gallagher and Laura waited anxiously for their release.

The linens were raised. Gallagher and Laura were welcomed to the sight of Miguel and a brown envelope in his hand. "*Buenos dias*," he said.

Gallagher worked to stretch his legs, which had gone numb after only a few minutes under the trolley. He saw that he and Laura were now in a laundry-room loading dock; the back of a truck was open and level with where they stood. "Miguel, good to see you. I didn't think we'd see you again."

"*Si*. Neither did I, *señor*. But I am glad I did." Miguel shifted his tone. "There is no time to waste. Your luggage is in those two laundry bags." He pointed to the inside of the truck. "Your new passports—Canadian, identity cards, and some additional cash are in this envelope."

"But we haven't even paid you yet. And now you're giving us cash? I don't understand."

"No time to explain, *señor*. Get into the truck. Father Avino told me we could not take your money and that we should provide you with this additional cash for your trip." Miguel walked over to Laura. "You take care of the *señor* now, *señorita*."

Laura hugged Miguel and kissed him on the cheek. "We can't thank you enough," she said. Miguel smiled and was noticeably touched.

"In you go, *señorita*," he said, ushering Laura into the truck. He turned to Gallagher. "Now you, *señor*. You take care of the beautiful *señorita* and then you come back to see me when you are able. I'll be waiting for you."

"Thank you." Gallagher was lost for words and held out his hand to Miguel.

"God be with you both." Miguel covered his two American friends with some empty laundry bags, shut the double doors of the service truck, and nodded to the driver, who watched through the side mirror.

The truck pulled away.

An hour later a small Cessna aircraft began its journey over Mexican airspace, toward its prearranged destination.

Chapter 39

"What do you mean, 'They're gone'?" asked a perturbed officer at the CIA headquarters in Langley, Virginia.

The station chief in Mexico City was almost at a loss for words but attempted to remain calm and professional with what he did know. "We've had eyes on them and ears listening during their entire stay in Mexico," the man said. "When they didn't show up at breakfast in their usual fashion this morning, one of our men checked the room. They're gone. Nothing left behind."

Silence pervaded the air between Langley and Mexico City. "Well, tell me what you do know," said the officer in Langley.

"The two had been checking out charter flights and boats at one point during their visit. They also withdrew a fair amount of cash from ATMs here in the city. We assumed they were looking to run. However, we've checked those travel leads, and there's no sign that they booked reservations or took passage using those sources." The station chief continued, "Surveillance logs over the last few days show nothing abnormal. The two used the hotel pool almost daily, took meals with a predictable pattern, and did common sightseeing. Our man inside the hotel reported nothing strange either."

"What about unusual contacts or rendezvous with anyone?"

"Again, we didn't pick up anything. We had men on their tail the entire time. If they had met with someone, we would have photographed it."

"You mean had they met with someone *in the open*."

The line went quiet again. "Impossible. They would have to have had help to slip our nets."

The Langley officer sat quietly and thought. "Check with the Mexicans again," he said. "Check with the air controllers, check everything, and then check again."

"Yes, sir." The Mexico City station chief jolted at the sound of the phone being slammed on the other end at CIA headquarters.

* * *

Ten minutes later, the CIA officer at Langley already had passed word to alert all Central and South American stations to be on the lookout for two Americans matching the photographs that would be sent out from Mexico City. He sat back in his desk chair and looked at the man who had just arrived.

"Well, Simon. Now what?"

The agent known as Simon hid his own ire, refraining from blasting the slipshod work of the Mexico City station. "They had help. We can be sure of that."

"Wonderful. From whom?"

"I don't know. If they did escape as cleanly as it would seem, likely it was professional help, someone who knew a bit about tradecraft."

The CIA officer grimaced. "You think the Church helped them?"

"It crossed my mind."

"How? For Christ's sake, the Church had no awareness of their travels out of the country."

"You want to bet your life on that?" said Simon coyly.

"No." The CIA officer sat quietly, waiting for Simon to speak.

"I'm not sure it matters."

"What? That the Church may have known?"

"Well, that, yes. But more important that they have assumedly left Mexican soil." Simon waited for his comment to register with his superior.

The officer smiled. "Humph. Odds are they're heading south. Only place they would logically go, based on what we know."

"Assuming they're still on the trail," said Simon.

"Let's assume they still are."

"That would be the safe assumption, sir."

The CIA officer stood and paced behind his desk. "You think this may cause any damage with the Hawk?"

"Can't say. If Vatican intelligence knew the two were heading to Mexico, they're just as guilty for not telling us as we are for not telling them."

"And if they didn't know?" asked the CIA officer, retaking his seat.

"Then we tell the Hawk we have indications that they're heading to Nicaragua. If they show up there, we'll look like the true partners that we claim to be; if not, we'll lose nothing."

"We'll lose the element of independence from the Vatican on this matter."

"Had the two Americans not slipped out so neatly, we wouldn't have lost that independence," responded Simon, finally feeling relief in taking a much-desired jab at the Mexico City station.

"Gallagher is a tricky bastard, isn't he?"

"It would seem so."

The CIA officer exhaled heavily. "Fucker," he said, tossing aside the pen in his hand.

Simon waited as the officer thought for a moment. "Meet with the Hawk," the officer finally said. "Time to get back into bed with the Vatican on this, although for a few days I thought we had it made."

"Yes, sir."

"Then we'll wait and see whether Gallagher and this schoolteacher find anything." The officer looked at Simon with a steely-eyed seriousness. "If they do find what we think might be down there, we get it, and then…" The officer went silent in mid-sentence.

"And then, sir?" asked Simon.

"And then we terminate the fieldtrip."

PART III

Chapter 40

The little Cessna aircraft had flown south, out into the Pacific, then tucked back around and landed in a remote airstrip in Guatemala before quickly unloading its passengers and their gear, refueling, then sprinting back to where it had come before nightfall.

Gallagher and Laura were greeted on the dusty tarmac with a handshake and a near-toothless smile from a greasy-haired man in ragged tropical shorts and matching shirt. "Welcome to Guatemala, *Señor* and *Señora* Smith," said the man, his demeanor unexpectedly friendly. "This way."

The businesslike man walked them to a small building in a compound of several buildings of similar size. Although the site appeared to be a remote jungle outpost of some sort, Gallagher noticed the military manner and orderliness of it all.

"Please, Mr. Smith, drop your bags," said the man, as he walked around the back of a bar in which they were the only patrons. "You must be thirsty."

"Where exactly are we?" asked Gallagher, his wits somewhat out of balance after the events of day.

The man walked back around holding two bottles of cold beer then placed them on the round table where Gallagher and Laura had seated themselves. "Please, feel welcome here. My name is Jorge Ramos, and that is all you really need to know right now. You will stay here tonight. We have running water, so you are welcome to clean up. We will have something ready for you to eat in a little while."

"Thank you, Jorge. You are most kind." Gallagher sipped at his beer.

Ramos smiled then pulled a folded map from his pocket. Sitting down, he opened it. Gallagher and Laura looked on curiously. "Another plane will arrive here tomorrow with the mail and other supplies we need to keep this place going. The story is that you are a married couple on holiday who need a lift back to Guatemala City." Ramos pointed to the city on the map. "A commercial flight is leaving the next day for Managua. With your new passports, you should have no problem entering the country."

"What do we do when we get to Managua?" asked Gallagher as Laura looked on.

"Oh, *señor*, that is up to you. Unfortunately this is not a 'packaged tour,' as you might say." Ramos laughed.

"I see."

"There is no need for worry," said Ramos, as he pulled another, smaller map of Nicaragua from his pocket and opened it on top of the other map. "The place you are looking for is here, we think. It is more of a village apparently. Too small to be noted on any map." Gallagher watched Ramos's finger move across the map a he provided his briefing.

"You think we can find it?" asked Gallagher.

"Most certainly, *señor*, if it is still there. These little villages come and go. My advice would be to rent a jeep and try. That is all you can do, *señor*, yes?"

"It would seem so."

"Good. There is also a contact in Managua whom I have been instructed to provide to you."

"What is his name?" asked Gallagher.

Ramos smiled again. "No names, *señor*. Only a phone number that I will show you and that you will need to memorize before leaving tomorrow. The number is not for general information, *señor*. It's only to be dialed if absolutely necessary. Do you understand?"

"Yes," said Gallagher. He and Laura were beginning to comprehend the stretch of the invisible network that spread across Central America.

"Very good, *señor*." Ramos went behind the bar and grabbed another beer for himself. He offered Gallagher and Laura a cigarette. Gallagher accepted, and Ramos lit it and then one for himself. "What you are looking for must be important, yes?"

Gallagher now smiled and exhaled smoke. "Need-to-know, Jorge. Need-to-know."

"You are learning, *señor*," said Ramos, raising his bottle of beer to the table and smiling. "You will do just fine."

Chapter 41

"I thought we were clear. You were not to call here."

The well-dressed man was calm as he cradled the phone in his hand. "The detective and the teacher have gone off the radar. We don't know where they are."

"You're being paid very well not to make such mistakes. First you remove the priest without permission, and then a second priest, and now you lose the only trail left? The client is not happy."

"Those deaths were unfortunate but couldn't be helped. Your client was the one pushing us for immediate results," said the well-dressed man, his ire growing but subdued.

"What do you want?"

The well-dressed man waited. "We need to know where they are. If they obtain the information out of our sight or reach, the game is over. And your client's agenda will be more than compromised, wouldn't you say?"

The man on the other end of the line didn't respond to the last comment. "I will see what I can do, but it dislikes me." The man waited then shifted in his line of questioning. "And nothing obtained from their apartments sheds any light?"

"I would think that would be self-evident. I didn't dial this number on a whim."

"I'll do what I can. But if we can't locate them soon, we may have to flush them out from wherever they may be."

"That wouldn't be wise," said the well-dressed man. "Doing so might never give your client the assurance that he's looking for. It could lead to blowback."

"They may be flushed out soon anyway. If the police move forward with their inquiry and formal charges are filed against the detective, we may be facing that scenario whether we like it or not."

"Then I suggest," said the well-dressed man, "you make sure that doesn't happen."

Chapter 42

Forty-eight hours after they had landed in Guatemala, Gallagher and Laura found themselves driving in an open-top jeep in the Nicaraguan countryside. Gallagher had been trying his best to dodge potholes on the dirt roads, while Laura struggled to navigate with a map in her lap and her hand clamped to an armrest in the jeep.

"Easy," said Laura, after a bump that nearly sent her over the side.

"These aren't exactly city driving conditions," responded Gallagher. "How much farther?"

Laura looked at her map and then at her watch. "We've been driving three hours. My guess would be another hour." The jeep hit another bump. "Or an hour-and-a-half, if this jeep makes it that far." Laura looked at Gallagher and smiled.

"Very funny," said Gallagher.

Despite the intrinsic danger of their situation, Gallagher and Laura were getting swept up in feeling of adventure. With all their gear strapped securely into the back of the jeep, they felt a sort of liberation. The lush, natural surroundings were free of any complexities, and the simple rural sites seemed to take them away from the serious and complex reason for their excursion.

The weather was hot and very humid, but the wind from the open jeep and the rise in altitude made it comfortable and added to the sense of freedom that they both found somewhat ironic.

Thirty minutes later, Gallagher pulled into a small country store with one rusted gas pump and a dirty sign offering Coca-Cola. An old man in a straw hat slowly got up from a metal chair in front of the store and approached the jeep.

"*Buenos dias*," said Laura with a smile.

"*Buenos dias*," responded the man to the beautiful "gringo" in the jeep. "*La gasolina, señor?*" said the man, looking across to Gallagher, who sat in the driver's seat.

Gallagher glanced at the fuel gauge. "*Si, por favor. Gracias.*"

The man hobbled to the gas pump and removed the hose. Laura leaned over to kiss Gallagher and said, "Another few weeks here, and you'll be a native speaker."

"I'm going inside to get us something to drink. I'm parched." Gallagher responded to Laura's kiss with one of his own. Then he pulled back and looked through his sunglasses at Laura's. "Ask your friend here about the village. Maybe he knows something." He got out of the jeep and walked into the store.

Five minutes later, Gallagher returned with two bottles of Coca-Cola and some candy bars. He paid the gas attendant, who tipped his straw hat and went back eagerly to his metal chair. Gallagher got into the jeep. "What did he say?"

"Looks like we made better time than I'd thought," said Laura. "The village is only twenty miles away. I have the directions."

Gallagher started up the jeep as Laura waved to the gasman, who raised his hand then plopped his hat over his eyes. The jeep kicked up dirt as it took off down the road and toward the little village of Caldera, the proximity of the location now bringing a serious silence for the first time all day.

Chapter 43

The jeep rolled into the tiny, one-street village an hour later. Small shacks with clay and iron roofs lined the road. Three children chased a chicken into a deserted alleyway. Few people were about, and there were no cars or buses to be seen.

Gallagher and Laura felt the stares they knew were coming from the shacks. Gallagher pulled the jeep to a stop in front of what looked to be a postal office.

"Now what?" he asked Laura.

Laura looked out on the town. There was a simplicity to it all, she thought, and she felt strangely at home. "Patience, Peter. I'm not sure these people are used to a couple of gringos waltzing in here." Gazing at the street, she caught the curious look of an old woman who was sweeping a front stoop. "Let's pull off this main road, and try to be a little more inconspicuous."

They parked the jeep near a large shade tree a hundred yards away, grabbed their bags containing the photos and other materials, and began to walk, Laura leading the way. Laura caught the eye of the woman she had seen and flashed her a smile. "*Hola,*" she said to the woman. "*Buenos dias.*"

The old woman curtsied and smiled back at Laura, not sure of Gallagher. "*Buenos dias, señora.*"

Laura, in fluent Spanish, instantly began to charm the woman and set her at ease. Gallagher watched from a few feet away, careful not to encroach on her interaction with the villager. After a minute, Laura turned toward him and relayed the gist of her conversation. "There's a small house about a mile down the road. This woman thinks the lady there may have some better information. Apparently the lady is rather reclusive."

Gallagher and Laura loaded themselves back into the jeep and took off down the road, leaving the old woman looking at a trail of dust.

They arrived not three minutes later at the old house, which was set back from the dirt road in a patch of land they assumed once had been used for farming but had clearly gone wild over the years. Smoke wafted up from the chimney.

"Wait here, Peter. If she's as shy as the old woman told me, you may spook her. Give me the picture you showed Father Symanski, the one of him with the other priests and the boy." Gallagher reached into his bag and riffled through its contents, pulling the now crinkled photo out and handing it to Laura. "I'll signal you if I find anything."

Gallagher watched as Laura made her way to the front door of the decaying house. She knocked on the door then looked back at Gallagher, who remained anxiously watching.

The door didn't open, but Gallagher saw Laura speaking to someone who was inside. He waited, his stomach churning. The door opened, and he watched even more anxiously as Laura was let inside. The door closed.

Ten minutes later, the door opened again, and Laura signaled to Gallagher to join her. Gallagher grabbed his mailbag attaché and walked slowly toward the house. His breathing grew noticeably heavy. He walked in behind Laura, his eyes adjusting to the low light and the sweet smell of burning wood. An old woman with white hair and a dirty house apron held the picture he had given Laura against her chest with both hands.

"Peter," said Laura, "this is Mrs. Bolanos. She's Tio's aunt." Laura turned to the old woman and introduced him as Peter Gallagher, which let Gallagher know she hadn't used their false identities.

The old woman nodded. "*Buenos dias, Señor* Gallagher."

"*Buenos dias, señora.*"

Mrs. Bolanos spoke directly to Laura and pointed to a small chest adjacent to a low table. Laura turned then spoke to Gallagher, again translating. "She apologizes for the tight space here. We can put our bags in that chest and use it to sit on."

Gallagher moved to the chest, placed his and Laura's bags inside it, and slid the chest next to the low table in the center of the meager two-room structure. He helped Mrs. Bolanos move a small stool then helped her to sit down. "*Gracias*," she said, breathing heavily as she took a seat.

The old woman looked at the two Americans then at the photo Laura had given her. She stared at it and began to weep. Laura took her hand and spoke to her again in Spanish. Gallagher silently looked on as the woman spoke to Laura again.

Laura turned to Gallagher and translated. "She said that seeing that photo brought back memories of past times, and that the sight of the little boy makes her feel very old." Mrs. Bolanos continued to speak in Spanish as Laura translated. "He was such a good boy, she says."

Gallagher looked at the woman warmly and began his line of questioning. Laura translated for him. "Mrs. Bolanos, do you remember when that picture was taken?"

The woman spoke. "She says it was many years ago," said Laura. "She says it was a very dangerous time. The rebels had just deposed the government, and her nephew was sent to her for safekeeping."

Mrs. Bolanos continued to talk. "She says the rebels used the village to wage war on the government, and then they waged war on the village."

"What about the other men in the picture?" Gallagher asked.

Mrs. Bolanos looked at Laura as she translated the question. Then she put her hands over her eyes and began to cry again. Laura worked to calm her and gently coax her to an answer.

"She says the priests…" Laura looked at Mrs. Bolanos and could tell she was growing noticeably angry. "She says the American priests came. They came to the village and…" Laura worked to translate through the emotion that was now growing in the old woman. "They…" Laura turned to Gallagher. "Something about the devil priests and how they stole from the villagers. They made them do and believe evil things. Unholy men, she says."

Laura turned toward Mrs. Bolanos and again tried to calm her.

"Ask her about the boy. Is he alive? Where can we find him?" Gallagher asked Laura.

Out of one ear, Gallagher caught the sound of an engine. He watched as Laura continued to try to get through to the old woman. He rose from his seat, headed to the window, and peered out. Two men wearing tropical apparel and dark aviator sunglasses were looking in the back of the jeep. Gallagher's internal alarm sounded, and he moved back toward the table. Laura looked up at him.

"Visitors," Gallagher told her. Without a second's thought, he grabbed the picture from the table and nudged Laura from atop the chest. He opened the lid, tossed the photo into the chest, and slid the chest back against the wall from where it had come.

Laura hurriedly spoke to the old woman, who looked confused as to what was happening. Gallagher watched as Mrs. Bolanos acknowledged the information that Laura was telling her in rapid-fire Spanish. Gallagher reseated himself on the floor and attempted to compose himself.

The door swung open forcefully. Mrs. Bolanos screamed at the sight of the two men, their dark aviator sunglasses staring imposingly at the group, who sat around the small table. The guns in the men's hands were very much at the ready.

Chapter 44

"I tell you again. We're tourists." Gallagher remained defiant. He sat in a hot and humid interrogation room somewhere in Managua, Nicaragua. Laura wasn't with him.

One of the arresting agents, who had raided the little house in Caldera, smiled and looked down again at the passport in his hands. "Mr. Smith, if that is your real name, we're not amateurs. Don't test my patience." The man lit another cigarette. He didn't offer one to Gallagher, whose arms remained tied behind his back.

Gallagher said nothing, as he continued to stare at the agent. As he did, he wondered what the man already knew or whether he knew anything at all. He also wondered what Laura was saying. They were in a prototypical "prisoners' dilemma," but he decided to stick to his cover story. To go back on that now would be tantamount to a very long prison term or even a death sentence.

"You still want to tell me you are a tourist, Mr. Smith?" said the agent, inhaling deeply on his cigarette. He stood and moved to where Gallagher sat. "Tell me the truth."

Gallagher worked to stall, answering the challenge as best he could without answering the question directly. "You tell me, *señor*. You assumedly impounded our jeep and our luggage. You tell me what you found in there. You found clothes for tourists who are on vacation. You found a razor and a comb. You can keep the sunscreen."

The agent swung hard at Gallagher's stomach, doubling him over. "Don't fuck with me, you arrogant shit." He pulled Gallagher's head up by his hair then slapped him across the face.

Gallagher coughed and gasped for air but then gathered his wits. If the agent could beat him senseless, it would at least stop the questioning, he thought. "Fuck you. I want to speak to the Canadian Embassy."

"You may want to speak to a priest, *señor*, because it may be the last conversation you will ever have." The agent spat into Gallagher's face then slapped him again before returning to his chair opposite his prisoner. "Shall we try again?"

Twenty minutes passed as Gallagher continued to lead the agent nowhere. He remained firm on his cover but wondered how long he could keep it up. Had Laura already confessed, Gallagher thought, they would have had him by now. He only hoped she continued to resist.

"Okay, *Señor* Smith," said the agent. "You give us no choice but to resort to other, more intensive efforts." The agent smiled sickly then lit another cigarette.

The door to the small interrogation room opened. Another agent summoned the interrogator. Gallagher looked on, his mouth and nose dripping with blood and his body dripping with sweat. The interrogator stood and walked out of the room. The door closed.

* * *

When the door opened again, the blood on Gallagher's face was dry and his mouth desperate for water. His head was now bowed, and he was starting to doze off, his senses losing focus.

"Mr. Smith?" said a voice, in near perfect American English.

Gallagher looked up, his eyes trying to adjust to the light and through the haze of the humid air that was mixed with lingering cigarette smoke. He caught sight of a tall, well-dressed gentleman in a tropical suit and tie. The man carried an expensive brown leather attaché.

"*Señor* Smith," said the man again, as he pulled out a chair and sat across from Gallagher.

"Are you from the Canadian Embassy?" asked Gallagher.

"No," said the man, watching as the glimmer of hope in Gallagher's bloodshot eyes faded from sight. "I'm a lawyer. I've arranged the release of both you and your wife."

Gallagher looked at the man—who appeared to be in his mid-40s, with a strong physique and kind, dark brown eyes—and then looked around the room, wondering whether this was a trick. "Is she okay?"

The lawyer looked at Gallagher closely. "Your wife is fine. I have just seen her, and they are readying her for release. Your luggage will be returned. However, as soon as you and your wife are ready, you've been asked to leave the country. If you do so quickly and quietly, no charges will be filed."

"Who are you?" asked Gallagher, dazed.

The man looked on sympathetically, his air polished and professional. "My name is Thomas Alfredo Orgeira Garcia." He stared sharply at Gallagher.

"That's quite a name," said Gallagher, managing a chuckle.

Garcia smiled back strangely, his eyes looking straight into Gallagher's. A gentle nod of his head signaled something. "Why don't you just call me by my nickname then, if that would be easier."

"And what would that be?"

Garcia replied, "You can call me Tio."

Chapter 45

Captain Drexler put down the phone in disbelief. He grew quiet and serious and peered through the blinds that hung on the glass walls into the precinct's common office. He wondered whether something or someone was out there waiting to strike. He shook his head to clear his thoughts then focused his gaze on Ty Johnson, who was at his desk filling out a mountain of paperwork.

Drexler sauntered over to him. "Johnson," Drexler whispered, while checking whether anyone else was taking notice of his location, "come see me in twenty minutes. I'll be in the cafeteria." He walked out.

Johnson, perplexed, lifted his head from his pile of paperwork. He looked nervously around the office to see whether any interested stares were being sent his way. There were none. *Oh, Christ,* he thought. *The game is up.*

* * *

Drexler was alone at a quiet table in the police cafeteria, sipping at a can of soda and pretending to make notes on a pad of paper.

Johnson approached guardedly then sat down. "What's up, boss?"

"What have you heard from Gallagher?" asked Drexler.

"What do you need to hear?"

"Don't fuck with me," said Drexler in a lowered voice as he scanned the room. "I just got a call from the mayor's office again. It seems no charges will be filed against Gallagher. He is to be reinstated immediately. Now where the fuck is he? I've called him several times myself, after I got tired of you—over the last few days—telling me you were supposedly ignorant as to where he is."

Johnson swallowed hard and appeared genuinely shocked. He said nothing but just looked at Captain Drexler directly.

"Johnson, I'm not going to jump down your throat on this one." Drexler was calm in his tone but clearly on edge. "The fact that I wanted to meet here, away from curious eyes, should be an indication to you that the matter with Gallagher is starting to seriously baffle me."

"What happened?" asked Johnson.

"The mayor called me directly, said Gallagher was to be reinstated. No questions asked. What the fuck is going on? Frankly, I'm getting worried about Gallagher. This whole thing stinks."

Johnson looked at Drexler and waited, sensing that the relationship had most definitely changed with Drexler over the issue. "I think there are some things we need to get straight on, boss. But let's just say you're right to be concerned."

"What do you have to tell me? No bullshit. We need to be straight up on this."

Johnson again waited then took a deep breath. "Do you want the short version or the long one?"

Chapter 46

Gallagher finally woke up a little before five thirty that evening in a plush guest room in Thomas Garcia's home in the hills overlooking Managua. A housemaid in livery placed a cold glass of water next to his bed and fresh towels on a chair nearby.

"*Gracias*," Gallagher said.

The maid smiled and pointed to the wooden valet on which hung fresh clothes that hadn't come from his luggage. "For you to wear, *señor*," said the maid in decent though heavily accented English.

Gallagher smiled back and nodded his thanks, watching as the maid slipped out and closed the door. His head and body felt sore and raw, but the sleep had been sound, and he was feeling much better. He got up, showered for the second time that afternoon, then got dressed, pleasantly surprised at the near exact fit of the white button-down shirt, blue blazer, linen pants, and brown loafers. He finished the water brought to him minutes before and walked out and down the home's commanding staircase.

"Ah, Peter," said Garcia, dressed in a light sport coat and slacks. "How are you feeling?"

"Still sore but much better. Thank you for everything you've done." He took in the home with more detail than when he had first arrived that afternoon: the clean, open floor plan; fine antiques; and breathtaking view from the large, clear windows of the Nicaraguan capitol below.

"It was the least we could do," said Garcia. "The clothes fit you well. I was right. I told Carolina that you and I were just about the same build." He smiled, a cocktail in his hand. "Come, let's get you a drink. The ladies are in the sitting room chatting away."

Gallagher followed Garcia outside and onto the massive, red-tiled terrace. The sun was starting a slow descent, the breeze of the hills cool and comfortable.

"Magnificent house you have here, Thomas."

"Yes, we are lucky. Here, gin and tonic with ice." Garcia handed Gallagher his drink. "Please, let's sit. We have much to discuss."

They walked across the terrace to an outdoor sitting area. Gallagher caught sight through the window of Laura and Carolina, Garcia's wife who was dressed in a chic, sleeveless blue dress, her soft dark hair cascading down over tanned and toned shoulders. They sat comfortably on a sofa inside, glasses of wine in their hands, deep in conversation. They turned and briefly waved when they saw him, Laura sending him a relieved smile that he was up and about and looking well, all things considered.

"Please, Peter, come and sit," Garcia said as he took a seat in a white wicker chair.

Gallagher joined him in an adjacent chair and scanned the view of the city. He took a deep sip of his drink.

Garcia looked at Gallagher and waited for him to get comfortable. "The woman you met in the village was, indeed, my aunt. She is my father's sister. She called me as soon as the police took you and Laura away."

Garcia reached into his sport coat and pulled out the dog-eared photo of himself as a small boy and handed it to Gallagher. "I was thirteen when the picture was taken. Must have been around '80 or '81."

Gallagher was stunned to see the small picture he had left behind in the village house. "How...?" he began to ask before Garcia interrupted.

"Someone from Caldera brought it with your bags. Everything is here. The government doesn't know about them. If they had found your bags and the contents, you wouldn't be sitting here."

"And your aunt? Is she unharmed?" asked Gallagher.

"She is fine. She told them nothing."

"We're grateful. How can we ever thank you and your aunt for all you have done?"

"She is a strong woman. I owe her my own life as well." Garcia grew quiet and sat forward in his chair, his elbows on his knees as he held his drink. "Peter," he began, "many things ran through my mind today as all of this went on—that picture for one. And why you are here in Nicaragua."

Garcia looked back through the window at his wife and Laura, who were talking and laughing. "There are things this picture brought back to me: memories I have long since hidden away, things that are unpleasant and that I would not want my wife to learn about…for her own protection and that of my children."

"I think I understand," responded Gallagher.

Over the next hour, Gallagher relayed the events that had led them to this place in time: the death of Edward Sachs, SJ; the investigation and discoveries at the parish in Washington; the conversation with and subsequent death of Clarence Symanski, SJ; the discovered surveillance at their Washington apartments; the events in Mexico City; and how one picture of a small boy taken thirty years ago had led him and Laura to a small village in Nicaragua.

Garcia listened intently, allowing Gallagher to move quickly through a recitation of events that Gallagher was very good at describing. The story resurrected feelings and memories that Garcia had hoped were dead.

Chapter 47

The sun was setting over Managua, the city lights beginning to twinkle.

Garcia rose and refilled their cocktail glasses with more ice, gin, and tonic. "It looks like the ladies are in no rush for dinner," he said, as he looked through the glass window and caught the sounds of his wife and Laura laughing and talking in Spanish over wine that flowed freely. "That's good. It gives us more time to talk." Garcia handed Gallagher a fresh drink. "And sneak a cigarette," added Garcia, again looking to make sure his wife wasn't watching before poaching a cigarette from a silver case next to their chairs.

Gallagher lit a cigarette with Garcia and sat back. His mind felt lighter, but perhaps it was the booze. Either way, he accepted the feeling without guilt. He waited for Garcia to speak.

"Peter, what I will tell you is between us, agreed? Some of this Carolina already knows, but other things I need to keep away from her. It is for her safety, as I said. Do you understand, my friend?"

"Of course."

Garcia inhaled deeply on his cigarette and exhaled into the cool evening air of Managua. "In 1978 my father sent me to the village of Caldera to live with my aunt. He was an army officer with the Somoza regime. He and Somoza had been good friends, classmates at West Point. Originally the plan was to get my sister and me out of the country. But by the time my father had determined we should leave, the net was already up, and there was no way out. The Sandinistas were only days away from taking the capitol." Garcia paused for a long moment. "So we were smuggled to the countryside, assumed new last names, and lived like other villagers. My father was executed by the communists, my mother raped and then killed, and my family home burned to the ground."

Gallagher saw deep pain in Garcia's eyes. He wanted to offer words of comfort but could find none.

Garcia got up from his chair and paced around. "The village was effectively a sanctuary, albeit a covert one. My father knew from his intelligence officers that the Sandinistas had taken over, and what better place to put children of the Somoza regime than in the last place the Sandinistas would suspect them to be living?"

Gallagher sipped his drink nervously. "It must have been terrifying."

"It was…and worse." Garcia sipped his own drink then sat back down. "This is much harder than I thought it would be, going back to those times in my head. I've tried not to do that."

"I'm sorry, Thomas. Should we stop? We don't need to do this tonight."

"We have to do this tonight. You need to know this. My sister, who was a couple of years older than me, had a much harder time. She was used to more comfortable living. My father had doted on her. He loved her so much.

"Eventually she adapted. For me it was much easier. The poverty and dirt did not bother me. My aunt and uncle helped as best they could to deal with the transition, although the fear of death helped drive home how crucial blending in was for us." Garcia smiled slightly. "I'm rambling on now. I'm sorry."

"Don't be."

"Let me cut to the chase. Your story and your theory about why Father Sachs was killed—I believe it is true. A number of Jesuits were supportive of the Marxist revolution. Cardenal, who you mentioned, was probably the most prominent of them here in Nicaragua. But there was also considerable support from other Jesuits around the world, the American Jesuits in particular.

"Beginning in the mid-1970s, American Jesuits began to show up in Nicaragua in noticeable numbers. There was support from these priests for the communist insurgents. They came down and used their positions as Catholic priests to convert the peasants to the Sandinista cause. They preached what they called 'liberation of the masses'—freeing the poor from the bondage of American imperialism that had, as they said at that time, been responsible for the plight of the Nicaraguan people."

Gallagher interjected, "And the priests in the photo?"

"Yes. They were part of it. We had maybe one or two American Jesuits who were in the village at any one time. Sometimes there were more. At first the villagers seemed to welcome the priests. They were kind, they worked in the fields with the villagers, and they tended to the sick."

Gallagher remained silent, watching as Garcia's demeanor turned more serious.

"There was an old priest. Father Dominguez was his name. He must have been in his late seventies when I arrived. Father Dominguez was just a poor village priest, and he did not see eye to eye with these American Jesuits who came down with their long hair and beards and were preaching things he viewed as heretical."

"What sort of things?"

"Oh, anything and everything, Peter. They told the villagers they needed to use birth control, that pre-marital sexual relations were a way of expressing God's beauty, that the Pope and the Catholic hierarchy were tyrants ruling like medieval princes. They sat around and smoked marijuana and sang folk music, often as part of what they called a 'people's Mass.'" Garcia looked at Gallagher's reaction. "Yes, you see what I mean."

"So what happened?"

"One day old Father Dominguez, after threatening to force the Jesuits out of the village, was taken by the Sandinistas—in full view of the villagers—and summarily executed. The complaints about the Jesuits stopped after that."

Gallagher absorbed the information with disgust. "What about the Jesuit priests? Didn't they respond with revulsion at the killing of a fellow priest? Christ almighty." Gallagher suddenly controlled himself. "I'm sorry for saying that. It was inappropriate."

"But understandable," said Garcia, sympathetically. "That was my reaction as well. No, the Jesuits did nothing. They simply walked over to the body of Father Dominguez and said prayers. Then they sat down with the rebels who had executed the old priest and ate dinner."

Gallagher was shocked, but he sequestered his emotions again, trying to stay levelheaded.

"When the Sandinistas actually began to 'govern' the country," Garcia said, "it got worse. Some of the Jesuits began to have sexual relationships with the girls in the village; they took the best food for themselves; the drugs were rampant. The whole time, these priests justified it all by saying this was part of the 'New Church'—the 'People's Church,' they called it."

"What about the priests in the photograph?" Gallagher asked.

"I don't remember much. I think I blocked most of it out." Garcia looked at the picture again. "This one—Father Thomas was his name. He was very enthusiastic about it all. He was the one who blessed the body of Father Dominguez that day. And this other one." Garcia looked as though he was trying to remember his name.

"That was Clarence Symanski. The priest at Georgetown University whom I met with and who I found dead a day later," said Gallagher.

"I don't recall seeing him more than once, maybe twice. I think he was just in the village for a short time. I don't remember anything else about him."

"And this one?" asked Gallagher, leaning over and pointing to the former pastor of St. Gabriel in Washington.

"O'Brien." Garcia stared at the picture, as his mind seemed to search for something. "I remember him. He was a staunch supporter of the communists. He was in the village many times. He came and went frequently, bringing supplies when he visited."

"What sort of 'supplies,' Thomas?"

"Food, medicine, and…" Garcia failed to finish his sentence.

"And what?"

Garcia looked back to see that his wife was still inside and out of earshot. He sipped his drink and looked at Gallagher. "Weapons…and cash, American dollars. Lots of both."

"Are you saying that Father—" said Gallagher before Garcia interrupted him.

"Father O'Brien was smuggling weapons and dollars from the United States. How he was doing it or who his sources were, I don't know exactly. But I can tell you with total confidence that this Jesuit was directly financing and supplying one of the most brutal communist revolutions in Central America." Garcia waited as Gallagher digested the revelation and then added, "And he was doing it, as he used to say, 'for the greater glory of God.'"

Chapter 48

Garcia and Gallagher were quiet through the first course of dinner, mostly listening as their respective better halves laughed and talked without interruption. It was the first time in a long while that Gallagher had seen Laura so relaxed and at ease.

Neither of the men shared at the table what they had discussed before sitting down to eat. They had agreed that the subject was best left for later that evening or deferred until the next day. But somehow both knew that they likely would be revisiting the issue sooner rather than later.

The evening was otherwise perfect. The Garcia home was warm and inviting, the epitome of sophistication and elegance. Inside the large dining room, the hosts and guests sat around a large table draped with fine linen, china, and crystal. The food was hearty and exquisitely prepared from the best local beef and fresh vegetables, the maid ensuring that the meal was properly served and the wine properly chilled. Garcia and Gallagher felt relaxed as the discussion of the previous hours now sat pleasantly in remission.

"Mama, Papa," said one of the two girls who had approached unnoticed.

Carolina looked over to see her two young daughters dressed in their white nightgowns and slippers; the younger girl held a small teddy bear. "Hello, my angels," she said in Spanish then shifted to English. "Laura, Peter, these are our daughters, Isabella and Lucia. Isabella is seven, and Lucia is five." Carolina turned to her daughters. "Are you ready for bed?"

"*Si*, Mama," said the oldest, who kissed her mother on the cheek, followed by Lucia. The girls moved to Laura and, to Laura's surprise, kissed her goodnight as well. *"Buenas noches, señorita."* The girls moved around the table with well-bred manners and also bid their father and Gallagher goodnight.

Laura smiled as she watched the two little girls give Gallagher a peck on the cheek before scampering off to bed with a giggle. "They're adorable, Carolina. You must be very proud of them."

"They're the apple of their father's eye," said Carolina, looking fondly at her husband through the candlelight.

Garcia smiled at his wife. "Those manners have been very expensive indeed. The nuns have been very good in their teachings."

"They're in Catholic school, then?" asked Gallagher.

"Yes," said Garcia, looking at his plate.

Gallagher noted the gesture and understood it perfectly, having just been made privy to the tenuous personal history that Thomas Garcia had with Roman Catholic institutions; the sadness of those recently revived memories on the house patio still painfully fresh.

Carolina interjected, as her husband grew silent. "More wine?"

Gallagher was nearly drunk but graciously accepted. "Please, that would be wonderful."

Garcia picked up the wine bottle and poured more for his guest and his wife. "Laura, as Carolina may have mentioned when you were talking, my history with the Church was somewhat strained in my youth."

"I mentioned it to Laura when we talked, darling," said Carolina. "Laura is a teacher at a Catholic school in Washington, DC."

Garcia smiled. "What are your thoughts, Laura, on Catholic education these days?"

Laura felt slightly defensive, but the multiple glasses of wine had numbed what would have otherwise been an uncomfortable question. "I think it remains very good. I mean, the quality of the basics remains first rate. To the discredit of the Catholic school system where I teach, however, there are some theological defects." Laura sipped her wine.

"Do you find that the Church is rather apologetic in terms of asserting the faith on the students?" asked Garcia warmly.

"I think that's probably true," said Laura. "The Church has failed in many ways to pull itself from its Vatican II mindset in which the only rule is that there are no rules. I don't think inculcating in young children doubt in the faith does them any service. In my opinion, there's a real benefit in theological confidence and in instilling discipline and tradition. But we're repeatedly told that those traditional teaching methods were abusive or archaic. Even so, they worked well for my parents. Yet my own generation, shaped by the 'rule of no rules,' doesn't seem to display the same sort of reverence and loyalty. Frankly it's a shame."

Carolina took a long draw of wine before saying, "We quite agree. Fortunately the nuns at the girls' school are very steeped in traditional Catholic teachings. I tend to think the mistakes of the past have been recognized for just that, although in Nicaragua there still remains a strong whiff of antiestablishment thinking. Some continue to see it as a threat, but it seems ironic to think of such ideas as truly 'established' anymore."

For nearly two hours, the dinner table was replete with lighter discussion and a celebratory atmosphere. The perfectly cooked beef and fresh vegetables from the Nicaraguan countryside were delicious and the wine continued to flow freely. By the time coffee and dessert were served, the guests and hosts were quite drunk and laughing constantly. Gallagher and Laura had remained thoroughly enchanted by the stories of their hosts—how Garcia had attended West Point and how he and Carolina had met on a blind date when Carolina was studying at Columbia. How they courageously had moved back to Nicaragua from Honduras in the late 1990s. How Garcia had gone back to study law then struggled to find a place among the most prominent of Managua attorneys.

Gallagher provided his own life story. He recounted how he had found and then lost a calling as an attorney. He spoke of how he had come to Washington, DC, and about his first cases as a police detective. Laura too had described her personal journey—her privileged upbringing in Washington as the daughter of a man mired in politics and her own educational path to public service through teaching.

By the time the coffee had grown cold, the wineglasses empty, and the ashtrays full, the two couples had charted a rich course across a multitude of topics from politics to religion to travel and to love. Personal philosophies were exchanged and debated, dreams shared, and disappointments recounted. It was with a sense of sadness for all that the night was drawing to a close and that pillows were now in order.

"We've had a wonderful evening," said Laura, her eyes growing noticeably heavy. "I think I'll sleep for days. Thank you so much."

"Oh, Laura, it's our pleasure," said Carolina. "We consider you and Peter family. We expect this to be the first of many evenings together over the years." Carolina turned to Peter. "Now, when are you going to make this lovely girl an honest lady?"

"Carolina," said Garcia, challenging his wife with a smile, "give him a break." He turned toward Peter. "Although my wife is quite correct," he added with a laugh.

Peter blushed and, through the candlelight, looked at Laura, who caught his eyes and smiled back. *Yes*, he thought. *They're right.* "Well, we'll have to see," he said.

"Oh, you poop," said Laura, flashing him one of the smiles he would never tire of.

"I mean, we'll have to see if she'll go along with the idea," said Peter.

Laura continued to smile. *Yes, I will,* she thought. *I certainly will.*

Garcia looked at Peter and Laura and then at his wife. *Yes, they will make a good couple*, he thought. He now only hoped that what he wanted to be true would be. But there were things that Garcia knew—and that he still had to tell them—that might place them in more danger than he wanted at that moment.

But what Garcia had left to tell could wait until the morning. The danger would still be there to face them; there was little doubt of that. And he needed more time, if only the night, to figure out a way to help them avoid it, if he could at all.

Chapter 49

At six o'clock the next morning, the CIA in Langley, Virginia, was notified by the National Security Agency of another intercepted diplomatic cable that had originated from Managua en route to the Nicaraguan embassy in Washington, DC. The agent, known as Simon, sat reading it a little after seven a.m., his CIA superior watching him as he did.

"It seems our missing Americans are in Managua," Simon said, as he sat before the CIA officer's desk.

The officer waited until Simon finished reading the cable, then said, "What were they doing in that village? How did they get out of Mexico City right from under our eyes? Who's helping them? What did they find?"

"Nothing," said Simon. "They found nothing."

"Why do you say that?"

"Why send the cable otherwise? My guess would be that Nicaraguan intelligence sent this to see if their contact in Washington knows anything that can shed more light."

The CIA officer rubbed his chin. "The parish housekeeper, Maria Rosario?"

"That would be my conclusion based on the fact that the first cable out was likely spurred by the housekeeper's own intelligence."

"Goddamn it," said the CIA officer. "Where is it? If the Nicaraguans don't have it, we don't have it, and the Hawk doesn't have it. Where is the book?"

"Perhaps the detective was looking for it." Simon looked down at the cable again. "At this village, Caldera."

The CIA officer pondered ending the game and sending a team to "terminate the fieldtrip" but then dismissed the idea for the moment. "Perhaps these spics have given us an opportunity."

"To do what?"

"To flush out the third force in this mess. We still don't know who was responsible for the deaths of those priests."

"Does that matter at this point?" asked Simon.

"I don't know," said the CIA officer, "but the alternative is to send a team down there, grab the detective and the girl, squeeze whatever they know out of them, and leave them by some dirt road for the peasants to find the next morning." The CIA officer thought for a moment. "While it's tempting, I'm not sure we can do that. It would only give the press a heads-up and sully the entire objective of the operation—to solve this quietly and avoid any embarrassment to the United States of America."

"Then what are my orders, sir?"

"Put a twenty-four-hour watch on the housekeeper. Arrange a tap on the parish phone and bug the rectory."

"Sir, we're heading into dangerous territory here," said Simon, aware that the CIA was legally barred from what it considered "domestic unpleasantness" of this sort. "We're on thin ice already in keeping tabs on the housekeeper. If FBI counterintelligence got wind of that fact alone, they'd cut our balls off."

"Just do it. Do you understand?" The CIA officer ground his teeth unconsciously. "If the information we're after isn't in the hands of anyone we can suspect, perhaps it's still in that parish somewhere. Also, run the name of the village against the computer and see what comes up."

"Yes, sir," said Simon, now wondering whether his government's interest was reaching irrational proportions. Or perhaps the interest was coming from the very top for some other agenda, he thought suspiciously.

The CIA officer sensed Simon's doubt. "Remember, Simon, there's always the alternative of direct action." He paused. "Are we clear on things, then?"

"Yes, sir."

"That is all then. I want constant reports back, and I want it done quietly." The CIA officer looked down at his desk then repeated, "That is all."

Simon stood and handed back the cable, placing it gently on the desk of his superior before walking out of the office. He returned to his cubical to undertake the order he was given, although his conscience and growing suspicions continued to call to him.

It was time again to confess his sins.

Chapter 50

It was nearly noon before the Garcia household began to show signs of life after the late and highly enjoyable dinner the night before. Thomas and Carolina Garcia came down the stairs together with slightly cloudy heads and a desperate desire for strong coffee. They were somewhat surprised to see Laura bright eyed and bushy tailed, sitting on the veranda, sipping coffee and poring over photographs that littered the table at which she sat.

"*Buenos dias*, Laura," said Carolina, holding her husband's hand as they joined her. "Have you been up long?"

"*Buenos dias*. I was up at nine. I apologize for the mess here."

"Have you eaten?" asked Carolina.

"No, just coffee."

"Melinda?" Carolina said, calling for her housekeeper as she turned and went back into the house.

Garcia smiled and moved to pour himself a cup of coffee. "Carolina will have Melinda get us brunch. Is Peter up yet?"

"No," said Laura. "He's dead asleep, I imagine. Between the ordeal with the police and the late night, he must be exhausted."

Sipping his coffee from a cup and saucer, Garcia looked down at the table that Laura had strewn with photographs. "So those are the photos you and Peter have been carrying around all this time?" He moved to the table, pulled out a chair, and sat down.

"Yes," said Laura. "Did Peter tell you about any of these?"

"Other than the one photo that brought you here, we didn't really talk about them," said Garcia. "These are from the parish then?"

"Yes. We haven't looked at them much since we left Washington. I thought this morning, with the house quiet, it would be a good time to pull them out again, although I'm not exactly sure what purpose they hold now."

Garcia and Laura looked up as Carolina approached with Gallagher in tow. "Look who I've found." Carolina turned back toward the kitchen. "Brunch in a few minutes."

Gallagher smiled sheepishly then moved toward the coffee. "That was quite a night. I slept like a baby, although I am a bit sorer than yesterday." He rubbed his jaw.

"Our secret police are very adept at making sure their interrogations produce no outward signs of interrogation, although I can imagine you're feeling the effects."

Gallagher touched his stomach. His ribs felt tender. "Very," he said. "Do you think the police were on to why we were here in Managua, Thomas?"

Garcia put down his cup. "I don't think so. My guess is that two foreigners arrived in the city and didn't have any hotel room, or a local address where they were staying, or a demonstrable itinerary. That was enough to trigger the interest and suspicion. If they knew your real identity or purpose, as I said, it would not have been so simple to arrange your release.

"Speaking of which, we should get you two on a plane at some point today or tomorrow at the latest. I would recommend that we get you a flight to Panama City. From there you can go back to the United States under your real passports."

"We'll be sad to go," said Gallagher. "We've really enjoyed our time here with you, even with everything that happened." He poured some milk into his coffee and took a sip then moved to the table and sat down with Garcia and Laura. "Ah, the famous picture album." He moved his hand over the top of the piles, scattering and spreading the photos across a wider area of the tabletop.

Garcia picked up his cup and sipped his coffee, as he scanned the photos with no appreciable interest. He sipped his coffee again, placed down his cup, and reached for one of the photos. "These men were in the village all those years ago."

Laura looked up as Gallagher recognized the image from one she had described that day in the parish archives.

"That's Senator something or other," said Gallagher, looking to Laura for more detail.

"Senator Forbes Raybeck," she said. "That was taken in the 1970s. Names are on the back."

Garcia examined the list of names on the flipside of the photo. "Yes, this man was in the village. He came with the priest, O'Brien, once or twice. He was also there as part of an American delegation at the invitation of the Sandinista government."

Gallagher and Laura looked on as Garcia scrutinized the picture. "Do you think the senator has anything to do with any of this?" asked Gallagher.

"I don't know," said Garcia, his look growing more concentrated and serious. He turned the picture over again and looked at the back then flipped it over again.

"What is it, Thomas?" asked Gallagher, drinking down more coffee.

Garcia looked up. "Richard Miller. Is this man related to you, Laura, by any chance?"

"He's my father. This picture was taken at a parish picnic of some sort. My family were—and are members—of St. Gabriel."

Garcia turned white, his eyes wide. "This man was in the village once when this senator was present. He was there. I remember him."

"Who?" said Laura, wanting to have misunderstood.

"Your father, Laura." Garcia looked at her with disbelief as he held up the picture to her. Gallagher went pale as well. "Your father was in the village too."

Chapter 51

Laura's reaction to what Garcia had said about her father was peculiarly cool.

"You don't look surprised, Laura," said Garcia.

She was silent, thinking. "No, I am surprised. I suppose the last few days have numbed my senses. Nothing seems to surprise me about any of this."

Gallagher interjected. "Laura? Your father was involved in politics for many years, at least on the periphery. Is it possible he was there for a legitimate purpose?"

"I would assume so. I certainly hope so." She turned toward Garcia. "You said Senator Raybeck was in the village with my father, Thomas?"

"Yes."

"You're sure?"

"Yes." Garcia's expression was quizzical.

"And how many times did Senator Raybeck visit the village over the years?" asked Laura.

"I don't know. Maybe half-a-dozen. Why?"

"How many times was my father present? I mean, was he there with Senator Raybeck each time he visited?"

"I just remember seeing him the one time." Garcia considered for a moment. "It was the first time the senator arrived. After that, your father wasn't there."

"Were these official American delegation visits, Thomas?" asked Gallagher.

"There were some official visits, yes. But only a couple while I was in the village—right after the fall of Somoza. This was when the Americans thought the Sandinistas were a benign political movement. Your President Carter thought very highly of the Sandinistas at first."

"Were the American priests there at that time? The Jesuits, I mean," said Gallagher.

"Yes. O'Brien was there and also another. Father Thomas, I believe. It was all very friendly," said Garcia. "The Sandinistas, the Jesuits, and the American representatives—all together." Garcia grew stern as he recalled the alliance. "I should go see how Carolina is doing with brunch." He excused himself and moved inside.

Laura looked at Gallagher across the table. "He's upset, Peter."

"Yes, but I don't think we should take this personally."

"What went on in that village?" asked Laura, looking into the house to make sure she wouldn't be overheard.

"It wasn't good." Gallagher was tempted to tell Laura about the weapons and cash that Garcia had informed him about the night before, but he stopped himself. He sat there, thinking.

"What? Tell me."

Gallagher realized there was no point in hiding the truth. "Guns, money, sex, drugs…" he said. "Shall I go into more detail?"

Laura looked him straight in the eyes. "Oh, Jesus."

"I'm not sure that even Jesus was in the minds of those who supposedly represented his ideals on Earth."

"You mean the priests," Laura declared. "You mean O'Brien and Thomas." She now understood the anger she had just seen in Garcia and the cryptic ramblings of Mrs. Bolanos during their visit to Caldera.

"And other Jesuits, yes. I think it's fair to say from what Thomas told me that the Jesuits failed in upholding their sacred vows."

Laura's mouth opened as if trying to ask something, but no words came forth. Gallagher looked at her and said nothing.

Thirty minutes later, brunch was served. The table had become a strategic roundtable of sorts as the revelation about Laura's father was openly discussed. There were no awkward moments, as one might have expected;

the four friends had established a seemingly impenetrable trust over the last twenty-four hours.

Garcia and Gallagher kept silent on some of the more salacious and bloody events that Garcia had shared the night before, but all other topics were freely discussed. The four had clearly come to the conclusion that what had transpired over the last few days and weeks was much more than a simple murder investigation. Most likely a political agenda was at play.

"We need to get you out of the country today," said Garcia. "I'll arrange to get you onto a flight to Panama City and from there into Miami."

"Why not just go straight to the American embassy here?" asked Laura.

"I'm not sure that's wise," said Garcia. "If this whole thing has to do with American intelligence in some way, going to the US government may not be in your best interest."

"Well, then, where do we go?" asked Laura.

"We need to get back to Washington," said Gallagher. "The DC police may be the best bet. Theoretically, they have no interest in these political matters. They're probably the only people we can trust until this whole thing gets sorted out. Once we're back in DC, we can get your father involved."

Unexpectedly, the maid walked onto the terrace and informed Carolina that someone from Isabella's school was on the phone. Carolina walked into the house and returned calmly a couple of minutes later. "It seems Isabella forgot her journal, Thomas. I need to run it over to the school." She turned to Laura. "Isabella's teacher has the children writing in journals as part of their Spanish lessons. I think it's been very helpful with improving her writing skills."

"That's a wonderful idea," said Laura. "I should think about implementing something for our students like that when the new school year starts." She added, snidely, "Well, if I still have a job."

Gallagher sipped his coffee. He noticed Garcia staring off into the distance. "Thomas?" Garcia didn't acknowledge him. "Thomas?" Gallagher repeated, louder this time, his raised voice causing Carolina and Laura to cease their conversation.

Garcia came back from his thinking and turned toward the others.

"Thomas, what is it?" asked Carolina, her concern apparent. Gallagher and Laura waited.

"O'Brien's book," said Garcia. The others looked on, not knowing what he meant.

"What book?" asked Gallagher, breaking the silence.

"The book," said Garcia. "It is the book."

"What book?" Gallagher asked again, his voice unconsciously fierce.

"There was a book that O'Brien kept with him at all times," Garcia explained. "He made notes in it at night. I saw him writing in it. It was like an accountant's book."

"Like a ledger or a diary of some sort?" asked Gallagher.

"Yes." Garcia looked over. "And I think it is the reason for all of this."

Chapter 52

Captain Drexler watched through the open slats of his DC office as Johnson walked toward his door. He waved him in and put down his mug of coffee. "What did you find out?" asked Drexler once the door was shut.

Johnson sat in a chair in front of Drexler's desk, ready to recount his conversation with his roommate from Howard University, Horace Holmes, who was an aide to the current mayor of the District of Columbia. "All this cloak and dagger is a lot of work. Horace was pretty jumpy."

"What did he say?"

"He said there was a call to the mayor from a lawyer in DC the day after Sachs's death—a guy by the name of Victor Campbell. Campbell is a parishioner at St. Gabriel. Horace said this Campbell asked the mayor to make sure this 'event' would be handled quickly in order to avoid any negative press about the parish."

"Well, that explains the first call," said Drexler. "What about the second call?"

"Yeah," said Johnson. "Horace got pretty nervous when telling me about the second call. Seems the second one came from a guy named Davis Malloy. Malloy is a heavy hitter on K Street. Lobbyist, political strategist, another lawyer."

"Fucking lawyers. The whole damn city is full of them." Drexler folded his arms. "This Malloy, he's a member of the parish too, I take it?"

"Actually, no. He's not. Apparently he didn't even mention St. Gabriel when he called. Instead he cited some bullshit about maintaining the credibility of the police department in the eyes of the public. He said that removing a good detective would put congressional support for the DC budget in jeopardy."

Drexler leaned forward. "I'm not seeing the connection, Johnson."

"Neither did I at first. Davis Malloy's firm works for the Raybeck campaign. Well, it's not yet a campaign officially, but the word is that Garret Raybeck is being touted as a possible presidential contender."

"Who?" Drexler asked.

"Garret Raybeck. Democrat. Governor of Massachusetts."

"You mean that good-looking white kid we've been seeing lately on the news?"

"Yeah. Actually he's about fifty, but he's young looking with a hot young wife. I've seen him on the Sunday talk shows. Seems like a pretty levelheaded guy. Horace says his approval numbers are through the roof in Massachusetts. He's taken some pretty conservative positions on American foreign policy. Even the Republicans reluctantly like him."

"So what?"

"Well, I checked some things before I came to see you. I tried to put some of these pieces together and all that."

"Johnson, get on with it."

"Garret Raybeck is the son of former US Senator Forbes Raybeck, also from Massachusetts. The old man was a parishioner at St. Gabriel. The young Raybeck is a current parishioner. Malloy's firm used to employ the elder Raybeck as some sort of political consultant and part-time lobbyist after he left office. And Victor Campbell? The guy that made that first call to the mayor? Guess who he used to be chief of staff for years ago?"

Drexler's eyes grew wide. "Not Senator Forbes Raybeck?"

Ty Johnson sat back and smiled. "Bingo."

Chapter 53

Across town in the confessional at St. Matthew's Cathedral, the Hawk and Simon had begun their typical exchange of information. The dialogue started slowly and deliberately, the cautious nature of both men more of a barrier to the truth than the physical barrier of the confessional screen that separated them.

"You sound different today," noticed Monsignor Sansevarino.

Simon didn't immediately respond. Finally he spoke. "I'm concerned for the detective and the woman. Langley is becoming unhinged, I fear. If the document isn't recovered soon, it wouldn't remain in the interest of the United States to keep the matter…shall we say, 'indefinitely unknown.'"

"I see," said the Hawk. "Perhaps that was the result of your agency having lost track of the two Americans when they ventured into Mexico. Or was it their arrival in Managua that made the difference? Or what they may have found there?"

Simon swallowed hard. He knew the Vatican spy who sat across from him in the confessional was aware of his agency's subterfuge, and there was no way to go back and remedy that.

"I take orders just like you do, Monsignor," Simon finally mustered. "We both are servants of much larger masters."

"But we need not be ignorant slaves in serving those masters."

"No, we don't," said Simon, "but I'm not sure where that leaves us."

The Hawk paused deliberately to make Simon even more uneasy. He then spoke. "There is a greater good that we must now achieve."

"It would seem so."

"Then tell me what you know. We don't have more time to play these games. If the lives of the detective and the woman are in danger from within, then we need to act quickly to avoid any unwanted results." The Hawk paused. "God is patient, Simon," he said, "but I am not."

Chapter 54

The commercial flight that would take Gallagher and Laura to Panama was departing from Managua in a little more than three hours. Garcia had made the reservations, using their false identities, as they had all agreed. Once safely in Panama, Gallagher and Laura would have no choice but to use their real passports during the next leg of their journey into the United States. That could not be helped. American immigration controls were too sophisticated to risk the use of forged documents upon arrival.

After Gallagher and Laura had packed their belongings, the Garcias had helped to sift through the pictures and other materials one final time. They would not be traveling any further. Garcia had assured the two Americans that the materials would be safely hidden and would remain in his control until they signaled for their safe return back to America. Now, after copies had been made on Garcia's office copier, only a few select photographs would remain with Gallagher and Laura on the journey ahead. If something were to happen, they had all reasoned, the pictures and other evidence would be safe and available to, hopefully, evidence the truth.

An hour later, Gallagher and Laura bade farewell to Carolina, who wouldn't be traveling with them to the airport. Thomas Garcia would drive them in his car and ensure that they safely made it aboard the plane.

Laura hugged and kissed Carolina as both women wiped tears from their eyes.

"You will promise to come and see us in Washington," said Laura, holding Carolina's hands.

"Yes, we promise," responded Carolina. "You two, please, be safe." Carolina walked over to Gallagher. "Take good care, Peter, and look after this beautiful girl."

"I promise." Gallagher smiled at Carolina then looked at Laura affectionately.

"We must go," interrupted Garcia.

The black BMW sedan moved gingerly down from the hills above Managua and into the city center. There was silence in the car, the tension palpable while the air conditioning worked to cool the interior.

Garcia attempted to break the tension by pointing out some of the sights as the car made its way through the city and toward the international airport. "This is the old quarter of the city. You can still see how beautiful it is, even with the poor condition of many of the buildings."

Gallagher and Laura gazed out the car windows. "Yes, it is lovely," said Laura. She looked at the people and the bustle of the city and longed for home. The plane from Managua couldn't leave soon enough, she thought, although pangs of sadness still resided at, once again, having to shed new friends that were now more important to her, it seemed, than any whom she called old.

The traffic slowed as the congestion of the city picked up and then began to thin as the BMW moved out from the denseness and toward the airport. Garcia honked his horn at a passing pedestrian who seemingly ignored the traffic lights in front of him. Garcia looked into his rearview mirror as his car continued on.

"You seem a bit jumpy, Thomas," said Gallagher. "We have plenty of time." He looked at his watch again.

Garcia didn't respond, focusing intently on his driving. He turned right at the next intersection and made his way back toward the city center. Gallagher noticed the turn but remained quiet.

"I'm going to see if we can make a bit better time," said Garcia. "I think there's a faster way around all of this chaos."

Gallagher looked into the passenger-side mirror, seeing Laura's face nearly pressed against her window. He looked over at Garcia. "It seemed like the traffic was breaking up a bit before, Thomas. Now we're heading back into more traffic."

Garcia said nothing, as he quickly looked again into his rearview mirror. He turned the car to the left and then down another street to the right. The car now stood waiting for another traffic light to turn green.

Gallagher looked in his mirror again and saw the beige Toyota sedan two cars behind. Two men, wearing the familiar aviator sunglasses, sat inside it. He turned slightly toward Garcia without looking obvious. "We have a problem, don't we, Thomas?"

Garcia looked in his rearview mirror, catching Laura's eyes. "We're being followed."

"I figured as much," said Gallagher. "Same sort of goons that picked us up at Caldera."

"Secret police," said Garcia. "The government does follow me from time to time. My past makes me a routine target. But somehow I think it isn't me they're interested in this time."

Garcia's car stopped at another light, behind two others in the queue. A white-gloved policeman directed traffic from the center of the intersection. He blew his whistle and waved through the traffic that now ran perpendicular to the waiting black BMW.

Gallagher grew tense. "They may be just making sure we leave the country as promised."

"That may be true. They obviously picked up on the travel plans. Your names were likely being monitored for such activity."

"Then we should just go to the airport and continue as planned," said Gallagher.

"Yes," said Garcia, watching surreptitiously through his rearview mirror. "But somehow I don't think that's what they're interested in."

"Why do you say that?"

"Because we're still sitting here in this stopped traffic." Garcia looked over at Gallagher. "At a green light that has been green for nearly thirty seconds."

Gallagher and Laura looked at the green light and the uniformed police officer in the intersection, one gloved hand holding back the traffic line they were in and the other holding an issue radio to his ear. Panic began to set in.

Garcia gripped tightly on the wheel as Gallagher and Laura looked ahead. "Also, my friends," Garcia said with an eerie calmness, "because the 'two goons' as you call them..." Gallagher and Laura looked toward Garcia. "...are getting out of their car."

Chapter 55

"Hold on," said Garcia, his eyes watching as the two Nicaraguan agents worked their way slowly toward the black BMW.

Gallagher and Laura threw themselves back into their seats and gripped the nearest armrest. "Oh, shit," said Gallagher.

"My thoughts exactly," responded Garcia, pushing in on the clutch and slipping the car into gear. "Hang on!"

The tires of the BMW screeched as Garcia nervously pressed on the accelerator. The agents, now only a few feet from the car, jumped and raced back to their own car, which was still running. Smoke from the BMW's tires filled the small street. The traffic cop ahead put down his arm and moved to grab his sidearm. Garcia released the clutch and commanded the powerful car around those in front of him by way of the cobblestone sidewalk that was, fortunately, empty.

The agents behind slammed the doors to their own sedan and took chase as the black BMW pulled back into the intersection, forcing the traffic cop to drop his gun and leap out of the way.

The BMW weaved in and out of traffic. The agents followed, watching as the BMW continued to dodge screaming pedestrians and numerous compact cars.

Gallagher looked back and saw people still clinging to lampposts or the security of shop entryways. In the car behind, he spotted one of the agents holding a radio. "We don't have much time, Thomas. One of the goons is calling for back-up."

Garcia kept his eyes on the road ahead and honked his horn repeatedly. The car turned left and right, zooming through oncoming traffic with wild abandon. "We're not going to be able to slip the net in the car, Peter."

In the backseat, Laura had turned green. "I think I'm going to be sick!" she screamed.

"Hold on!" said Garcia again, pulling the car into a hard left turn and back onto another sidewalk to move past more traffic. "And Laura, don't throw up in this car. Carolina will kill me." The car veered back onto another road, slamming down from a high sidewalk curb.

"Oh, my God!" said Laura, again closing her eyes as the car nearly ran down a mother and the baby carriage she was pushing. Fruit from a street vendor's stall peppered the windshield of the BMW as it sideswiped it. Garcia turned on the windscreen wipers, trying to remove the sticky juice that labored down the glass.

Gallagher's stomach was now beginning to churn too. "What are we going to do?" He looked back, seeing the agent's car struggling to keep up through the chaos that the black BMW was leaving in its wake. He heard sirens approaching.

"Hold tight, you two," said Garcia through gritted teeth, as he shifted the car into higher gear and picked up more speed. "I have an idea."

Marked police cars entered the chase, coming in from side streets to follow the unmarked car of the secret police.

"We have more company, Thomas!" Gallagher said.

The BMW rolled on without any particular route in Garcia's mind. He moved the car down more side streets, left and then right and then another left. Laura's knuckles had gone white from her grip on the armrest, but she managed to keep down what was in her stomach.

Gallagher continued to keep tabs on the growing number of cars in the chase behind while trying to assist Garcia with avoiding collateral damage ahead.

Garcia worked to explain his idea to his two passengers as he continued to drive with ferocious aggression through the dirty and cramped streets of downtown Managua. Gallagher and Laura took deep breaths and readied themselves.

The car took another hard right into the red-light district and down another small street, finally losing the government cars that continued their furious pursuit.

The BMW slowed after taking another abrupt turn. Garcia gave a wink and a nod to Gallagher and Laura, waited, and then pulled the car out of the small street and back into full throttle. The chase continued as the government cars reestablished contact and followed the BMW toward a major road, across the city, and back into a small neighborhood on the other side of town.

Garcia looked into his rearview mirror, watching with amazement as no less than five marked and unmarked cars worked to catch him. He turned left and then down another street.

The BMW moved toward a highway before slamming on its brakes and coming to a full stop before the sight of a hastily assembled roadblock. Automatic weapons took aim. Garcia gently raised his hand from the wheel after turning off the car.

The car with the two plainclothes agents pulled to a screeching halt next to the BMW's driver-side door. The agents leapt out, guns drawn, and took out the BMW's tires. The agents threw open the driver-side door and hauled Garcia out and onto the ground while looking inside. Another agent released the latch to the car trunk and opened it fully, revealing an empty space.

"*Americanos?*" said one of the agents to Garcia, who lay prostrate on the hot asphalt as the smell of his overheated car engine wafted over him.

"*Que?*" responded Garcia, taking a kick from an agent. "There is no one else," he added in Spanish, mustering a small smile through the pain in his ribs.

The agents began to frantically relay the situation into their radios, calling for an immediate search of all surrounding areas.

Peter Gallagher and Laura Miller were gone.

Chapter 56

The police net around Managua had gone up quickly in the hours after Garcia's car had been stopped and searched. Garcia had been arrested and taken to police headquarters and his car impounded. While he was questioned thoroughly, his own stature as a prominent member of the legal community shielded him from the more ruthless and painful interrogation that the Nicaraguan secret police desired for having been so brazenly challenged earlier that day.

Now sitting outside in the cool air above Managua, Garcia was back home. He again looked at his wife, who was curled up by his side on the outdoor sofa. "It will be okay," he said as Carolina continued to try and calm herself from the ordeal of the last six hours. "The government knows nothing. There is no way they will find the package Peter and Laura left with us." Garcia waited a moment. "But we should be wary of the phones and what we say to each other in the house. They will be watching and listening now."

"Should we leave? Fly out?" asked Carolina.

"We can't. We have to stay. If we leave, they win." Garcia gently touched his wife's face. "But now we too are wrapped up in Peter's investigation. We need him to succeed. We do need *them* to get out."

"But what can we do to help them now?"

"Nothing. We can do nothing." Garcia put his arm around her and held her closer. He looked down over the city and at the twinkling lights that were so familiar, thinking that his friends were down there, somewhere—their lives hanging in a balance that he could no longer sway.

"We can only wait now…wait and hope and pray." Garcia looked over to see his wife asleep in the crook of his arm.

* * *

Gallagher and Laura were startled by a large brown rat that boldly attempted to chew Gallagher's leather shoe. He kicked it away and held Laura a bit more tightly with his arm.

Thus far, Garcia's gamble had kept them from capture by the Nicaraguan secret police, although they were far from being free. The two Americans sat in the basement storage room of a small barbershop in a dirty and poor quadrant of Managua. The shop was owned by a distant cousin of Garcia's who once had served as an enlisted man in the army of General Ernesto Somoza. The owner wasn't a friend of the current government and was more than willing to help anyone who was in unfavorable graces with it.

The shop basement door opened, a light shining down onto the stairwell. Gallagher rustled Laura from her doze.

"*Señor* Gallagher?" said the voice as the shop owner worked his way down the creaking stairwell.

"Yes, *Señor* Lopez. We are here."

Jaime Lopez laughed. "Where else would you be?" He laughed and flashed his light into the eyes of Gallagher and a groggy Laura.

Gallagher reached forward and moved the light to the side. "Are we safe here? We thought we heard a commotion earlier."

The old man chuckled again. "The secret police were here. They have been combing the city for you. They came, they broke some things, and then they left. But there still remains a tight net around the city."

"And the man in the barber chair when we arrived? He will remain quiet?"

"*Si, señor,*" said Lopez. "That was my old squad mate from the army. He will not say a word." Lopez paused. "As for the rest of the neighborhood, it is largely whores, drunks, and peasants—none of whom care at all for the government and their empty promises. This accounts for the shear frustration of the agents when they searched this part of the city, since no one will cooperate." Lopez looked around the room. "*Señor*, you and the *señorita* will need to stay here until we can figure out how to get you out of the country. They will not knowingly allow you to leave Nicaragua alive. You know that, *Señor*, yes?"

"We've figured as much."

"I will bring you some blankets and more food."

A loud snap interrupted the conversation. Lopez shone his light toward the floor of the damp basement and walked toward a crate. He looked around the corner. "Ah, ha!" He reached down and picked up the large rat trap and the fresh kill, which still twitched. He raised it and showed it crudely to his guests. Laura looked away in disgust. "Be advised, *señor*, we need to get you out of the city quickly." Lopez waited. "The longer we wait, the more likely you will find yourself in a similar predicament."

Gallagher took a few seconds to recognize the analogy that he and Laura had, thus far, avoided a similar fate. "All I need is the phone. Do you think it's safe to go upstairs to use it?"

Lopez lowered his kill. "*Si, señor*. That can be arranged now."

Chapter 57

"It would appear that the situation has changed," Simon told his CIA superior, a hint of antagonism in his voice. He leaned forward and nonchalantly threw a manila folder onto the desk.

The CIA officer sitting behind the desk sensed the confidence of the agent but ignored his tone and opened the file. His eyes grew wide, his lips terse. He looked up and across the desk at Simon. "Where did this come from?"

Simon smirked. "Records."

The officer looked back into the folder, knowing now that he had been saved from a professional catastrophe. "I see."

"Richard Miller was one of ours. Nonofficial cover. As you see there, he's the father of Laura Miller, the schoolteacher with Gallagher." Simon paused and waited for his superior to say something, but the room remained silent.

The CIA officer attempted to cover his tracks and the arrogant judgment that had almost seen the woman killed by an order he had considered giving. "You didn't think I wasn't aware of this, did you? It was no coincidence that my decision was made to avoid any harm coming to Ms. Miller or Mr. Gallagher."

Simon smirked again, the message clearly sent across the desk to the superior who again allowed it to go unchallenged. "Richard Miller was sent to Central America on a number of official visits. His involvement in Nicaragua was especially relevant. He was the primary source for the agency's knowledge of the weapons, supplies, and funding filtering into that country to support the Sandinistas."

The CIA officer remained silent.

Simon continued, "In short, Richard Miller was the first to suspect the involvement of senior US officials involved in this illegal arrangement and the existence of the smoking gun we're interested in finding."

"Yes," said the officer, looking back down into the file before him. "And he has been out of the game for some time."

"That is irrelevant." Simon shifted gears. "The surveillance order that you gave has panned out."

"Again, as I knew it would."

"Perhaps," said Simon, smirking again and successfully needling his superior. "It would seem that Gallagher and Miller have been identified by Nicaraguan intelligence. A search is underway in Managua." He threw another manila folder onto the desk. "NSA intercept."

Simon continued as the officer looked quickly at the cable. "The phone taps on the rectory picked up a call from the parish pastor, Father Damien Thomas, a few hours after that cable was intercepted. The call went to a pay phone. Who was on the other end of the line, we don't know. The recipient of that call barely spoke."

"And what was conveyed?" asked the CIA officer.

"Basically the content of the cable you're looking at. We think the housekeeper and the priest are connected in this. We know the housekeeper, Maria Rosario, is an agent of the Nicaraguan government." Simon threw another manila folder across the desk.

The CIA officer again opened the folder and glanced at the photographs. "What am I looking at?"

"Our team followed the Rosario woman last night. The photographs show her at a café two blocks from the Nicaraguan embassy. The man sitting with the woman is Hector Cortez, chief of station for the Nicaraguan government in Washington. We assume the cable contents were passed to Rosario during that meeting. The info was then passed to Father Thomas."

The CIA officer looked up directly at Simon. "My hunch was correct then?"

Simon sat back in his chair and crossed his legs, his previous and careful professional deference now excised from within. "Enough of the bullshit."

"Excuse me?" said the CIA officer, attempting to reassert his authority.

"Go fuck yourself," said Simon. He pulled his chair forward and propped his elbows on the desk of his superior. "I'm going to forget the 'termination' issue and the illegal wiretaps for the moment, but I won't put up with the intra-agency, political bullshit. Are we clear?" Simon pulled out a tape recorder and played back the spliced conversations that evidenced his superior's questionable orders of the last few days.

The officer said nothing, grinding his teeth.

Simon looked at his superior directly. "Gallagher and Miller are now being hunted. Odds are they know the whereabouts of the diary. The problem we now have is that they're nowhere to be found. They may even be dead now, thanks to how we've played this whole thing."

The CIA officer looked at Simon and waited; the tables were now turned.

"And so here's what we're going to do," said Simon.

Chapter 58

The air was warm and humid when Ty Johnson ventured out for his routine morning run. As was his custom, he had driven over to Rock Creek Park en route to work, parked his car, got out, and stretched, watching the other runners. He threw on his earphones, dropped his keys and his cell phone into his pocket, and slowly moved toward the running-path entrance.

His pace picked up after the first half-mile, as he felt the sweat begin to pour from under his gray Howard University T-shirt. *Three miles to go*, he thought before his mind shifted back to the fate of his friend and partner, Peter Gallagher. He tried to dismiss the issue for the moment and turned up the volume on his MP3 player.

Venturing farther into the wooded park, Johnson's feet pounded the path in a steady motion; his eyes kept lookout for loose rocks that would love to turn his bad ankle for yet a fourth time this year. He looked up and saw a middle-aged black man wearing a gray hooded sweatshirt and shorts overtake him and move quickly ahead. Johnson had admittedly seen very few African Americans jogging in Rock Creek Park; instead it was a steady sight of white urban professionals that he usually found running with him—and none of whom he'd ever seen wearing a sweatshirt during this time of year. A sense of ethnic embarrassment took hold for a moment, as he realized the prejudice that even he, as an African American himself, had yet to fully exorcize for his fellow blacks. His thought subsided as another runner passed him and began to gain on the hooded black man who was now well ahead of Johnson.

The morning light continued to grow brighter as Johnson moved along the path, his breathing heavier. A few minutes later, he looked up again, seeing the path before him clear of any fellow runners. His police instincts took over, and he glanced through the trees. The second runner who had passed him was now winding his way through the trees as the path weaved its way back and forth through the foliage. Johnson stopped suddenly and pulled off his earphones. The black runner, whom he had taken a particular interest in, was nowhere to be found.

A year ago, Johnson and Gallagher had investigated the death of another Washington jogger—a young congressional intern who had ventured into Rock Creek Park on a similar morning, only to be raped and killed; her body had been found crudely buried and badly decomposed. Ever since, Johnson had yet to fully relax in the place. There was nowhere that was safe anymore, Johnson thought, his hands on his hips as he looked around.

He spat then wiped his mouth with his sleeve. He took a deep breath and repositioned his earphones, picking up a Smokey Robinson song in mid track. He looked around once again then continued on his run.

Twenty-five minutes later, Johnson began his last descent down the path in front of him as it wound its way back to the parking lot. Pushing himself, he picked up speed. *Another two hundred yards*, he thought. His thoughts were broken as a runner from behind tried to work himself around and past him. Johnson picked up more speed. He'd be damned if he'd let another runner pass him this morning and only a few short yards from the finish. He glanced to his right, now seeing the runner who was on his heels; the gray sweatshirt hood masked the black face. Johnson swung around instinctively and into an attack stance.

"Back off, brother!" said Johnson, pulling off his earphones. "I'm a cop."

The man behind him stopped, remained calm, and kept his hands visible as he slowly reached for the hood of his sweatshirt. Johnson looked curiously as the very black face was revealed, only a slight sweat on the brow but nothing more. The face was somehow familiar.

The man looked at Johnson then spoke. "Actually it's 'Father,' not brother," said the man in heavy African English. "My name is Father Michael Benjamin."

Johnson stood breathing heavily, still trying to take in the moment. His mind snapped back. "The Ugandan priest?"

"Yes," said Father Benjamin, looking about the area cautiously.

"I've been looking for you for the last few weeks."

"Walk with me," said Father Benjamin.

Johnson looked around, suspecting a trap. "Are you here alone?" he asked, turning around and cautiously walking back down the path with the priest.

"Yes. I apologize for frightening you. It was the only place I knew would be safe to contact you." Father Benjamin wiped his brow. "When your office contacted the American embassy in Kampala, I suspected something had gone wrong here in Washington."

"Why would you suspect that?" asked Johnson, still keeping an eye on the tree line, not sure what to expect next.

"I heard about Edward Sachs." The priest looked around then stopped. "His murder doesn't surprise me."

Johnson looked at him quizzically. "Why do you say that? What do you know?" He turned and looked around again as his breathing slowed. "How did you get in the country?"

"How I got into the country isn't important right now," answered Father Benjamin. "Your partner, Mr. Gallagher, and the girl with him are in grave danger."

Johnson looked at him closely. "I realize you're a man of the cloth, but enough of the mystery. What the fuck do you know?"

Father Benjamin looked at Johnson closely but without malice, a great seriousness in his dark eyes.

"I know everything."

Chapter 59

"The arrangements have been made, Excellency," said Monsignor Sansevarino, while walking with Archbishop Lucessi in the garden of the Washington Embassy of the Holy See.

Archbishop Lucessi walked at a snail's pace, his hands behind his back. "And your opinion on whether we can trust the Americans to hold up their end of the bargain you reached?" he asked.

"I must say that I am not sure, but Simon understands that without a partnership, this matter will not resolve itself satisfactorily."

"We must certainly have faith then, yes?" Lucessi stopped and looked over at his chief intelligence agent in Washington.

"Yes, Excellency."

The two men continued to walk again down the brick path. "What about the deaths? Did Simon have insight that he was willing to share?"

"When we spoke last, the only suspects remain the Nicaraguans. However, it seems unlikely, given what we know. With Rosario inside the gates—their own agent—the last thing they would have wanted was for Sachs to have died. His death only blew her cover."

Lucessi said nothing then shifted again to more pressing matters. "What is your plan to make contact with Gallagher? He is on the run, yes? Does Simon believe that American intelligence can track him and bring him in?"

Monsignor Sansevarino looked up toward the embassy, a sense of confidence taking hold that he worked to subdue. "No, Excellency, but perhaps we can."

Lucessi stopped and looked toward Sansevarino then turned and looked toward the Embassy, watching as another priest, wearing a black cassock, walked toward them gracefully.

The priest reached Lucessi then genuflected while taking his hand and kissing his episcopal ring. "*Pax vobiscum*, Excellency," said the priest.

"*Et cum spiritu tuo*," responded Lucessi. "It is good to see you again, Father."

"And you, Excellency."

"And what news do you have to bring to us?"

Father Michael Benjamin smiled respectfully and said nothing, although there was much news he indeed had brought with him.

Chapter 60

An hour after making his phone call, Gallagher and Laura were on the move again, under the cover of darkness. Gallagher had attempted three times to remember the number that Jorge Ramos had given him in the Guatemalan compound those few days before. With all that had occurred since then, it was lucky he had. The voice on the other end had been without emotion and not surprised by the call that had come in the early hours of the morning.

Laura was now asleep under the crook of Gallagher's arm in the backseat of a well-appointed Range Rover as it headed toward Nicaragua's northeastern coast. The ride had been a long one, thought Gallagher, as the sun began to rise again and spread its rays over the mountains. In reality, it had been only a short four hours.

The two men sitting in the front seat had said few words during the drive. There was little they were interested in, other than getting their cargo safely to the destination—a destination their passengers weren't made aware of for their own safety and for the security of the operation that would hopefully see Gallagher and Laura on their way back to the US.

Gallagher continued to look out the window but had finally stopped turning back to peer out of the rear of the vehicle. He felt safe now, if only for the time being. The ride from the barbershop and through two police checkpoints had nearly done his heart in. But the men in the front had seen to those impediments with thick wads of US dollars and friendly handshakes. Who was funding their escape, Gallagher had no idea, but he suspected that whoever it was wouldn't see the cost of this escape as anything but a drop in the bucket and business as usual.

The man in the front passenger seat finally turned around for only the second time that morning and looked at Gallagher. "Two more hours," he said, before turning back around.

"Where are we headed?" asked Gallagher.

There was no reply.

Wherever they were going, it was of little import compared with his desire to return to the US. Tired, bruised, but not yet broken, Gallagher and Laura had at least something—a realization that the prize was likely back at the very place where their journey had begun.

Until they returned home to come face-to-face with the answer to the mystery, there would be no peace and no real chance for a return to any normalcy, if they could ever find that again.

Normalcy, thought Gallagher as the Range Rover moved deftly over the country road. Was there any normalcy to begin with? Likely not. Life was not normal. The only certainty was the true lack of normalcy.

However, the one thing that was certain was the truth. Somewhere a few thousand or so miles away in Washington, DC, the truth sat somewhere waiting for revelation. There was at least that one certainty, no matter how difficult it may be in life to actually come across it.

Gallagher, after having spent so much time searching, was now, more than ever, determined to find it.

PART IV

Chapter 61

The well-dressed man was behind his desk, looking across at the giant that once again sat before him. "The police have been asking more questions."

The giant sat quietly and didn't respond. He hadn't slept in two days.

"Are you sure the parish is now under watch?" asked the well-dressed man.

"Yes, sir." The giant didn't move in his chair. "Four men, round the clock on twelve-hour shifts. They're located in a utility van down the street from the rectory."

"And you are sure you weren't spotted?"

"They didn't see me."

"Good."

The well-dressed man stood and walked to the window. "The police have closed their investigation on the detective. There is no reason that he should not be returning. The question now is: How will they bring him in?"

"Yes, sir."

"These men watching the rectory..." The well-dressed man turned and looked at the giant again. "No doubt they are intelligence agents looking for the same thing we're searching for. How to get the detective back into the country quietly—that is the question."

"Yes, sir."

The well-dressed man sat and thought quietly, before finally saying, "If American intelligence is on one side and the Vatican on the other, there is only one way for the detective to find assistance."

The giant looked impassively and said nothing.

"You will shift focus now, do you understand?"

"As you wish, sir," responded the giant.

"You will focus on the police now, do you understand?"

"As you wish, sir."

The well-dressed man looked down onto his clutter-free, well-polished desk and then up at the eyes of the professional killer who sat before him. "Follow the nigger, do you understand?"

"The nigger," said the giant. "Yes, I will follow the nigger."

The well-dressed man smiled. "He will lead you to his partner and the girl."

"Yes, sir."

"Once you find them, you kill them. Do you understand?"

"I will kill the nigger," confirmed the giant.

"No," said the well-dressed man. He waited and then clarified his intentions. "You kill them all."

Chapter 62

There was a ship waiting to depart from the Benjamín Zeledón Port, near the town of Prinzapolka, when the black Range Rover rolled in at a little after noon. The ship's captain was watching from the bridge, the ship now loaded with fresh produce and destined for the port of Miami. He watched as the three men and one woman got out and walked into the port authority office. He knew they would soon be arriving to take their place on board his ship for a trip that he was being paid very well to make without any questions. He had done the same before on many other occasions and fantasized about how to spend his earnings.

Gallagher and Laura looked around furtively as the two men who had ferried them across the country made the necessary arrangements to have the ship manifest and crew list forged to allow them safe passage on board. The driver of the Range Rover waited with them as the other man worked to seal the deal with the easily corruptible port manager on duty.

Gallagher looked at the driver and tried to muster a smile. The man nodded courteously then watched as his partner and the port manager walked into a back room to complete their transaction with a briefcase full of more American dollars.

"I need to use the phone," said Gallagher to the driver.

The driver grew nervous and rattled off something in Spanish that Gallagher couldn't translate. Laura quickly intervened. The driver smiled, looked around, and then dismissively waved Gallagher toward the phone that rested on the port manager's cluttered desk.

Gallagher picked up the phone, dialed the number in Maryland, and waited anxiously, hoping Uncle Larry would again be there to take his call.

Chapter 63

The call that had gone out from the port near Prinzapolka, Nicaragua, had, by this time, set off alarm bells for the competing powers in Washington; the man who possibly held the key to the long-awaited treasure that each was searching for was now en route back to the continental United States.

The tenuous concordant between the CIA and the Vatican was holding for the time being by an even more tenuous nexus made possible by, of all organizations, the police department of the District of Columbia.

Captain Drexler sat across from Ty Johnson at the greasy spoon known as Ben's Chili Bowl, trying unsuccessfully to work his way through a hot dog and a cold soda.

"Not hungry, boss?" asked Johnson, before taking a sip of his ice water. A large bowl of chili sat below his hands.

"No." Drexler looked down at Johnson's bowl. "I see your appetite is about the same." He took a final drink of his soda. "Let's go."

It was still hot in Washington. The humidity of the summer was thick and relentless as Drexler and Johnson walked down U Street with their ties loose around their necks and their shirtsleeves rolled up. Both slipped on their sunglasses.

"You know they're using us," said Johnson.

Drexler picked his teeth with a toothpick. "If it gets Gallagher back in one piece, who cares? I don't think we have a choice. This whole goddamn situation is out of control."

"It's pretty fucked up, I'll give you that," said Johnson. "And I'm more than nervous. I'll be honest. I got the wife and kids out of town this morning.

I'm not sleeping well." He looked through his dark lenses and scanned the street. His senses had now gone officially into overdrive. "How is this going to come to any real closure?"

Drexler continued to pick his teeth while watching through his own dark lenses, scrutinizing every parked car and pedestrian that flashed before him. "It was smart to get the family out of town. Get a bag packed. You can stay with us."

"Thanks, boss," said Johnson. "How are we going to play this out?"

"Fuck if I know. We got spies and Vatican priests running around. We got a dirty department playing politics. And we got one of our best detectives out there trying to come in safely." Drexler stopped and looked at Johnson. "What do we really know at this point? You trust that Father Benjamin?"

"Can't say I do, exactly. But it's like you said… What choice do we have?" Johnson pulled off his aviator sunglasses and looked at Drexler. "The Feds have the lead now. All we need to do is help bring Pete in so they can wrap this up."

"I keep saying that to myself too, over and over again. But it doesn't feel right. No matter how much pull the Feds have, there's still a killer out there somewhere. I don't think the Feds have a fucking clue who it is."

"Do we?" asked Johnson, placing his sunglasses back over his sweating face. He mopped his brow with a handkerchief.

"No, we don't, and that's what bothers me. The Feds get what they want from Gallagher and the girl once they return, and who knows what happens. For all we know, Gallagher and the girl will disappear. Who's to say we might not be next? We could all be fucked." Drexler thought deeply then shifted gears. "Get your stuff and get back to the office."

"Roger, boss."

"How many days do you think before Gallagher shows up?"

"Not sure. His call to Jefferson's was pretty cryptic other than it was the only place he would agree to come in. Two or three days. I don't know."

"Like I said, get a bag and get back to the office. Lock your place up."

Johnson shot his boss a quizzical look. "What is it?"

Drexler threw down his toothpick. "We have to carve our way out of this one. If the spies want to play more games, we'd better have our own escape plan ready."

Johnson stopped. "Not sure I follow."

Drexler looked at him and smiled. "Don't worry. You will."

Chapter 64

The small fishing vessel had made its way from Cape Hatteras before sunrise, its course due north. Gallagher and Laura were asleep below deck after a two-day nonstop journey since leaving Nicaraguan territory. The Panamanian-flagged freighter that had sailed from Nicaragua and moored in Miami had offloaded its cargo of fruit along with two American citizens without incident. They easily were able to land in US territory without a second glance.

Upon arrival in Miami, Gallagher and Laura had been shuttled up the coast in another Range Rover. They slept most of the way and had dispensed with asking any more questions. Arriving at the small fishing dock in North Carolina eight hours later, just after one a.m. Eastern Daylight Time, they were led aboard the small fishing boat that would take them—and several crates of black market cigarettes—on the last leg of their journey home, before the boat proceeded farther north to offload its contraband.

Gallagher was rustled from a hard sleep as the small boat hit a swale and lurched suddenly to starboard. He quietly wished for a time, very soon, when he finally could get some meaningful rest. He looked over to Laura, who remained deeply asleep in the rack below his own. He threw his legs onto the deck, pulled on a T-shirt, and walked carefully topside.

"Good morning," said the ship's captain, who sipped at a mug of coffee while keeping a careful eye on the sea. Another crewmember stood watch in the wheelhouse.

"Good morning, sir," responded Gallagher, as he reached for a solid handhold for balance. "Looks like we have a bit of rough sea."

"Nothing to worry about," responded the captain. "She's a small girl but a strong one." The captain sipped at his mug. "There's fresh coffee in the galley. Why not get yourself a cup?"

Gallagher looked on with trepidation as his stomach began to turn.

The captain laughed gently. "You'll get your sea legs soon enough. Storm coming."

The sky was clear and the air warm. Gallagher peered out at the horizon and wondered where this intelligence was coming from.

The captain answered Gallagher's silent question. "Looks clear, but the sea is picking up. Message came in over the wire that we have a cold front that's likely to bring some rain and rough seas in the next few hours. I suggest you and the lady take care of anything now. If you need to shower, we have fresh water for the time being. You should also get something to eat. It's likely to get a bit rougher before too long."

Gallagher smiled to himself. "Great," he said.

"Oh, don't worry, Mr. Gallagher. You leave the sea to me. We'll get you to Maryland in one piece, rest assured, although the journey may be a bit of a bumpy one."

The journey already had been a bumpy one, thought Gallagher as he took in more of the sea air. He only hoped the journey would smooth eventually.

Somehow he sensed that not to be the case.

Chapter 65

Ty Johnson sat in the small dive known as Jefferson's Crab Shack finishing off the last of the scrambled eggs and crabmeat that had been prepared for breakfast that morning. He had arrived after leaving Washington around midnight, pulling up to the small Maryland seaside restaurant around three a.m. He was tired but more confident now that things might be moving in the right direction. Earlier that morning, word had come in over the radio that Gallagher and Laura were en route and would arrive late in the afternoon. He was looking forward to the reunion with his partner, whom he had truly missed these last few weeks.

Johnson sucked down more orange juice in silence as his father-in-law, Larry Sylvester, walked in.

"Weather report doesn't look good, Ty," said the old man. The Coast Guard issued a weather advisory for the routes along the East Coast—from South Carolina to New Jersey."

Johnson looked on with concern. "What does that mean?"

"It means your friends are in for a rough ride." The man was calm in delivering his information. "They'll be fine," he added, reassuring his son-in-law. "We need to batten down here as well. I've got to go tend to our own boats. You going to be okay?"

"I'll be fine."

"What time are your government 'friends' supposed to arrive?" asked the man, now well briefed on the fact that US government representatives of some type were to take custody of Gallagher and Laura once they eventually landed.

Johnson looked at his watch. "Around noon or so."

"Plenty early," responded the old man. "If this storm is bad enough, they may be headed for a long wait." The old man paused. "I suggest you get some sleep. It's going to be a long and rough day."

Johnson looked at his father-in-law apprehensively.

"Go on," said the old man. "We got plenty to do around here, and you'll just get in the way. Go get some rest now, you hear?"

"Yes, sir," said Johnson with a smirk.

"Don't you sass me," said the old man. "You get on now and get some rest. I'll let you know if we get anything in over the radio."

Johnson got up reluctantly and walked outside to get some air en route to the small house that his father- and mother-in-law called home. His eyes were sore and tired, but the humid air of the Maryland summer eased the pain just a bit. He turned and looked out toward the sea, now praying that the winds would be fair and the seas forgiving that day. He walked on and shifted thoughts as his body and mind forgot about all of that for the moment and instead longed for a cool pillow upon which to lay his head.

* * *

The giant looked through his binoculars as Johnson emerged from the restaurant and sauntered toward the little white-siding house that stood only a short walk away. He had followed his target carefully since the man had departed Washington, DC.

He picked up his phone and dialed.

"Yes," said the well-dressed man.

The giant laid down his binoculars and focused on the call. "The detective drove through the night to a fishing compound."

"Wait and see where he goes. Do you understand?"

"Yes."

"Move to a place that's inconspicuous but where you can assure yourself that if he leaves, you'll see him. Do you understand?"

"Yes," said the giant.

"If his partner should arrive there, you know what to do."

"Yes, sir."

"Good," said the well-dressed man. "Check in with me in a few hours."

"Yes."

The phone went dead, as the well-dressed man cut the call off.

The giant placed his phone next to the silenced, high-powered rifle and automatic pistol. He waited for Johnson to enter the little white house, ensured he wasn't being watched, then moved his car to another location well out of clear sight.

There he would patiently lie in wait for his targets to arrive. The time to strike would come, he knew. There would be no failure, the giant assured himself.

Chapter 66

From the backseat of a US government-owned SUV en route through Maryland's Eastern Shore, Father Antonio Mancini took notice as the sky outside began to darken and the driver was forced to switch on the windshield wipers to remove the drops of rain that had slowly accumulated on the windshield over the last few minutes. The weather was certainly deteriorating, he thought. Father Mancini, dressed in civilian clothes and with a Beretta secured in his shoulder holster, shifted in his seat. The man sitting next to him looked over.

"Looks like the weather is getting bad," said the man, a CIA field agent named James Tanner who, like his Vatican counterpart next to him, was well armed.

Father Mancini looked at Tanner and grunted yes, then turned away.

Tanner turned back toward his window. *Asshole*, he thought.

For the two men in the SUV, there was no love lost. They had been fully briefed on why they would be traveling together and what the operation meant for their respective governments. It was an arrangement of necessity, both sides having been forced into an unwanted partnership that neither man had a choice but seeing through to completion. The rest was all over their heads. It had gone on so for many years now.

Nearly three decades before, both American and Vatican intelligence had become aware that the parish of St. Gabriel potentially contained a dark secret. Inside the walls of the prosperous Washington congregation, more than just spiritual comfort was being provided to the communist movement in Central America. The CIA had known about the political bent of the parish members for years. It watched with a careful eye as its priests vocally expressed their political proclivities then ventured into the communist revolution in Nicaragua with apparent abandon. How deep the network was, however, hadn't come to light until years later, although no hard evidence had ever been uncovered, until now.

For the Holy See, the Jesuit parish in the heart of the affluent Georgetown section of Washington, DC, was one of the many Jesuit-run institutions that had raised its ire in the years when the Society of Jesus had waged open rebellion on the very Church it had been formed to defend. But it wasn't until the CIA had reluctantly decided to share what it knew that the Vatican had become fully aware of just how active the Jesuits were in waging war. By that point, the Vatican and the CIA had become intimate partners—the Vatican having been pivotal in bringing down communism in Europe, effectively ending the Cold War.

The rumors of a "smoking gun" had circulated for many years within the walls of Langley, Virginia, although there were actually very few at CIA headquarters who dared to mention or act on it. St. Gabriel was the parish of American senators and representatives, powerbrokers, and others within the highest levels of the US government—some of whom were outright hostile to the CIA and others who were suspected as potential conspirators. For the CIA, the idea of US officials and radical Jesuits conspiring to support communist revolutionaries was a political time bomb that no one wanted to see go off. It was conveniently ignored, until the rumors of the so-called smoking gun became more real and more serious.

If the rumors were true, the deceased parish pastor, Father Francis O'Brien, had been in possession of a diary. According to other assessments, based on factual intelligence gathered over the years by agents and informers in Nicaragua, the diary contained a complete record of transactions made in support of the Sandinista revolution over a period of nearly two decades: bank accounts, wire transfers, material shipments, overseas couriers, and arms brokers; it contained a detailed history of an American-run-and-supported illicit covert operation orchestrated from within the boundaries of Washington, DC, itself.

It wasn't these facts, however, that raised the most concern for the CIA. It was the other information that this so-called diary contained: the names of high-ranking US government officials who had aided in the planning and funding, many still in positions of substantial power and influence. It contained names and information that, if obtained by a foreign government, could be used as perpetual blackmail against those high-ranking officials.

It was here that the confluence of US national security and the Vatican's theological war with the Jesuits existed. Both sides were willing to partner to finally quash the temporal and spiritual rebellion of a wayward order—the Americans providing the intelligence and the Vatican providing the operatives that could get access into the highly guarded world of the Roman Catholic Church.

Yet no matter how informed both American and Vatican intelligence may have been as to the suspicions of aid and comfort going to communist revolutionaries, there was never a true ability by either side to uncover the facts alone. For the CIA, there was little hope of penetrating the walls of an American church without help. The Vatican, needing the resources and intelligence the CIA provided, was quite willing to assist when the offer was presented.

Now, inside the cool SUV, American and Vatican agents sat side by side to complete the decades-long operation. They would collect their prize soon enough, Tanner and Father Mancini thought separately. But who, ultimately, would keep it, was still to be determined.

No matter how long the agreement had been in place between their two governments, both men were all too aware that the endgame still remained—most certainly—uncertain. Both men had been tasked, in unambiguous terms, to make sure the ultimate victory would be their own respective government's to claim.

Chapter 67

Inside the pilothouse, Gallagher clung tightly to a handrail with one hand and threw up into a plastic bag held by the other. Laura was down below decks; she too was nearly dehydrated from seasickness.

For the last three hours, the small fishing boat pitched and rolled as the waters of the Atlantic Ocean pummeled its hull. Water spewed over the bow as it dipped again, ever deeper. The winds howled and the rain came down relentlessly. The captain, drenched in sweat, stood watch over the ship, commanding the man at the wheel to hold steady and his second crewman to man the radar.

With great skill, the captain moved to the chart table and checked the GPS. "Right ten degrees rudder," ordered the captain.

"Right ten degrees rudder, aye," responded the man at the wheel.

"You going to make it, Mr. Gallagher?" said the captain toward the nearly green face of his passenger.

Gallagher tried to swallow. "Not sure. Are *we*?"

When the captain didn't respond, Gallagher grew increasingly concerned that the situation was getting critical.

Another wave came over the bow, smashing to pieces the wooden net box that was fastened to the deck. The captain peered through the pilothouse window, watching as the remaining bits of wood were washed overboard.

"Gallagher!" said the captain, his stress beginning to show now. "Go below and check on the status of the cargo."

"What?" Gallagher responded with disbelief.

The captain moved toward Gallagher, grabbed the bag of vomit from his hand, and threw it onto the deck. "When I give you an order, you follow it!

You understand me? I've got a hundred thousand dollars in profit sitting down there, and I'll be damned if I see it destroyed." He looked at Gallagher closely. "Go down there and see if we have water inside the cargo hold!" He pulled a flashlight from his belt and authoritatively shoved it into Gallagher's hand.

"Yes, Captain," responded Gallagher.

"The correct response is 'Aye, aye, Captain,' Mr. Gallagher."

"Aye, aye, Captain."

"Good. Now go. Check on Ms. Miller as well. I want both of you up here as soon as you've checked the cargo hold."

Gallagher moved down the small ladder that led below the deck. The captain watched Gallagher's head disappear then turned toward the man at the wheel. "Come left five degrees rudder."

"Coming left five degrees rudder, aye," said the sailor.

The captain looked ahead through the pilothouse window, the windshield wipers barely able to keep up with the rain. He turned and looked at the man at the wheel. "We've got to hold course now and hope."

The two crewmen said nothing while the captain looked at the charts, radar, and GPS again in rapid succession. The waves continued to batter the boat, slowing ripping it apart, the captain knew.

The conditions would remain brutal. Of that, he was certain. But just how long they could stay afloat? Of that, he wasn't sure at all.

Chapter 68

Using all the balance and coordination he could muster, Gallagher made his way down and into the cramped cargo hold. The flashlight revealed an inch or two of fresh seawater on the deck; the pitch and rolls of the boat made the water lap up against the crates secured to it. How much damage the water had done to the cargo, he couldn't tell, nor did he care at this point. He wished they could've just been driven north to Maryland, instead of being ferried in this tiny vessel. But the network had been firm on the arrangements; the fact that they were lucky to have been driven as far north as the Carolinas was the only thing close to an explanation given.

Gallagher waded into the water and identified a small starboard crack in the wooden hull. The water continued to seep in steadily.

Soaked to the bone, he finally made it up the cargo hold ladder and opened the hatch to the sleeping quarters, finding Laura curled in a ball and wrapped in a damp wool blanket. She wasn't doing well, he could tell.

He moved closer toward her then found the overhead lights and switched them on. They hummed reluctantly to life. Laura cringed in fear when they did.

"Laura," he said, attempting to comfort her, "the captain needs us in the wheelhouse." She cried to herself and curled up even tighter.

"Laura," he said more forcefully, "we need to go now. We're taking on water. I'm not sure the ship is going to hold together. We have to get topside. We don't want to be down here if we begin to break apart."

Laura didn't react.

"Damn it! Did you hear what I said? We need to go now!" Gallagher turned and began to gather their bags that, miraculously, appeared bone dry.

He worked quickly, finding some plastic to waterproof the few pictures and other materials contained inside.

He turned back to Laura when he was done, finding her looking at him with pure fear. He grabbed her and held her close, brushing the wet hair from her eyes and gently caressing her face. "We'll be okay. I promise," he said, trying to sound convincing. "But we need to go now."

Laura looked at him and then was suddenly snapped out of the place she had been, screaming as the boat rolled again and Gallagher fell away from her, smashing his head against the bulkhead.

"I'm okay," said Gallagher, his head bleeding. He wiped at it with his hand, realizing he had a bad gash.

Laura rolled out of her rack and tried to keep her balance as she helped Gallagher place a crude bandage, fashioned from an old T-shirt, on his head.

After strapping the bags onto their backs precariously, they moved from the sleeping quarters and up to the pilothouse, along the tight ladder that led from below. The boat suddenly rolled again. Gallagher and Laura worked their way up to a landing located between the lower spaces below and the ship's bridge high above.

"You all okay?" came the voice of a crewmember in the bridge, yelling down the ladder.

"We're here!" said Gallagher, steadying his feet against a windowed hatch that led to the ship's outer deck. The wind and rain were relentless, he noticed, looking through the window. He pushed Laura up the next ladder and into the wheelhouse; the bag was strapped to her back, making it difficult for her to climb.

Gallagher watched Laura being pulled up by a crewman. He reached for his bag and handed it up to the man.

"Forget the bag," said the crewman angrily.

"Take it!" said Gallagher. "It goes where we go! And I can't make it up with it on."

The crewman acquiesced reluctantly. "Come on, then," he said, after grabbing and throwing the bag onto the wheelhouse deck.

Gallagher reached up the ladder as yet another swell sent the small boat violently pitching and rolling. His wet shoes slipped, and he tumbled down, hitting the deck below with a thud.

Dazed and losing more blood from the gash on his head, he attempted to stand, his mind foggy. As he got to his feet, the ship rolled again. Gallagher reached for a handhold without thinking, grabbing the latch to the door adjacent. The ship rolled again. The latch moved downward.

In an instant, Gallagher was swept out onto the deck, the wind and sea violently washing into the space where he had stood only a second before.

Chapter 69

How powerful the force of nature was at that time was apparent, given the ease with which it swept Gallagher from the small confines of the fishing boat.

"Man down!" yelled the crewman, watching as Gallagher's hand attempted, unsuccessfully, to cling to the hatch that his body was being forced from. "Man down!"

Water continued to pour into the space below as the crewman above in the wheelhouse instinctively slid down the ladder after Gallagher.

The captain leapt toward the starboard window, looking for signs of life below. The rain prevented his seeing much beyond a foot or two. He turned and caught the fear and horror in Laura's eyes but ignored it.

"Keep her steady!" yelled the captain to the other crewman still behind the wheel.

"Aye, sir!" responded the crewman, his own stomach now finally turning in a fit of uncharacteristic anxiousness.

The captain, dressed in foul weather gear, forced his way out onto the small outer deck that led off the bridge. He moved to the floodlight and flipped it on, hearing the subtle screams of the crewman below working to save Gallagher.

The wind and rain beat hard into the captain's face, making it difficult for him to see. He focused the floodlight on the deck below. The light quickly revealed the situation, and the captain gasped.

"Hold on!" yelled the crewman toward Gallagher, who was now caught on the deck rigging by a mangle of his legs and arms.

Gallagher remained dazed, the wind and rain seemingly muted as if he were looking at a silent film of the chaos that surrounded him. Had he been fully aware, he would have seen himself only a few short feet from a watery grave.

The captain struggled to hold the light in position as his crewman below bravely made his way toward Gallagher. Tempted to yell an order, the captain was unable to provide any further direction, watching as Gallagher's body began to untangle itself. The captain knew there were but a few more seconds to save him.

The boat rocked to starboard, sending the crewman sliding toward the edge of the deck. He caught himself a few short feet from Gallagher. The two men now both stood exposed to a certain death together.

Another wave came over the bow, washing more seawater over the two men. The crewman shook his head, trying to sweep the wet hair from his face and regain his focus. He gasped for air. "Hold on there, mate!" he yelled, grabbing Gallagher's arm.

The hard grip of the crewman's hand on his arm shocked Gallagher into reality, the sounds of the weather now suddenly blaring in full stereo. He looked over to the crewman and noticed his struggle. *Come on, Peter*, Gallagher told himself. *Help the man.*

With all of his strength, Gallagher pulled himself toward the crewman. The heavy metal rigging cut into his hand as he did.

"Keep pulling, you son of a bitch!" yelled the captain from above, releasing his wrath on the storm and the bad luck of the voyage that had befallen him. "Goddamn it, pull!"

Gallagher moved his leg, catching a foothold on a piece of rigging. He pushed with all he had, the crewman still pulling on his arm. Laura remained on the deck of the pilothouse, clutching a handhold and listening to it all unfolding below her.

The ship pitched forward, the sea spewing warm saltwater over everything in its path. Gallagher lost his handhold and slid forward along the slippery deck toward the bow. Grabbing more rigging, he found himself behind the crewman, who coughed and retched seawater from his chest.

The captain locked the floodlight in place and rushed inside the wheelhouse, bringing with him rain and a powerful wind.

"Hold her steady, goddamn it!" yelled the soaking wet captain as he whizzed by the man at the wheel and jumped down the ladder into the space below.

The captain forced the hatch open and again took a face full of water and stinging rain. He looked down and saw Gallagher's legs below him as Gallagher worked to pull the crewman to safety.

After propping open the hatch, the captain took to his knees and grabbed Gallagher's legs, pulling with all the might and furor he had left. The train that was Gallagher and the crewman moved toward the hatch. The captain looked to his left. He saw the waves ahead and sensed they had only seconds. He pulled again.

Gallagher's head and upper torso now sat astride the hatch deck plate, halfway in and out of the enclosed space. With his left arm, he pulled again on the crewman's legs as the captain assisted.

The captain looked left again and saw the bow begin to rise. Another few seconds and the waves would be over them. He turned back and pulled, screaming with anger.

The crewman's body moved to a point just outside the hatch. The captain stepped over Gallagher and grabbed the back of the crewman's wet clothes and hauled him inside. The crewman landed with a thud and coughed up water from his lungs.

The bow had reached its crest and began to move down. The captain could see the wave ahead. He grabbed Gallagher by the pant seat and pulled. Gallagher struggled for the deck space adjacent to the crewman. The captain fell backward as Gallagher landed with a second thud and retched.

The bow moved down to its nadir, as the captain watched the water begin to come over. He kicked Gallagher's legs aside so he could slam the hatch into place just as a wave of water rolled past in a massive force.

The boat lurched again to starboard. The captain shuffled back up the ladder to the pilothouse, leaving the two exhausted men below to their own devices. "Hold her steady, my boy!" yelled the captain to the man at the wheel.

The crewman drew strength from the victory his captain had just won against the hostile sea. "Aye, Captain!" he yelled back with seafaring solidarity.

"You all right, Miss?" said the captain to Laura.

Laura looked up and registered in her eyes both a thankfulness and glimmer of hope drawn from the captain's demeanor. "I'm okay. Thank you, Captain. Thank you."

"There. We'll be okay." The captain gently patted Laura's head as he shuffled by and toward the radar.

He looked up after examining the radar, the GPS, and then the horizon. The rain was beginning to wane and the sky beginning to lighten.

"I'll take the wheel," said the captain to his crewman at the helm. "Go below and tend to Braxton and Gallagher. Then I need a full damage report."

"Aye, Captain," said the crewman, turning over the helm with a smile and descending the ladder to take care of the two waterlogged men.

"Leave the sea to me," said the captain to Laura, who still remained on the floor. "She's a tough little ship."

Laura looked up at the salty fishing captain, letting go an unexpected burst of laughter through her tears.

"Next stop will be Maryland," the captain told her, "but I think we all may need a bit of a drink before that, hey?"

Laura smiled again, wiped her nose, and stood with newfound sea legs. "Yes, Captain," she said. "I think that would be a very good idea."

Chapter 70

At the Washington Embassy of the Holy See, Archbishop Pio Lucessi stood looking out his large office window at the heavy rain and wind that was finally abating after nearly six straight hours. He turned as his resident intelligence officer, Monsignor Sansevarino, entered after a perfunctory knock.

"Excellency," said Sansevarino, "the teams are still awaiting the arrival of the ship."

Lucessi glanced at his watch. "The boat is very late."

"Yes, Excellency. The storm was more than expected. If the boat makes it at all, it will be a miracle."

The Papal Nuncio looked at his resident intelligence officer. "Well, then we must pray that they do. We've come too far to have this operation fail."

"Mancini will not fail us, Excellency."

"Humph," said Lucessi. "We shall see." The Archbishop moved toward his desk, lit a cigarette, then continued. "The safe house is an American one, yes? We play this game on American soil and with American agents to rely on." He exhaled a stream of blue smoke. "I would say the odds are greatly in favor of the Americans."

Sansevarino remained calm and cool. "The debriefing will take place on American soil and in an American safe house, yes. But the diary may not be with the detective. If it isn't, the Church retains the key to its retrieval. The Americans cannot just barge into St. Gabriel—should it reside there—and remove it." Sansevarino paused. "If its location at the parish is discovered, Mancini will relay that information to us. The Americans have no idea that Father Benjamin is one of our assets nor that he is even back in the United States."

"Where is Benjamin now?" asked Lucessi, inhaling on his cigarette.

"He returned to the parish yesterday. He is ready to strike when the time comes."

Lucessi walked to the window and peered out. "What if the diary is with the detective, should he arrive at all?"

Sansevarino said nothing, his sharp eyes focused on the Papal Nuncio.

Lucessi knew the answer to that question and accepted the silence of his intelligence officer's gaze. He knew well that the Holy Church hadn't survived these many centuries without decisive action when absolutely required. And if the endgame demanded such action, Lucessi was prepared to deal with the result, should it come to that.

For the sake of his own soul and the Holy Church, however, Archbishop Pio Lucessi prayed to himself once again that it would not come to that.

Chapter 71

Hours earlier, the giant had watched with interest when the large black SUV had arrived right before the worst of the wind and rain had descended.

Now, with the sky beginning to clear more rapidly, the giant picked up his cell phone and dialed his superior.

The well-dressed man picked up his phone quickly. "Yes?"

"An SUV arrived a few hours ago. Four large men."

"Then our gamble was right," the well-dressed man told the giant.

"It would seem so, but the detective and the woman haven't yet been seen."

"They must be arriving by boat."

"It would appear so."

"You weathered the storm well, then?" asked the well-dressed man, not really caring either way as long as the work was done.

"Yes."

The well-dressed man rose from his desk and pondered the next steps. "Will you need more men?"

"Yes," responded the giant. "I can't do the work alone with this many present."

"How many men will you require?"

"I need three, each with his own car. They also need high-powered weapons with special munitions and other supplies."

The well-dressed man glanced at his expensive watch. It was nearly six p.m. "I'll arrange to have a team to you in three hours. One car will drive to meet you. The others will stage at a rest stop two miles from your position. The man who will meet you will provide the communications information needed to run the other assets. Do you understand?"

"Yes, sir."

"This storm has delayed the arrival, if they're coming by boat. The darkness will be of added benefit," said the well-dressed man, making notes on a piece of paper he would burn once the operational arrangements were made in the next few minutes.

"Yes. It would seem to be."

"You've done well thus far, but you must complete the assignment cleanly. Is that understood? There can be no traceability." The well-dressed man buttoned his expensive suit jacket.

"Yes," said the giant, feeling the adrenalin of the hunt surging again and reviving him. "I understand. It will be clean."

Chapter 72

The CIA men parked outside of the St. Gabriel rectory listened intently as the rectory housekeeper, Maria Rosario, engaged in a curious conversation with the pastor, Father Damien Thomas.

"I go to my mother's now, Father," said Rosario.

"Do you think she is very ill?" responded Father Thomas, according to their prearranged coded dialogue.

"Yes, Father. I am afraid so. I must go and see her."

"God be with you, then. I will pray for you both."

There was a pause and then the sound of a door opening. The men in the van watched as the woman walked down the rectory stairs carrying what appeared to be an overnight bag. She turned right at the bottom of the stairs and headed down the sidewalk.

One of the two agents in the CIA van listening turned to his partner with a look of curiosity. "Her mother's? What the fuck is that about? What do we have on a mother?" He continued to watch the woman as she walked down the street.

The other CIA agent looked through his notes, stopping on a page halfway through his thick binder. "The woman has no relations here in the United States that we know of."

"Shit," said the first agent. "Pull the phone log for calls into the rectory."

The agent worked his computer furiously. The screen popped up in a few seconds. Both agents studied it closely, the first pointing to two incoming calls in quick succession five minutes before.

"You remember any phone conversations?" the first agent asked.

"No, but if the phone wasn't picked up, the computers wouldn't have kicked in."

"Fucking technology," said the first agent. "Pull the rectory audio from the last ten minutes."

The second agent worked the computer again while the first notified a nearby team to track the housekeeper.

"I got it!" said the second agent.

"Put it on the speakers and dial down the ambient noise."

The agents listened intently to the audio recording of the rectory five minutes before. The muffled sound of a telephone ringing three times was heard. There was no answer. The agents continued with the recording, listening again exactly thirty seconds later as another three rings were heard, again without any conversation having taken place.

"Phone records show the two calls originating from a payphone on Massachusetts Avenue," said the second agent.

"Fuck me," said the first. "The bitch is making a run for it." The agent picked up his phone and dialed Langley.

The agent, known as Simon, picked up immediately. "Yes," he said.

"Looks like the Rosario woman is making a run. Two unanswered phone calls, three rings each, came in a few minutes ago. Source of the calls was a pay phone across town."

"Christ," groaned Simon. "Not fucking now." He took a few seconds to think. The intelligence coming in from Nicaragua was clear that alarm bells had sounded in Managua, with the fleeing of two suspected Americans in the days before. The assumption was that Nicaraguan intelligence smelled a rat, had started putting some pieces together, and pushed the panic button.

"Pick her up quickly," said Simon, "before she finds herself in a diplomatic car on the way back to Managua. Hold her and get her confined, quietly. Call me back when you're confirmed."

"Roger that," said the first agent before he hung up the phone.

Not three minutes later on the dusky streets of Georgetown, the housekeeper known as Maria Rosario was deftly swept into a nondescript vehicle and driven off with nary a sound. The operation was so swift and flawless that even the few pedestrians remotely near the woman at the time didn't realize what had happened.

Back in Langley, Simon waited in his office, thinking. "Christ," he said to himself again. "Why now?" He knew the operation to bring Peter Gallagher and Laura Miller back safely into the country was underway. His men, along with those from Vatican intelligence, were in place and awaiting the exchange.

How much time they had, Simon wasn't sure. The weather that had delayed their scheduled arrival had been unfortunate but inconsequential up until the last few minutes.

Now there was more to consider. How connected was the parish pastor to all of this? If he was connected, would he be expecting a signal from the housekeeper at some pre-planned point in time? What was happening inside the rectory? What about Father Benjamin? The CIA didn't have video from inside the rectory. Would the pastor call the press and expose the conspiracy? Was there a conspiracy at all? The list of questions that ran through his mind was varied, but there was little to go on, other than speculation and suspicion. He needed to remain focused on what they did know. The rest would have to be dealt with as the situation developed.

All of that said, Simon was now growing more concerned about the planned debriefing and what might follow should the location of the diary be revealed. He didn't trust the Vatican, but sharing intelligence had gotten them this far. It also had likely saved the lives of two innocent Americans, one of whom was the daughter of a former CIA operative and a current US ambassador. Of that, he was certain.

Simon picked up his phone again and called his field operative, now stationed with the team awaiting the arrival of Gallagher and Laura. The message he would provide was clear—the stakes were now markedly raised.

It was up to the team now in Maryland to ensure that Simon's personal and professional gamble would pay off for himself and, more important, for the United States of America.

Chapter 73

The sun was beginning to rise over the warm waters of the Atlantic. The sea was soothing and gentle, no clouds to be seen across the horizon.

The storm the day prior had sent the small fishing vessel some fifty miles off course and done more than a fair amount of damage to the ship's hull. One crewman along with Gallagher had sustained relatively minor injuries, but they were still serious enough to prevent their assistance with the damage repair, an effort that had gone on for most of the night and into the early hours of the morning that followed.

All things considered, the captain knew it was extremely fortunate that they had weathered the storm mostly intact. Nevertheless the planned rendezvous at the small Maryland port was now significantly behind schedule—nearly twelve hours, he conservatively estimated. The captain sipped his coffee and brushed the delay aside. There was nothing he could have done to prevent what had occurred.

Gallagher and the crewman, Braxton, lay below deck fast asleep. In addition to the cut on his head, Gallagher had most of the skin from the palm of his right hand taken off and several bruised ribs. Braxton sustained a concussion and trauma to his right arm, which was now held in a sling.

The cargo hold was secure. The breached bulkhead had been patched sufficiently for the time being to prevent any further leaking, as long as there was no further rough weather along the way. Half of the illicit cargo was ruined. All in all, any profit that the captain now hoped to reap would likely go right back into the repair and refitting of his battered ship. That said, he was sure his seafaring heroics in getting his special passengers to their destination in relatively one piece would be richly rewarded by the network with whom he was secretly connected.

Laura sat on deck now, her blond hair blowing in the morning breeze. The captain walked down the outside ladder from the pilothouse.

Laura turned to greet him. "Hard to believe this is the same ocean as last night," she said.

The captain looked out over the bow and took in the warm salt air. He sipped his coffee. "Yes, the sea is a funny thing. A lot like life. Tumultuous one minute, serene the next."

"How true," said Laura, looking back to take in more of the moment.

"Mr. Gallagher is a tough man. He's had a rough ride, but he's got some fight in him. I'll give him that." The captain looked at Laura as she turned back toward him again.

"I'm in love with him," said Laura. "I've never told anyone that. I'm not even sure I've told Peter that properly since we started this trek."

"I'm not usually one for asking questions of my passengers, Miss Miller. Oftentimes it's better that I not know too much. But I can tell that you and Mr. Gallagher have been through quite a lot recently."

Laura smiled. "You might say that."

"Well, I think it's times like these—in the calm after a storm—that I feel most happy. It's the challenge and the hardship that makes life worth it. It's the hardship that makes the time after the most satisfying."

Laura looked at the captain and smiled. "I think that's true, Captain." She looked out over the sea again and felt the rising sun and salty breeze hit her face. "Very true."

The captain sensed it best to take his leave and return to the pilothouse. "We'll be heading toward the coast soon. I'll leave you to the morning again." He walked toward the ladder that led up to the bridge. He turned back. "Oh, and Miss Miller?"

"Yes?"

The captain waited. "Nothing," he said. "I'll be in the wheelhouse if you need me."

Laura registered a quizzical look as the captain turned and strode up the ladder and into the pilothouse.

Upon his entry, the captain looked at his able crewman behind the wheel, gave a reassuring wink, then moved to begin the final navigational preparations needed to make it to the coast in the next couple of hours. He moved to the bridge window and looked down again at Laura, who was alone on the deck. He said to himself a quick sailor's prayer that fair winds and following seas would find her and Gallagher once they landed.

But the old captain sensed that whatever Gallagher and Laura were caught up in was far more difficult than anything the sea might throw their way. No matter how fair the winds or following the seas, the captain somehow could tell that, even once they got to dry land, their journey wasn't over by a long shot.

Chapter 74

For the last eight hours, the giant and his team had been assembled and ready. They now waited for the arrival of the detective and the woman for their plan to go into action.

On a remote bluff some three miles away, a man with high-powered binoculars scanned the sea. Few boats had ventured out from their berths since sunrise. He put down his binoculars as the radio next to him rattled. He picked it up and listened.

"Boat leaving from docks. Looks like it'll be an at-sea transfer of cargo," said the giant from his concealed position. He had waited to send the message until he had been sure. Radio communication was to be kept to a minimum.

"Roger," said the man on the bluff. He picked up his binoculars and searched until he saw a small boat make its way out to sea. "I've got her."

"All units should be ready to move. Radio check, over," said the giant.

The three other men, located in their carefully staged locations, each responded and confirmed their readiness to the unit leader.

The giant took another look through his own binoculars before beginning his final preparations.

* * *

Inside Jefferson's Crab Shack, the CIA and Vatican teams attempted to stay awake with more hot coffee after a long and tense night for which they hadn't planned. Tanner and Father Mancini remained cool to each other. Even with the long hours they'd spent together, they seemed to have made little progress in breaking the animosity.

Johnson was also on edge but was somewhat more composed with the sleep he had managed to get the day before. He sat with the two sides and said little. He knew both the CIA and the Vatican resented the fact that it was he who had arranged the arrival of Gallagher and Miller and the specific arrangements that prevented the handoff until both were safely brought onto dry land by his father-in-law and crew.

Thirty minutes before, the radio from the fishing vessel off the coast had sent Johnson and his father-in-law the precise coordinates where the man and woman could be found. The information wasn't shared with the others, as had been reluctantly agreed—only that the vessels were now ready for the highly anticipated exchange.

* * *

Ten miles out to sea, the small fishing boat sent from the Maryland seaside still hadn't gained sight of the boat they were expecting. The captain checked the coordinates again. "Where are they?" said Larry Sylvester.

A crewman looked through his binoculars. "No boat out here," he said before his eyes caught the small hard rubber raft. "Shit! There they are! Off the starboard bow. Man and a woman. About a mile out, I would say."

The captain grabbed the binoculars from the crewman, confirmed the position, then ordered the boat to make haste. "Must have dropped them off and pressed on. Smart, if you ask me. Gave the agents the slip."

The captain looked through his binoculars again, watching the man and the woman waving at the approaching vessel. "Welcome home," said the captain before adding, "I hope."

Chapter 75

A stately and imposing beach house stood tall and strong above the Atlantic, its prominent position surrounded by green acreage, a tennis court, a swimming pool, and various outbuildings that made up the cloistered compound in Nantucket.

Sitting on a white wicker chair, an old man gazed across a green rolling lawn that sloped down gently to the sea below. He watched as his grown son kicked a soccer ball with his grandson and the dogs ran to and fro, giving chase. The breeze from the sea was cool, but the sun warmed his face. His lower body was covered in heavy tartan blanket.

Life had been good to him, the old man thought pleasantly. He had achieved everything that most could have only dreamed about. He had gained power, title, influence, vast wealth, and stature, but he had sold part of his soul to attain it.

The man coughed. A nurse, lurking close by in a white uniform, rushed to his side, attempting to place the oxygen mask over his wrinkled face. The man struck out at the nurse, who retreated as she usually did when the scene repeated itself during the course of her workday.

Life is very short, thought the old man, as he regained his focus on his son and grandson in the near distance. The nurse moved back to her perch a few yards behind in the shade and retook her seat to monitor the man.

Yes, thought the old man. His son would carry on his name and his legacy when he was gone from this Earth. All that the father had done—all the regrets and mistakes—would be wiped away, the slate wiped forever clean.

As the old man continued his musings, a fellow in a dark blue suit and dark sunglasses stepped out from the house and onto the brick patio. Gathering his bearings, he searched and caught sight of the old man in the chair a few yards beyond. He took a deep breath and slowly walked toward him. The nurse looked up as the man walked by and continued on without acknowledging her.

"Sir," said the man.

The old man tilted his head and adjusted his eyes to the man in the dark suit standing next to him and casting a shadow over his face. He looked back toward the view of his son. "You will tell me this matter is being resolved now, won't you?"

The man in the blue suit waited. "The detective and the woman have arrived. They were brought in by sea to a small dock in southern Maryland. How they made it into the country, we don't know exactly. We do know they're now in government custody."

The old man picked up a glass of ice water and sipped it slowly. "It will all be cleaned up now?"

"We expect it to be."

"I didn't pay five million dollars for mere 'expectations.'" The old man looked again at the man in the suit, who said nothing. "I didn't pay for this sort of uncertainty and chaos."

"No, sir."

The old man coughed again, sending the nurse springing again from her chair. The man in the blue suit moved aside as she placed the oxygen mask over the face of the old man, who slowly caught his breath. The nurse retreated again after being shooed away. "Finish this, do you hear me?" said the old man in a raspy voice. He spat onto the ground next to him. "Finish this."

The man in the blue suit looked down at the old man, who was focused again on his son and grandson.

"Yes, Senator," said the man in the blue suit. "It will be finished."

Chapter 76

If there was any word that Gallagher could use to describe his state of mind, it was most certainly "surreal." Even that word, however, didn't adequately capture his feelings regarding everything that had happened.

Plucked from the middle of the ocean, Gallagher remembered little: the blanket thrown over him and Laura as they sat watching the Maryland coastline, the reassurance of Ty Johnson's smiling face, the rush from the small fishing port into a cold SUV, and the hour-long drive to the house where he and Laura now were held. Everything had happened so suddenly, so quickly, that there had been little time to take it all in. Nor, thought Gallagher, was there much room left in his rattled head to capture it all without some loss of detail.

The mobile medical unit that had greeted the SUV provided Gallagher and Laura only cursory treatment then left. They were told they would be shipped off to a hospital once the debriefing was complete.

Gallagher rose from a bed inside the government house and dressed himself in the fresh clothes provided. A man waited while he finished and escorted him to the dining room of the small country house located, Gallagher assumed from the length of the drive, somewhere in Maryland. The house stood back in the woods, surrounded by trees. Some sort of safe house, Gallagher figured. It seemed to fit his idea of one.

"Mr. Gallagher," said Tanner, pointing to a chair around the table, "please sit. Can we get you some coffee?"

"Yes, that would be good," responded Gallagher, looking on as another man, wearing a headset over his ears, swept some sort of detector over the walls of the room. The heavyset SUV driver now doubled as a waiter and brought Gallagher a cup of hot coffee.

"Ms. Miller is still asleep," said Tanner, answering the question he knew Gallagher would be asking.

"Don't you want to question us together?" asked Gallagher.

"In time," said Father Mancini, slipping into the room from the shadows. Gallagher looked up.

"I'm sorry," said Gallagher, his mind still cloudy. "Can we go over the arrangement again? I'm afraid, in all the commotion of the last few hours, I've missed the details."

James Tanner, the CIA's man, took over. "Detective Gallagher," he began, "this debriefing is being done jointly. The US government and the Holy See have seen it in both our governments' interests to do this together. This house we're in is part of that arrangement. The man you see sweeping for listening devices is with Father Mancini. To avoid any lingering doubt between our two governments, we've thought it best to allow each side an opportunity to verify the true secrecy under which this discussion will take place."

Gallagher sipped his coffee and tried to appear relaxed, watching intently as the Vatican operative continued his security check.

Father Mancini took the handoff from Tanner and continued the description of the arrangement. "There are only six of us here in this house, Mr. Gallagher. You and Miss Miller and two members each from the US government and the Vatican."

"And Ty Johnson?" asked Gallagher.

"He's heading back to Washington, DC," said Tanner. "There are things that need to be done to allow you to get back to normal once we're done here. Detective Johnson is assisting us with those matters, including getting your files cleared so you can resume your duties with the police department." Tanner paused. "Your little escapade has created quite a mess of paperwork that will need to be, shall we say, reorganized."

Gallagher took another sip of coffee. "Can we get on with it, then?"

"Of course," said Mancini, getting a nod from his own operative that the sweep was complete and the house was clear of listening or recording devices. Both sides were now on truly neutral ground. "Why don't we start at the beginning, then?"

* * *

The giant and his team had tracked the black SUV without notice. The team of four men and four cars that he oversaw had been careful not to attract the attention of the intelligence teams that likely would have shadowed the SUV to its final destination. The leapfrogging of his own team's cars had been carefully orchestrated. He was quite confident there was little surveillance now on the house, other than his own.

The giant picked up his radio while looking through his binoculars toward the house. "Five men, one woman inside. Confirm."

One of the giant's operatives, watching from another position, looked down at his notes, and then picked up his own radio. "Confirm. Black Bird departed. One SUV, two blue, two purple, two green all remain. Over."

The giant smiled. "Roger. Phase One complete. Move to Phase Two positions. Repeat…Phase Two positions. Begin birdsong tracking. Make ready the hounds. Confirm."

The men from the team responded in the affirmative, moved with precision to their planned locations, and awaited the next order.

Chapter 77

It took nearly seven hours before Gallagher, Laura, the CIA, and the Holy See had concluded the debriefing.

Gallagher and Laura had been interviewed separately then together. Their stories were consistent, factual, and yet still unsatisfactory to both sides.

The accounts had covered the moment that Father Edward Sachs had fallen from the rectory window; the police investigation; the discussions with, and death of, Father Clarence Symanski; and then the entire journey through Mexico, Central America, across the Atlantic, and back into US territory.

Both the CIA and Vatican representatives had grown perturbed by the lack of information regarding who actually had helped Gallagher and Laura from beginning to end. Neither would reveal the names nor the logistics of the secret network that had dodged American and Vatican intelligence over the course of the couple's many days on the run.

For the CIA, what was known was that a diary *did* exist—a diary that, if found, revealed nearly two decades of names, dates, and other highly sensitive data that could compromise the national security of the United States. For the Vatican there existed the keys to striking a crucial blow in their decades-long theological struggle against the Jesuits.

Yet the vital treasure remained elusive, as did the answer to the question of who was behind the murders and wiretappings that had prompted the situation to reach the point where it now was.

Gallagher rubbed his head again, as Tanner and Father Mancini sat back in their chairs and exhaled in utter exhaustion. "You mind if I step out and have a smoke?" asked Gallagher, as Laura got up and declared her need for more sleep.

Tanner winced, revealing his own exhaustion. "No, Mr. Gallagher. Be my guest," he said, scanning the room. "Looks like our men may be out there as well."

Father Mancini grew alarmed, knowing that his own man from Vatican intelligence didn't smoke. He watched as Gallagher moved to the sliding doors off the kitchen.

Gallagher stepped into the night air and pulled out a cigarette. Tired, he fumbled for his lighter and dropped it onto the brick patio below his feet. "Shit," he muttered, reaching down in the darkness to feel for the lost lighter.

His hand moved over the hard brick then stopped when it hit a warm, thick liquid. His eyes adjusted to the darkness; the sight of the dead Vatican and CIA operatives made him fall back. He scrambled back like a crab, the cigarette clamped in his mouth. "Oh, Jesus," he said. The cigarette dropped to the ground not a second before he saw Father Antonio Mancini walk out the sliding door. Gallagher didn't have time to react.

Father Mancini had only a second to look down and see what had happened before a silenced bullet dropped him in place and sent the back of his head into the kitchen from which he had just come.

Chapter 78

The house went dark just as Gallagher scrambled over the bodies of Father Mancini and the two other CIA and Vatican operatives. After throwing himself back inside, he moved to secure the door. Tanner was already waiting with his gun drawn.

"Gallagher!" yelled Tanner. "Get the girl!" He pulled his phone from his pocket, taking cover behind the kitchen island. "Fuck!" he called out. "They're jamming the lines."

"Who?" yelled Gallagher, as a bullet blew through a window and landed near Tanner's feet.

"Get the girl, goddamn it!" screamed Tanner, his eyes trying unsuccessfully to ascertain the assailants' location. Another bullet landed dangerously close to him.

"Laura!" cried Gallagher, as he moved across the floor and out of the kitchen. He hugged the floor, making his way toward the bedroom where Laura had retired only a few minutes before.

"Peter?" said Laura. "What's going on?"

"Laura, get down!" Gallagher reached up and forcefully pulled her toward him. Gallagher held her tight and didn't move.

When the front door came crashing down a second later, Gallagher held Laura even more tightly and prayed for the first time in many years.

* * *

The two men dressed in all black and wearing night-vision goggles moved quickly to where Gallagher and Laura now sat clinging to each other on the floor. They carried silenced, short-barreled, fully automatic rifles.

Gallagher looked up as one man stood guard over them and the second moved like a cat toward the kitchen.

From the kitchen, a burst of muffled rifle fire followed, as the second man sent fifteen rounds into the body of James Tanner.

It took only ten minutes before the armed men, along with Gallagher and Laura, were gone.

From start to finish, the entire operation had taken less than twenty minutes.

Chapter 79

"Tanner has failed to check in, sir," said a CIA man assigned to Simon's group, who was calling from an operations center located in the CIA compound at Langley.

"How many minutes late?" asked Simon, his pulse quickening.

"Thirty, sir, and all previous checks have been on the dot."

Simon hung up the phone without a word and immediately dialed another number. The alarm was now official.

* * *

The Hawk rested his head in his hands and rubbed his eyes. He assumed the worst but would wait for his own team to link up with US intelligence at the Maryland house before facing the fire of the Papal Nuncio and then Archbishop Dietrich and Vatican intelligence itself.

While the thought that the CIA would betray him flashed again through his head, he seriously doubted it to be likely; there was just too much to lose by the CIA carrying off something brazen that would permanently cut itself off from the healthy working relationship with the Holy See. It would be absolute madness, if true.

But the final determination would depend on what was found at the house and who provided answers—that is, if there was anyone left to provide answers at all.

Chapter 80

Ty Johnson and Irvin Drexler had been informed about the raid in Maryland only after the CIA and Vatican intelligence had seen fit to do so. The message had therefore come some four hours after the "incident" at the Maryland "safe" house had been discovered; the whereabouts of Peter Gallagher and Laura Miller were unknown.

The two Washington detectives sat in their DC police precinct, waiting and on edge.

"Should we call the press?" Johnson asked his boss, who sat behind his desk. "We could go public with this thing. Blow it wide open."

Drexler looked back at Johnson and raised his eyebrows. "We could. Probably would save our own asses. But we'd be out of jobs and likely sued. Not to mention it would probably get Gallagher and Laura Miller killed, if they're not dead already."

"I guess that's true."

"Even if we did, what the fuck would we say? That a disgraced detective came up with an unproven theory behind the accidental death of a priest?" Drexler sat back in his chair and exhaled. "Fuck. We got nothing to say because we have nothing: no evidence, no witnesses, nothing. You think they shut down Gallagher quick? How quickly do you think they'll take down two black cops casting dispersions on the Washington white 'elite'? I don't give a fuck how 'liberal' these people claim to be. They would lynch us no differently than the KKK and not lose a second's sleep over it."

Johnson reluctantly laughed. "You're right, you know. All those lawyers and powerbrokers, congressmen, and sen…" Johnson stopped talking in mid-sentence.

Drexler looked across as Johnson's face registered curious concentration mixed with enlightenment. "What you got, Johnson?"

Johnson looked back at his boss. "I think we still have one thread to pull on."

"What thread?"

"The one that's been sitting in front of us for days."

Chapter 81

The first thing that struck Gallagher was the damp smell. The second was the closed fist of the hooded man who stood over him.

"Wake up!" said the man, his voice gravelly and distinctly foreign.

Gallagher slowly tried to open his eyes. "What the—?" Another blow came across his face followed by a hard splash of cold water.

"Get the girl up," said the hooded man to another, who worked to refill his bucket.

Laura sat in the corner and was doused into consciousness. "Peter?" she said, spitting water from her mouth. "Peter, where are you?" Her eyes opened fully and came upon Gallagher sitting across the room.

"Shut up, both of you!" said the hooded man. "Boss wants to talk to you."

Gallagher moved to wipe his eyes. His wrists and ankles were shackled with heavy metal bands connected by chains. The chains on his feet were secured to the stone floor with a large padlock. He looked over at Laura and saw she was secured in a similar fashion.

The room was cold. Earthen walls surrounded a hard cobblestone floor. A heavy wooden table sat in the middle of the room. Industrial floodlights were attached to the high ceiling and along the wall in front of them where a steel door stood closed, although none were illuminated. Gallagher watched as one of the hooded men opened the door and exited. The other guard waited and watched with his arms folded, as he stood next to it.

A minute later the floodlights flashed on, blinding Gallagher and Laura and forcing them to cover their faces with their arms. They heard the heavy metal door clank open but could only see vague shapes through the harsh light.

Under the cover of the floodlights, the well-dressed man moved into the room carrying a dossier. He pulled a handkerchief from his pocket, ensured that the seat at the wooden table was clean, then sat down. He glanced through the dossier.

"Who's there?" asked Gallagher boldly.

"You will be answering questions, Mr. Gallagher. Not asking them. Do you understand?" said the well-dressed man. "If you do not answer my questions or if you get out of line, this discussion will end very badly for you both." The well-dressed man grew stern. "Do you understand?"

"Yes, we understand," responded Gallagher.

"Very well," said the well-dressed man. "You and Miss Miller have caused me a great deal of trouble, time, and money. I will get what I want. How cooperative you are will determine how painfully this will go."

One of the well-dressed man's goons brought him a glass of water. He sipped it slowly. "Tell me where it is."

"Where what is?" asked Gallagher.

The well-dressed man snapped his fingers, sending one of his henchmen toward Gallagher. The man kicked him in the face, sufficiently enough to break his nose.

Gallagher screamed in pain, and Laura began to cry. "Leave him alone!" she said, before receiving her own kick.

"Now let's try again, shall we? The next time will not be so delicate." The well-dressed man remained impassive and took another sip of water. "You failed to inform your masters about the location of the diary. Why?"

Gallagher didn't respond then rethought the silence. "There's nothing to find."

"Bluff, Mr. Gallagher. Bluff," said the well-dressed man. "We have your debriefing on tape. We know it exists. Where is it? Tell me."

"I don't know where it is. I told you just as I told them. *I* don't know!" said Gallagher. "If I did, I would have gone and gotten it."

"Yes, we know," said the well-dressed man. "We were tracking you for a while, until you left the US. If you had found it, you wouldn't have gone on that little jaunt of yours. But that isn't to say you didn't hand it off before returning."

"Then why don't you ask the people we met along the way?" asked Gallagher defiantly. "Especially if you know so fucking much?"

The well-dressed man sent his goons to deliver more punishment for the profanity. Gallagher riled in pain as the message was delivered, his face covered with blood.

"You can scream all you like, Mr. Gallagher. Please do, in fact. I rather enjoy it. But you'll find there will be no benefit. Abolitionists used this room to hide fleeing niggers from the South. They built it well." He sipped his water, left the glass on the table, and stood up. "How long this goes on will be up to you. How difficult will be up to me." He moved toward the heavy metal door. "I suggest you get your wits about you and think hard and quickly. When I return, I'll need the location. If you continue to persist, I'll have no choice but to fry your brain with the medicine needed to force it from you."

The door shut hard, leaving Laura and Gallagher alone inside. Outside the room, the well-dressed man turned toward one of his hooded men. "They may talk if left alone. We'll be listening. Keep an eye on them, cut the lights, and switch on the microphone. The darkness may provide them a false sense of anonymity."

"Yes, sir," said the hooded man.

"And get the psychedelics ready." The well-dressed man moved off, leaving one guard to prepare the deadly chemicals and the other to watch and listen through the small slat on the heavy metal door.

How close Gallagher and Laura were to death, the guard watching most certainly knew. *Poor girl*, he thought. *So young and so pretty.*

* * *

Laura sat on her side of the now pitch-black room. She was cold and in pain. She thought first about pleading to their captors and then trying to communicate with Gallagher. But none of those options, she knew, would have helped.

Gallagher too sat in the dark and didn't speak, realizing that every word and every sound would be analyzed and then exploited in the minutes and hours they had left. He sat and waited, feeling her presence across the dark room.

The guard outside the cell had turned off his own lights, so as not to reveal his face, which was pressed against the metal door slot. He listened closely but heard nothing. The silence, he thought, was unusual. Most people, when placed in a similar scenario, would talk quite freely and quickly after the lights had gone out.

Laura sobbed gently.

"We'll be okay," said Gallagher. "Hang in there."

"If it wasn't for you, Peter, we wouldn't be in the position!" yelled Laura, trying to initiate her plan.

Gallagher was shocked at her outburst. "Laura? What's wrong with you?"

"The only thing that's wrong is my own judgment in having put up with you. I should never have talked to you when you walked into my classroom at the school."

Both the well-dressed man, now in an outer room, and the cell guard immediately picked up the outbursts and dialogue with express interest. The guard smiled to himself, relishing in the quarrel and the rebuke the woman had given the man.

Gallagher sat in the dark, puzzled at first, then understood the play. "I should've left you behind. You've been nothing but a distraction. If it hadn't been for you, I would've solved this case already."

"I should have seen at once that you weren't a real man."

Gallagher remained silent. Laura quietly sobbed again.

The guard, who was listening just outside the damp and dark cell, grew increasingly pleased.

* * *

The well-dressed man continued to go through the few pictures and other materials his goons had found during the Maryland raid. Aside from the faces of those he recognized, nothing gave any insight into the location of the item he was tasked to recover at all costs.

"The serums are ready, sir," said the senior guard after entering the room.

"Good. We'll wait a little longer. Perhaps this dissent we're hearing from the girl will provide us a lead." The well-dressed man looked back at the materials in front of him. "You can leave and take your post."

"Yes, sir," said the guard before heading to wait outside the room of the giant.

In a room above the cell, the giant slept deeply. He had been granted the privilege by the well-dressed man, who, while disappointed with the direct action required by the giant and his team, knew that his top assassin had executed his orders with absolute loyalty. The well-dressed man would need him rested.

After preparing the truth serums, the senior guard pulled a chair outside the room wherein the giant slept. He would now wait for the order from the well-dressed man. When the time came, the guard would need to wake the giant to assist with administering the drugs. In the meantime, the senior guard would sit quietly. But as he did, now well worn from the many hours without sleep, his eyes too began to close.

Chapter 82

The guard looked at the luminous hands on his military watch. It had been nearly two hours. The girl inside continued to sniffle from the steady sobbing she had displayed before. The man hadn't made a sound.

The guard looked back behind him and didn't hear anything. His superiors must be asleep, he thought angrily, his own lack of importance feeding his resentment. He turned again and caught the sound of the woman weeping.

Moving back from the door, the guard procured a small towel and wet it with cold water. He carefully filled the bucket, remembering the glass that remained on the table inside the cell.

The only sounds were of the woman crying. He would comfort her, the guard determined. He'd wipe her face, give her some water to drink, and ease her fears.

Carefully and quietly, the guard removed his hood, took his keys from around his neck, turned off the microphone to the room, and opened the door. The light from the room where he came fell across the face of Laura, who looked up and cringed in fear.

"Don't worry," said the guard. "I've brought you some water and a towel to wipe your face."

Laura continued to sob and curled into a ball as the guard approached softly.

"Don't fear. I'll make you feel better, and then you'll do the same for me."

Laura watched the eyes of the guard as he drew close to her face. She could see the lust and retreated.

The guard, tired and on edge, grew stern at her rebuff. He grabbed her face and attempted to force his "kindness" on her.

Laura spat in his face.

The guard snapped and struck her across the face. "Whore!" he raged. His emotions now in full heat, he grabbed Laura's face and kissed her on the mouth.

Gallagher was roused to consciousness by the noise and worked to comprehend what was happening. "Laura!" he said.

"Peter!" Laura yelled, trying to fend off the guard. Finding her chained arms behind the guard's neck, she snapped. Suddenly she felt herself outside of her body, a flood of adrenalin surging. Her eyes widened as she wrapped the chains of her bonds around the neck of her attacker and squeezed.

"Laura!" yelled Gallagher again. "Laura!"

Bracing her feet against the guard's body, she tightened her grip. "You sick creep!" she screamed, squeezing all the harder.

The guard reached for his neck to try to relieve the pressure. His hands fumbled but couldn't break free, his eyes looking in amazement toward Laura. The guard gasped and squirmed.

"Laura!" yelled Gallagher again. He could see the guard's body begin to slow.

Laura continued to squeeze long after the guard had succumbed to her rage. Then, without knowing why, she stopped and released her grip. The guard slumped at her feet. "Oh, God! Peter!"

"Laura, calm down! Calm down! Quiet now. Quiet." He tried to soothe her into a rational state of mind and then saw the window of opportunity she had created. "Laura, I need you to calm down and check his pockets."

Laura didn't move, her body and mind slowly moving into shock over what had happened. She looked toward Gallagher but couldn't see much but a muffled shadow.

Gallagher worked to try and direct her. "Laura, I need you to check his pockets."

Laura sat stunned but then finally responded, closing her eyes in revulsion as she patted down the still warm but motionless body of the guard. Suddenly she vomited and began to cry.

"You're okay. Just stay focused. Find the key ring." Gallagher looked at the open door of the cell, wondering why no alarm had been sounded. He looked back toward Laura.

Grunting, she pulled the chain from the guard's pocket on which was hung several keys of various sizes. "Here!" she said, holding them up for Gallagher to acknowledge as tears ran down her face.

"That's my girl," he said. "Everything is okay. Find the large key they used to lock these shackles." He looked back at the open cell door. Nothing. The sound of the heavy metal shackles hitting the floor snapped his eyes back toward Laura. "Good!"

He heard another rattle of heavy chains hitting the floor, as Laura worked to free him.

Gallagher and Laura were free from their bonds but still very much prisoners lost in another maze, not knowing the way out.

Chapter 83

The room outside the cell was small and cramped. Some sort of anteroom, thought Gallagher, as he held Laura's hand a little too tightly.

He listened, heard nothing, and then opened the door that led from the small anteroom. A low-ceilinged hallway made of reinforced earthen walls sat outside. A line of light bulbs connected by rudimentary electrical cord ran along the top.

"We must be well below ground," Gallagher said.

The tunnel ran both right and left. He moved off to the left without reason, his ears listening for any signs of life.

They walked quickly along fifty yards of corridor before finally reaching the end of the tunnel, which opened into a high-ceilinged room that measured only twelve feet by ten. A metal spiral staircase sat in a corner and ran up several feet to a landing next to which another heavy metal door stood. Under the staircase sat a smaller metal door, locked with a padlock, and resembling a large coal-shoot hatch.

Gallagher let go of Laura's hand and took to the stairs, slowly climbing with as soft a step as he could muster. His hand, nose, and body were painfully sore. His head remained cloudy.

He placed his ear to the door and listened. No sound. Looking over the rail of the stairwell, he glanced down at Laura, who looked up with trembling legs and her arms trying to hold her body calm. "Throw me the key ring," he said.

Laura took the ring from her pocket and tossed it poorly up toward Gallagher. The keys bounced off the stair rail, the sound echoing throughout the small room.

* * *

On the other side of the door, the muffled sound of the bouncing keys subconsciously caught the attention of the well-dressed man. He looked up from the array of photos and other materials on his desk and turned to the speaker nearby. He looked at his watch. It had been some time since he had heard anything; the prisoners were unusually quiet, he thought. He listened again, the marked silence triggering his own alarm. He hurried from his office after grabbing his own silenced automatic from a drawer.

Chapter 84

Father Damien Thomas hadn't received the planned call from Maria Rosario. It was to have come no later than one hour after she had departed the rectory building. Something was wrong, he knew.

He sat in the chair of the pastoral study, thinking. He heard a sound of footsteps moving slowly along the stairwell. He stood silently from his chair, his mind and heart racing.

The sounds stopped. Father Thomas picked up the phone on his desk and dialed a number. The weather recording picked up in mid-forecast. He listened for only a second then engaged in a mock conversation. "Hello," he said. "Yes, I think so." He continued the conversation after placing the receiver softly on the cradle. He moved around from where his chair sat. "I understand," he said.

Slowly, Father Thomas moved toward the door of his study and flung it open.

"Oh, hello, Damien," said Father Benjamin. "I didn't know you were in." The Ugandan priest held aloft his Bible. "Just reviewing the readings for tomorrow." Father Benjamin glanced into the study and caught sight of the phone on its cradle.

Father Thomas looked at the Ugandan priest disapprovingly. He knew the man was a spy. Out to destroy him, thought Father Thomas. His mind raced even faster now. "Yes, of course," Father Thomas said. "Of course."

"I'll leave you in peace. I apologize if I've frightened you," said Benjamin with a nervous smile.

Father Thomas said nothing, closed the door, and returned to his desk. His breathing grew quick. Panic had found him. He reached for a glass and some whisky from a nearby tabletop. He gulped it down and refilled the glass. He sat behind his desk again, his hands shaking. The old priest cupped his head in his hands and tried to draw himself back from the edge. Forty years of secrets, lies, deceit, and hypocrisy flooded him. He had kept them at bay this long; there was no reason now not to hold firm.

Outside the door to the study, Father Benjamin listened and grew nervous. The man inside knew, he thought. He hurriedly moved up the stairs to his room to gather his things. He would need to get out now and back to the embassy. The Church would understand.

As he worked quickly to gather up a small bag with enough to get him through the night, he failed to hear the sounds coming up the stairs.

"I didn't want this. Do you understand? I will pray for your soul, and then I will pray for mine," said Father Thomas, his eyes slightly glazed and his mouth dry. "But God will understand, won't he? He must."

Father Benjamin dropped his bag. "Forgive them, Father, for they do not know what they are doing."

* * *

"What do you mean, a gunshot?" said one of the CIA agents in the surveillance van located down the street from the rectory.

"I mean a fucking gunshot!" said the man listening with headphones still over his head.

"Oh, Christ," said the first agent. He picked up the phone and dialed Langley.

Chapter 85

The well-dressed man moved swiftly from his office and up the flight of stairs to where the giant slept. His rage at the sight of the sleeping guard on duty was controlled but apparent. He kicked the chair out from under the guard, who tumbled onto the hard, wood floor. "You incompetent!" he barked at the stunned guard before opening the bedroom door. The giant was already awake and at the ready.

The guard, the giant, and the well-dressed man moved down the stairs and toward the basement far below street level.

They moved quickly, descending several flights of stairs and a ladder before reaching the metal door that led to the spiral staircase. "Open it," said the well-dressed man to the guard he had just reprimanded. "Hurry, you idiot."

The guard did as told and opened the heavy metal door. The well-dressed man and the giant rushed by him and moved down the spiral staircase, down the tunnel, and into the anteroom. The guard followed close behind, arriving in the cell just as the well-dressed man and the giant digested the escape of the prisoners. The guard took off his mask in a primal plea for mercy.

The well-dressed man looked at the giant.

The giant turned, raised his own pistol, and leveled it at the guard. Another second later, the guard dropped dead on the floor of the cell, the punishment for his dereliction swift and final.

"Find them," said the well-dressed man to the giant. "If they try to escape, kill them."

"Yes, sir," responded the giant before running out of the cell and toward the tunnel.

The well-dressed man looked down at the two dead guards, turned, and moved hurriedly up to his office. There would be little time. His escape plan was already in place. All that remained would be to destroy the materials, sanitize the building, and prepare to leave. It would take only one final action to sever the last knot.

The giant had done well, thought the well-dressed man. He almost regretted having to kill him too.

Chapter 86

Gallagher had estimated that in the few minutes he and Laura had been on the move, they had traversed no more than fifty yards.

Seconds after the keys had bounced upon the metal stairs, Gallagher had shuffled down the spiral staircase, grabbed them and then Laura. Together they had found the key to the small metal door located below the staircase and jumped into the cool black darkness that lay beyond it.

Once inside, it took Gallagher only a minute to feel blindly along the walls and toward the ceiling to determine that yet another tunnel lay before them. He spread his arms left and right to find that neither touched the sides; nor could he touch the ceiling. Where the tunnel led, they had no idea. Even so, it seemed the only safe option—as if the word "safe" really meant anything at this point.

"We need to move faster," said Laura, her hands clamped to the back of Gallagher's shirt. The sounds of her words seemed to magnify themselves when she spoke, traveling down the apparent corridor.

"I'm trying," responded Gallagher. He held his arms out in front of him like a zombie, although he couldn't see them. The tunnel was large, he thought again. The dimensions making their progress slow, as he unintentionally zigzagged back and forth against the sides while trying to continue a forward progression.

The air inside the tunnel was stagnant. They heard no sounds other than their own fumbling. Gallagher tried to pick up speed but stumbled to the floor.

"Peter!" Laura whispered fiercely, losing connection with him.

"I'm okay. I'm here." He stood and reached back to ascertain where Laura was. He found her then took her hand. His other hand remained extended before them as their only sensor.

* * *

Inside the room with the spiral staircase, the giant had heard the muffled sounds come through the small metal door below it. He looked over, saw the lock hanging free, and knew his targets were on the move.

He pulled his gun out with one hand and with his other reached for the small penlight in his pocket. He switched off the room light then peered into the tunnel that lay behind the small metal door.

After listening for a second, he knew they were inside. How far ahead, he wasn't certain.

The giant had traversed the tunnel many times. It would take but a few short moments to catch them.

Chapter 87

Simon moved down the hallway from his office in Langley as quickly as he could without appearing as if anything was wrong. In reality, things had spiraled totally out of control.

His men outside the parish rectory had called minutes before with the report that a gunshot had been heard from inside. He had given swift orders that the surveillance team should vacate the area immediately. There was no time to send his men into the building and remove the evidence of the illegal listening devices and phone tap. That mess would have to be cleaned up later, if it could be cleaned up at all. There were now far too many things that needed to be cleaned.

From inside the CIA car, Simon's phone buzzed. He picked it up. "Yes?"

"Sir, the Rosario woman has been tough. She was obviously well trained," said an agent who had been involved in the Georgetown operation. "Even with the medications, she didn't say much. However, we did get something from her."

"What did she tell you?"

"There's some sort of house that she kept rambling on about once we administered the drugs."

"What house?" asked Simon, his frustration rising.

"Not sure, sir." The agent paused and looked down at the transcript again then read from it. "Something about a 'rich man's house,' 'house of the rich man,' 'old house.'" The agent paused. "Then it says something about 'a subway.' The analysts are trying to put the pieces together now."

"Is she still conscious?"

"For the time being," responded the agent. "Not sure how much more we're going to get out of her at this point."

"Well, keep trying. Do you hear? Get whatever she has. Don't do anything with her until I provide you with the authority. Do you copy that?"

"Yes, sir. We understand."

Simon ended the call, thought for a second, then dialed the number he now had well memorized. There was little more he could do from his side without more information. But having to throw himself now on the mercy of the Vatican was the last thing he wanted.

However, it appeared at this point, that it was the only option now available. And perhaps the Vatican would be just as interested to do whatever was in their power to make this entire episode go away as quietly and quickly as his own government most certainly did.

He was sure the Hawk would see things his way. After all, no matter how pious a man he was, he was still human. And both their careers now hung in the balance, along with so much more.

Chapter 88

Gallagher continued to move forward, now at a much quicker pace after having become accustomed to the space. They had traversed two hundred yards or more, he estimated. How far it went on remained a tense mystery as the minutes passed.

The gradient of the floor slowly began to rise, Gallagher could tell; the air had started to smell and taste slightly different. He hoped that their subterranean journey would be nearing an end.

Laura moved behind Gallagher, her hand hot and wet, having been attached to Gallagher's for some time. She again turned her head back toward where they had come from, watching and waiting for something she knew was likely back there in the darkness. The remaining guards would, at some point, get their scent. It was just a question of when.

The flicker of a light caught Laura's eye as she turned. She continued to watch, as the familiar pitch darkness behind her grew slightly grayer. "Peter," she said in a hushed voice.

Gallagher hadn't heard his name but stopped when Laura squeezed so tightly on his own fragile hand that he winced in pain. "I think we're almost there. What is it?" He stopped and stood quietly.

"Some sort of light." Laura stood deathly still. "Shush," she said.

The two listened carefully. The muffled sounds of footsteps were evident. Someone had indeed caught their scent.

"Come on," said Gallagher, pulling Laura forward. "We have to keep moving."

Thirty seconds later, Gallagher's left hand hit something solid. His quickened momentum carried him face first into a wall upon which a piece metal of some sort was impaled.

Laura's body followed into Gallagher's back. She stopped, stunned by the abrupt halt. Laura looked back again, more concerned with who or what lurked behind than what now lie ahead.

Gallagher examined the wall quickly. He let go of Laura's hand, allowing himself to make a more complete examination. He reached up. His hands hit the ceiling of the tunnel. A hole above, he could sense. "It's a ladder," he said.

Laura didn't hear him. The light from behind them grew significantly brighter. "Peter…"

Gallagher looked back down the tunnel they had traversed, now seeing the light himself. "Let's go. Take the lead," he said to Laura, grabbing her and lifting her onto the ladder. "Up. Now!"

Laura began to shimmy up the metal ladder.

"Faster, Laura. Faster!" Gallagher's heart was beating harder, and his breathing grew heavier.

The sounds of the footsteps behind picked up in pace. Gallagher looked again, seeing the light behind shining clearly. He took to the ladder behind Laura and moved through the hole in the tunnel ceiling through which the ladder led. "Move, Laura!" Faster!"

The spark and ping of a silenced bullet hitting the metal ladder below his feet jolted Gallagher. He tried to ignore it to keep pace behind Laura who was scrambling above. Her own fear propelling her upward, she was a petrified cat seeking safety from the baying hounds below.

* * *

Seven-and-a-half-minutes prior, Ty Johnson and Irvin Drexler had broken down the door of a five-story, brick, antebellum Georgetown mansion. They carried no warrant.

The house sat on a corner on N Street. A large and well-manicured English garden, a four-car garage, and a guesthouse sat behind. A tall brick wall surrounded it all.

Inside the well-appointed residence, the smell of burning paper hung throughout. Having followed it, Johnson and Drexler crashed through an office door and traded gunfire with a well-dressed man who hadn't expected any more visitors that evening.

Chapter 89

The CIA and the Vatican teams had reached the same conclusion—this matter needed to be cleaned up, and cleaned up quickly.

Simon and the Hawk had spoken for only a few moments while Simon continued on his way to the McLean location where his team tried to make sense of Maria Rosario's curious ramblings.

Both men had come very far in this mission. To see it now in tatters left neither side satisfied. But no matter how determined both sides were to find the elusive truth, both were now far more determined to cover up the operation that had failed on so many levels and that placed both their governments in the most precarious of positions.

The operation would now be "mopped up," as Simon had said, using the same partnership that had been leveraged since the beginning. The site of the Maryland raid already had been secured. A special team from Langley was now finishing that job. The Vatican had taken the bodies of their own operatives from the scene, both of which would be flown back to Rome on a diplomatic transport within the hour.

Meanwhile, the CIA, with Vatican assistance, had dispatched a second team to the St. Gabriel rectory. While the Hawk was livid over the CIA's unapproved surveillance operation there, he had again absolved them of fault. The joint team would have one last chance to search the premises before another police investigation might bring the whole sordid matter into public view.

And when it was over, the sides knew, all would be as it was before. It wouldn't be the endgame for which either had hoped, but at least one where there was potentially an opportunity to fight again another day.

As for the detective and the woman, little could be done now. While their likely demise would remain painful to both sides, these things sometimes couldn't be helped. There was a greater and higher purpose that their deaths would serve, both sides rationalized—a greater good and glory that must be preserved.

Chapter 90

Ninety feet. That's how far it took for Laura to reach the summit of the rusty iron ladder that led from the tunnel below. There she saw the rectangular outline of light directly across from where she stood. It was faint, but it was light nonetheless.

Right behind her, Gallagher struggled up. The man below him moved up too, his gun pocketed in order to allow him to climb unfettered.

Laura reached toward the outline. "It's some sort of door!" she screamed, not caring about alerting their unknown pursuer of her discovery.

Gallagher looked below his feet. The man who followed them was large, he could tell. The heavy sounds of the man's feet on the ladder gave evidence to his sheer size and weight. The man was now halfway up. "Look for a doorknob!"

"I don't feel one!" she screamed back in fear. She reached farther and examined the area more closely. "Wait! I think I feel something. It's a latch."

"Well, pull the damn thing!" yelled Gallagher, looking down to see the man's head below nearly at his feet.

The ladder shaft suddenly filled with light as Laura's hand triggered the latch and the door opened above.

Gallagher looked up as Laura began to move into the space that led from the door. As he did, he felt a hand grab for his leg. As he peered down, the giant man below looked up, his hand working to pull the gun from his pocket.

An "Oh, God," was all that Gallagher heard from Laura—now having penetrated the door and fallen into the space above into which it led. Gallagher took a firm hold on a rung two below the one he currently had hold of and dropped himself down on top of the giant, kicking hard with his feet.

The giant grunted and struggled to keep hold on the ladder. The free hand that had reached for the concealed weapon instinctively clamped onto the ladder. The gun that he fumbled with dropped below. The sound of the clanking metal on metal echoed up and down the tunnel.

Seeing the opportunity, Gallagher didn't wait to exact another offensive move but instead raced upward on the ladder, the pain from his wounded hand not even registering. His adrenalin trumped any physical discomfort he may have otherwise felt.

Five feet later, Gallagher reached the summit of the ladder. His eyes focused on the door and the light shining from it. His eyes caught sight of the space into which it led, and then he spotted Laura waiting for him on the floor.

Shocked into utter stillness, Gallagher froze at the sight of the room before him. It took all of Laura's remaining strength to pull him in.

Chapter 91

The room of Father Edward Sachs looked no different than it had when Gallagher had first seen it the night of Sachs's death. The small desk, the bed, and the wardrobe all were there—a sharp but distant memory. Gallagher, sitting on the floor, looked at the passageway through which he had just been pulled. The built-in bookshelf panel now swung open, revealing the access used by whomever had pushed Father Sachs to his death. There was no doubt; this was the answer that had eluded him those many days ago.

The sound of the giant moving up the ladder shocked him back to the present. Now just a few inches from the secret door, Gallagher pulled his legs toward him while still on the floor. At the sight of the giant's head, he released his legs. The sheer force of his feet and legs sailing against the giant's face made the man recoil and lose his footing again on the ladder.

Gallagher sprang up, slammed the large section of the bookshelf closed, and slid whatever he could find in front it. Sachs's desk was the smallest and easiest of the pieces to put into position. A small nightstand was added. "Laura, help me with the wardrobe!" he said.

Laura pulled herself to her feet and worked futilely with Gallagher to try to budge the heavy wooden wardrobe. It was no use, thought Gallagher, thinking the piece must have been in place since the beginning of time.

The giant, now recovered from the blow he'd received from Gallagher, pushed against the secret door from his position on the other side, fiercely working to get to his targets in the room beyond.

* * *

Two floors below in the rectory, Father Thomas remained almost in a trance. He had heard the noise above as if almost expecting it but didn't react. Calmly he finished his prayers, took the gun from his sideboard, and slowly made his way toward the chaos above.

But not even the struggle that was taking place could shake him from where his mind finally had gone.

Chapter 92

"Let's go!" yelled Gallagher. He grabbed Laura's hand as the giant began to succeed in his attempt at penetrating the now-blocked door.

Gallagher looked at Laura, her eyes now fixed and her feet planted. He turned, seeing the figure of Father Thomas now standing in the doorway, a rosary in one hand and a gun in the other.

Just at that moment, the giant breached the hidden door of the bookshelf. His massive frame and hands instantly clamped down on Gallagher, who had stood frozen by the bizarre and haunting sight of the old Jesuit priest before him.

Father Thomas said nothing, remaining without emotion as the giant tossed Gallagher across the room. Gallagher's body slid across the floor with a tremendous force, dislodging a small and threadbare Oriental carpet from its neat position on the hardwood floor. Gallagher struggled to regain his senses as the giant threw Laura in a similar fashion toward him.

Father Thomas remained expressionless, the gun still clamped in his wrinkled hand.

The giant looked at the priest as if to request permission to issue the coup de grace and then moved slowly toward his targets.

Paralyzed by fear, Gallagher and Laura didn't hear the sound of the bullet that struck the giant in the back. They looked up in wonder as the giant stopped in mid-step. The expression of disbelief registered on the giant's face as blood dripped from his mouth.

The giant tried to take another step forward. He froze, laughed, then fell to the floor with a loud thud. The sound and force of the giant's massive body seemed to shake the entire building when it landed, sending books tumbling off their shelves and jolting the doors to the heavy wardrobe open.

Laura, screaming, buried her face in Gallagher's chest.

Over the body of the giant that now lay before him, Gallagher saw what had happened.

Ty Johnson stepped through the secret bookshelf door, having discovered the underground tunnel leading from the Georgetown townhouse. "You okay?" he said to Gallagher, while not taking his eyes or aim off Father Thomas.

"I'm not sure," responded Gallagher, garnering a cautious look of relief on this face, "but it's good to see you."

Chapter 93

"Put the gun down, Father," said Johnson, his own gun pointed straight toward the catatonic parish pastor. "It's all over now."

Father Thomas didn't move but looked toward Gallagher, who held Laura tightly against his body. "Life is short, Mr. Gallagher. Too short," he said.

The room went quiet.

"Put the gun down, Father," said Johnson again, sensing the unsettled nature of the old Jesuit. "We can all just walk away now. Put down the gun."

Father Thomas remained focused on Gallagher. "We can never just walk away. Our sins and our regrets stay with us forever. While they may have been justified for the best of intentions, eventually they awake and find us, no matter how well we may have suppressed them with logic and reason."

Gallagher looked up at the old priest, pleading with his eyes. "Father, please do as Detective Johnson says. Put down the gun."

Father Thomas's eyes glazed over as he continued. "It was all meant to be for God, Mr. Gallagher. All of it. That, I want you to know."

"I know, Father. Now put the gun down, please!" said Gallagher again, knowing the lingering standoff was only making their situation more perilous by the second.

"You will tell them, won't you, Mr. Gallagher? You will tell them I did it all for God? For the greater glory of God?"

Gallagher now knew what the old priest was saying and what, tragically, he was doing. "I will tell them, Father," he said calmly. "Yes, I will tell them."

Father Damien Thomas smiled subtly then nodded. He looked toward Johnson then returned his focus a final time on Gallagher. He said nothing more, and then he moved to raise his gun.

Ty Johnson fired only one bullet.

Chapter 94

The smell of cordite filled the room, which had grown incredibly hot. Displaced dust from the giant's fall mixed with it all; the room was almost hazy now.

Gallagher looked on as Johnson checked to see whether either of the still bodies had any signs of life. Johnson's reaction after checking the pulses verified the finality of it all.

"Come on, Laura," said Gallagher, forcing her head from his chest. "It's over now."

Laura lifted her head and opened her eyes, looking at Gallagher before breaking down and crying.

Gallagher hugged her closely while sharing a look with Johnson. "Easy now, Laura. It's okay. Everything is going to be all right."

Johnson picked up his radio and called for backup and an ambulance. He walked over to where Gallagher sat on the floor holding Laura in his arms then squatted next to him. "You okay, partner?"

"I think so, but it's going to take some time," said Gallagher. "How the hell did you—" he began to ask.

Johnson interrupted him. "Yeah. We found the house where you were taken. Drexler and I must have busted in shortly after you slipped into that tunnel."

Gallagher continued to try to ask more questions, only to have Johnson continue to answer them before he could finish. "Who—"

"We traced those calls from the mayor's office. All were sourced back to former aides or individuals who knew Senator Forbes Raybeck." Johnson waited a few seconds. "We traced the house through a series of holding companies owned by the senator."

Gallagher and Laura said nothing.

"You don't look surprised," said Johnson.

"No," said Gallagher. "He was involved with it. Must have been neck deep in it."

"In what, exactly?" asked Johnson, his own pieces of the puzzle still not completely pieced together.

Laura had stopped crying, quieted by the revelation that Johnson had begun to provide. She wiped her eyes then worked to stand up. Gallagher was too tired to get into the intricacies of his partner's question. They would delve into all of that later, he knew.

Laura walked toward Johnson and hugged him. "Thank you," she said.

Rubbing his eyes, Gallagher remained seated. He looked around the room. "What a mess."

He turned on his side and prepared to push himself into a standing position. The carpet he had dislodged when the giant had tossed him across the room remained rumpled against his back. He turned around, while still on the floor, and pushed it away.

If there were anything more that could have shaken Gallagher at that point, the sight of a loose floorboard wouldn't have been on the top of his list.

But the sight of the two small crosses cut into it most certainly was.

Chapter 95

It wasn't a single diary that Gallagher, Laura, and Johnson discovered hidden under the floorboard. Instead, there were three volumes—each one covering a period of anywhere between five and ten years—each laying out, in meticulous detail, the names and events that had transpired during the respective period. The dates covered by each volume were noted in faded black ink.

"Christ almighty. Sachs had them the whole time," said Gallagher, stunned, while leafing through one of the volumes.

"But why?" asked Laura, looking up, one of the volumes in her hands.

"I don't know," said Gallagher resignedly. "I don't know."

The sound of Johnson's radio crackling into life suddenly interrupted them. Johnson listened, responded into the radio, then looked at Gallagher. "They're rounding the corner, Pete. I'd say we have about sixty seconds to figure out what we want to do here."

Gallagher didn't need sixty seconds. He had pondered this moment for weeks. Yes, thought Gallagher. He knew exactly what needed to be done.

Chapter 96

Simon walked down the hall of CIA headquarters at Langley with a slight but unwanted spring in his step. He wore his best suit, and his shoes were perfectly polished.

The director of the CIA stood when Simon knocked on the door. "Come in," he said.

Simon walked in smartly. "Mr. Director," he responded then handed him the single volume across the massive oak desk.

The men sat down in unison.

The director looked at the volume, leafed through it quickly, then placed it on the desktop. "I guess congratulations are in order, although several of our men died because of this."

Simon held a calculated pause before finally saying, "Hundreds or thousands died because of what is in it, sir."

The director allowed the remark to go unchallenged, although he didn't appreciate the lecture. "I suppose that might be true," he grudgingly conceded.

"I'm not sure the president wants to know about this," said Simon.

"No." The director held back his ire. This whole event, he knew, was better left conveniently unresolved. He secretly cursed the fact that it had ever come to light, no matter how "quiet" it was to remain within official circles. A great deal of political fallout was still possible if it did see the light of day—a concern more for his highly influential personal connections, who were now exposed, than any national security imperative.

"Is that all then, sir?" asked Simon, looking across at the feckless leader of his own agency.

"What about the DC police detective and the woman? Will they remain quiet?"

Simon stared sharply at the director. "The arrangement was that in return for the book there would be no further involvement of the agency."

The director said nothing.

"Make no mistake. This is over." Simon looked forcefully at the man. "Are we in agreement, sir?"

"Watch yourself now." The director grew visibly stern. "I can have you out of this agency in about three minutes."

Simon rose to the challenge. "You want a congressional investigation, sir? You be my guest." He waited for a moment. "And if I, or any of my men, or the detective, or the woman should have one hair on their heads harmed, professionally or personally, you mark my words, it will be as if a bomb went off."

The director again composed himself and remained quiet.

Simon stood from his chair and began to walk out of the office. He turned around. "There is a great hypocrisy in all of this, don't you think?" he said, intentionally dropping the "sir." "For nearly thirty years, the 'best and brightest,' the affluent, the connected, those who were supposed to *defend* the American way of life were out to undermine it. Even now there's little apology in the face of the glaring evidence—only quiet resentment at it having been unearthed."

"You expect me to apologize for something I had no involvement with? Is that what you're telling me, you impertinent shit?" The director rose sharply from his chair and leaned over his desk toward the man in front of it.

Simon walked back up to the desk and leaned over it as well, his face just a few inches from the director's. "In some ways I pity you," he said. "Too cowardly to admit that your own kind was wrong. It doesn't go past my attention that some of those mentioned in that book are personal and political friends of yours. If it was up to me, I'd feed the lot of you to the newspapers, but I have almost less confidence that anyone else would care than I do in your own limited interest in the truth."

The director stood back.

Simon continued, "I guess there is a 'greater good' that comes from hiding the truth, right? The kind of 'good' that keeps people content in not having to honestly examine their own beliefs, or face the reality of their own delusional perceptions, instead of desperately clinging on to carefully constructed rationales that were only formed to suit their own damn purposes."

Simon stopped speaking and looked at the director closely again. "Of course there is," he spat with contempt. "Men like you don't change." He took a few steps toward the door and turned around. "You just rationalize."

The director said nothing as Simon turned and walked out without another word. He resignedly sat down in his chair when the door shut, looked at the book in front of him, and for the first time in many years, began to listen again.

Chapter 97

Falling to one knee, Archbishop Hans Dietrich, the head of Vatican intelligence, kissed the ring of the cardinal who had awaited his arrival. "*Pax vobiscum*," he said reverently to the man known as *Dottrina*, the title indicating his powerful role as the man in charge of maintaining the integrity of Roman Catholic doctrine across the globe.

"*Et cum spiritu tuo*," responded the cardinal, who wore magnificent scarlet vestments in contrast to Dietrich's violet apparel.

Dietrich stood up and handed the small book to the cardinal. The cardinal looked at the book and smiled. "Please Archbishop, do sit down."

"Thank you, Your Eminence."

Dottrina placed the book in front of him. "You have done well, Archbishop."

"Thank you, Your Eminence," said Dietrich. "However, I must express my regret that two of our priests perished in our attempt to obtain it."

"They are with The Father now," said *Dottrina*. "The deaths of the other Jesuits were also unfortunate."

"Yes," said Dietrich. "Unfortunate."

Dottrina was quiet. He looked down at the book and then finally spoke. "Well, then. It would seem that this operation is finished." He waited for the head of Vatican intelligence to rise and depart. The audience was now over.

Hans Dietrich sat but didn't move. He remained perplexed by the reaction from the powerful cardinal, given the sheer importance with which the Vatican had undertaken the operation to recover the vital information. Four priests of the Church had lost their lives as a result. More important, thought Dietrich, the Jesuits, who had been a thorn in the side of the Holy Church and *Dottrina* himself for many years, were now exposed and vulnerable.

No matter which protocol should be followed, Dietrich rose to challenge the cardinal, as deftly and delicately as he could. "Eminence, may I be permitted to ask the course that will now be followed? The work of Vatican intelligence will likely be impacted on the way forward."

Dottrina noted the challenge but showed no outward signs of his inherent displeasure with the questioning. "These things must be handled very delicately, Archbishop, as you must know. However, the Holy Father will act in time. *Cunctando regitur mundus.*"

If you can outwait all, you can rule. Dietrich knew his Latin well. He also knew that at the highest levels within the Vatican power structure, the principle of *Romantia*, the concept of "Roman power," was almost a religion within a religion. Yes, he thought, understanding that the Church would now wait and do nothing.

Dottrina worked to try to analyze the face of the Church's chief spy but saw nothing. Dietrich was also very adept at the concept of *Romantia*, although *Dottrina* also knew that the concept grated on the hardline German as a necessary facet of his role. The cardinal remained silent then worked to provide the additional information he was, reluctantly, willing to share.

"There are rumors within Jesuit circles that the Vatican is now in possession of damning evidence of their treachery," *Dottrina* said. "The Jesuit Father General may now be more malleable not knowing for sure whether we possess the truth. He can now be used to suit our purposes. We will allow the Jesuits some latitude and, in return, we will gain political leverage in many countries."

"I see," said Dietrich, remaining impassive.

The Jesuit Father General, although viewed as a renegade by many within the Vatican hierarchy, remained a powerful figure within the Church. His power and black robes were responsible for the moniker "The Black Pope."

Dietrich was now aware, through the code of *Romantia*, that no matter how deserving the Jesuits were of swift justice by the Holy Church, careful deference would remain the chosen course of action. The thought repulsed him. Three Jesuits and one other priest had been murdered. Hundreds or thousands of others had been killed in Central America. The Church had been undermined, the faithful led astray like sheep to the slaughter as a result of decades of Jesuit modernism. Didn't the truth of those atrocities deserve to come to light?

Dietrich looked across at *Dottrina* and knew the answer. Even so, he had faith that God would see fit to make right what he, as a servant of his Church, wasn't tasked with doing. Yes, thought Dietrich, he would obey. To do otherwise would make him no better than the very Jesuit Order that had sparked the operation that was now officially accomplished.

Dietrich rose from his chair, moved toward the cardinal, and again kissed his ring in obedience. "*Pax vobiscum*," he said a final time.

The cardinal looked down at the Archbishop who knelt before him; his mind quivered for a second; his own conscience stirred with some angst as well. But there was a greater glory to be achieved, he rationalized. He too recognized in himself his own desire for the truth but accepted the unsettled need for it to be suppressed once again.

"*Et cum spiritu tuo*," said *Dottrina*.

Chapter 98

Gallagher again sat out on the large balcony as the sun began to rise again over the sea. Although he and Laura had been married only a few days, the long and overdue rest from the trials and tribulations of the preceding months had still yet to fully exorcise themselves from his mind. Even so, the morning solitude had become a welcome routine in trying to fix that.

The small wedding in the side chapel of the Metropolitan Cathedral of the Assumption of Mary of Mexico City had been an intimate yet solemn Nuptial Mass. Father Luis Avino had presided, as immediate family and a close circle of old and new friends looked on. Thomas and Carolina Garcia had flown in from Managua for the occasion and had joined Miguel as well as Ty Johnson and his wife. Gallagher and Laura were truly blessed in having such good friends.

After the two days of celebration that had followed, Mr. and Mrs. Peter Gallagher had retreated to a well-appointed Mexican resort for an extended honeymoon. By now the guests had flown back to their respective homes to resume life as it was. But Gallagher knew, as did all of the others, that life wouldn't be the same. Too many thoughts and ideas and beliefs and challenges and events had forever altered life as it once was. Yet the change still remained unfinished.

But Gallagher had seen to that.

While the world hadn't yet heard of Father Edward Sachs, Father Clarence Symanski, Father Michael Benjamin, or Father Damien Thomas, they soon would. They would learn all about them. So too would they learn the truth of St. Gabriel and Senator Forbes Raybeck and Francisco Cardenal and James

Francis Carney and Gustavo Gutierrez, the little Nicaraguan town of Caldera, and the very secret wars of the Society of Jesus. *Yes*, thought Gallagher, *the world will know.* No matter how painful the truth might be, how many feathers it would ruffle, how many perceptions it would refute, how many legacies it would debunk, how many institutions it would embarrass, how many people it would anger, it was infinitely better that it come to light.

Gallagher had given US and Vatican intelligence what they were after some weeks ago; both sides had been allowed time to digest it and to act. But he had known deep down that neither side would have the courage to act, the temporal prerogatives of the powerful always at the fore.

So Gallagher had taken the third diary volume. It now rested in a safe place that only he and Ty Johnson knew about. Its contents, however—and that of the two other volumes—had been carefully replicated. Packages had been sent out to various media outlets. Who would publish the story and make it known to the world, he didn't know. But someone would, he hoped.

Now, looking over the sea, Gallagher wondered what impact the truth would have when it traversed the globe. Tomorrow would, most certainly, be different.

A greater glory indeed existed, he had come to recognize, as the sun began to grow brighter. He realized it is the one certain thing that transcends time and space and the self-interested rationality that seems so powerful an elixir during earthly life.

Yes, there was indeed a greater glory, thought Gallagher.

And life was much too short not to embrace it to the fullest.

Printed in Great Britain
by Amazon.co.uk, Ltd.,
Marston Gate.